Swag Bags
and
Swindlers

Books by Dorothy Howell

HANDBAGS AND HOMICIDE

PURSES AND POISON

SHOULDER BAGS AND SHOOTINGS

CLUTCHES AND CURSES

TOTE BAGS AND TOE TAGS

EVENING BAGS AND EXECUTIONS

BEACH BAGS AND BURGLARIES

SWAG BAGS AND SWINDLERS

Published by Kensington Publishing Corporation

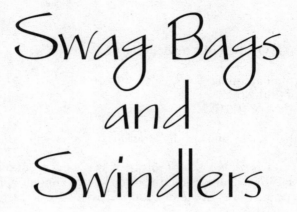

Swag Bags and Swindlers

DOROTHY HOWELL

KENSINGTON BOOKS
http://www.kensingtonbooks.com

KENSINGTON BOOKS are published by

Kensington Publishing Corp.
119 West 40th Street
New York, NY 10018

All Kensington titles, imprints, and distributed lines are available at special quantity discounts for bulk purchases for sales promotion, premiums, fund-raising, educational, or institutional use. Special book excerpts or customized printings can also be created to fit specific needs. For details, write or phone the office of the Kensington Special Sales Manager: Attn. Special Sales Department. Kensington Publishing Corp., 119 West 40th Street, New York, NY 10018. Phone: 1-800-221-2647.

Library of Congress Card Catalogue Number: 2015937826

ISBN-13: 978-0-7582-9498-2
ISBN-10: 0-7582-9498-0
First Kensington Hardcover Edition: October 2015

eISBN-13: 978-0-7582-9499-9
eISBN-10: 0-7582-9499-9
First Kensington Electronic Edition: October 2015

10 9 8 7 6 5 4 3 2 1

Printed in the United States of America

With love to Stacy, Judy, Brian, and Seth

Acknowledgments

The author is extremely grateful for the love, support, and encouragement of many people. Some of them are: Stacy Howell, Judith Branstetter, Brian Branstetter, Seth Branstetter, Martha Cooper, Christine Ridgway, and William F. Wu, Ph.D.

Many thanks to Evan Marshall of the Evan Marshall Agency, and John Scognamiglio and the talented team at Kensington Publishing for all their hard work.

CHAPTER 1

With age comes great wisdom.
Or was it power?
Or was it great responsibility that came with power?
But maybe that only applied to Spider-Man.

Anyway, I was staring head-on at birthday number twenty-five and was feeling pretty darn responsible. Truthfully, this wasn't a trait I'd ever noticed in myself—nor was it something my friends or family had commented on—but there it was.

I, Haley Randolph, with my tall-enough-to-model-but-I-don't five-foot-nine height, my *Vogue*-cover-worthy dark hair, and my too-bad-they-weren't-more-dominant beauty-queen genes, had fully embraced this new phase of my life because, really, it totally benefited me to do so in the best way possible.

This unexpected turn was unfolding courtesy of my job as an assistant event planner with L.A. Affairs. While the name of the company made it sound like a call girl service, it wasn't.

L.A. Affairs was an event-planning company that catered to the elite of Los Angeles, the stars of Hollywood, the well connected, the power players, and the industry insiders. I'd come aboard on the heels of a couple of other jobs that hadn't worked out as well as I'd have liked—long story.

If I do say so myself, things have gone great for me at L.A. Affairs. Well, okay, there've been a few unfortunate situations—none of which were my fault—but every job has an occasional hiccup, right?

The upside to all of this was that my probation period would come to an end in mere weeks, which meant I'd then be given a job performance review. Once I had the HR seal of approval, I would be deemed worthy of permanent, full-time employee status.

Since I'd done such a great job—except for a glitch or two here and there—I wasn't sweating it.

I pulled into the parking garage that adjoined the building that housed L.A. Affairs. It was a beautiful early November morning. Really, the only way to know the seasons changed in most of Southern California was to look at a calendar. Our weather was always mild, the breeze calm, the sun shining, and today was no exception.

I swung my Honda into a spot near the elevators. Our location was on the prestigious corner of Sepulveda and Ventura boulevards in Sherman Oaks, one of L.A.'s many upscale areas. Nearby were other high-rise office buildings, banks, apartment complexes, plus the terrific shops and restaurants across the street at the Galleria.

I grabbed my handbag—a classic black-and-white Chanel that perfectly complemented my black business suit—and took the elevator up to the third floor. The hallway was quiet as I headed for the entrance to L.A. Affairs, but that was because I was running a bit late this morning—which had absolutely nothing to do with any sort of responsibility issue that might impact my entire future.

Okay, maybe it did.

And, really, I was sweating my job performance review—big time. I had a lot—*a lot*—riding on it.

Permanent full-time status meant that I would be eligible for L.A. Affairs' benefit package, which included medical coverage—thus my new look-at-me-I'm-responsible mode. That, in turn, meant I could cancel the medical coverage I presently had through my crappy part-time sales-clerk job at the seriously crappy Holt's Department Store. And beyond that, it meant *I could quit my job at Holt's.*

I did a mental backflip just thinking about it.

"Are you ready to party?" Mindy, our receptionist, shouted as I walked into the L.A. Affairs office.

Mindy was pushing fifty, a little on the full-figured side, with blond hair that resembled one of those glass balls people decorated their gardens with. I was unclear on how she'd gotten this job, and even more unclear on why she was allowed to keep it.

She giggled and fluttered her lashes. "They make me say that."

Nor was I clear on why L.A. Affairs insisted she chant that ridiculous slogan.

"I know," I said. "It's me. Haley."

"Oh, so it is," Mindy said, chuckling. "It's just so busy around here this morning."

No one was seated in the reception area. None of the lights on her telephone console were lit.

"Oh, have you heard?" Mindy asked, doing her own version of jazz hands. "Big news today—"

Her phone rang. Mindy recoiled, twisting her fingers together.

"Oh, would you just look?" she said, shaking her head. "Another call already today."

Mindy lifted the receiver and pushed a button on the

telephone. "Are you ready to party . . . hello? Hello? Oh, dear." She punched another button. "Are you ready—? Hello?"

No way could I wait around for Mindy to answer the right line before I heard the big news of the day. I left, walking past the cube farm, the interview rooms, and turned down the hallway.

I'd taken the Holt's job about a year ago when I'd been desperate for some Christmas cash and my credit card balances had crept to troubling levels—plus Gucci had a fabulous new tote that I absolutely had to have. As things in life often do, Christmas had come and gone, my credit card balances had gone up and down like a bathroom scale before and after bathing suit season, and while I'd gotten myself that Gucci tote, it had soon after been relegated to the cool-a-month-ago-but-now-I-need-the-newest-style handbag repository in the closet of my second bedroom.

But I'd kept the job at Holt's, and not only because they provided medical coverage.

Anyway, a new, more responsible phase of life was upon me. All I had to do was ace my upcoming job performance review. And in the meantime, I had to make sure that all the events I planned came off flawlessly, without a single hiccup or glitch—or, at least, no hiccup or glitch that L.A. Affairs found out about.

Even though I'd just arrived at work, there was, of course, no way I was going straight to my office. Instead, I went into the breakroom where several employees were lingering over coffee before starting the day.

For me, one of the best things about working for L.A. Affairs was that absolutely nothing mattered more than outward appearances. Everybody dressed in fabulous business suits and awesome shoes and carried designer handbags. L.A. Affairs had a reputation to uphold, and we employees were expected to project a certain image at all times—which I was totally on board with.

I spotted Kayla, one of my L.A. Affairs BFFs, helping herself to coffee. She was about my age, tall, curvy, with dark hair. She'd worked here longer than I had and knew the inside scoop on almost everything that went down.

"Big news," Kayla said as I walked up. "Suzie went into labor."

This came as no surprise. L.A. Affairs was staffed by women, dozens of women, most of us in our prime life-is-going-to-change-big-time years. That meant somebody was always going into labor, or announcing a pregnancy, or getting engaged, getting married, dating some hot guy, or dumping some jackass.

Still, if Kayla deemed today's news *big*, something was definitely going on.

She glanced over her shoulder and leaned in a little. "Suzie's baby wasn't due for another two weeks," she said. "That means her events are up for grabs."

Even though I had yet to pour my first cup of coffee, I knew where this was going—someplace great for *me*.

"I'm calling dibs," I said, "on everything."

Wow, this was just what I needed to prove to HR that I was worthy of permanent, full-time employee status. I could swoop in, take over Suzie's events, and save management the headache of trying to divide up the work. What better way to demonstrate my commitment to the company and cement my I'm-the-greatest rating on my job performance review so *I could quit my job at Holt's.*

"Dibs on everything?" Kayla asked.

"Heck yeah," I said.

"Well, okay, if you're sure," Kayla said. She lowered her voice. "You'd better jump on it. One of Suzie's parties is being eyed by you-know-who, if you get my meaning."

"Damn," I muttered.

I knew full well who you-know-who was. Vanessa Lord, senior planner and captain of the Raging Bitch squad.

When I'd first come on board at L.A. Affairs I'd been assigned to work under Vanessa as her assistant planner. We hadn't exactly hit it off—long story. Since then, I'd been handling my own events and she'd farmed out her events to several other assistants, thereby spreading her venom among many employees. No way would L.A Affairs get rid of her, though. Vanessa brought in the biggest clients—which made her the biggest bitch—so we were stuck with her.

"I'm going to talk to Priscilla right now," I said.

"Let me know how it goes," Kayla said, and left.

I filled my coffee cup, then dumped in a few sugar packets and topped it all off with a generous splash of French vanilla creamer. I was facing a make-it-or-break-it moment. I needed all the help I could get.

I left the breakroom, then circled back and grabbed a bag of M&M's from the snack cabinet, dumped the whole thing in my mouth, and headed out again.

Priscilla, the office manager, had an office down the hall. As I passed I saw that she was elbow deep in file folders—already. So what could I do but dash into my office, drop my handbag in my desk drawer, and hurry back?

"Hi, Priscilla," I said, as I paused in her doorway. "Can I get you another coffee? I'm on my third cup. Wow, this morning is flying by."

"I know what you mean," Priscilla said, looking up at me.

Priscilla was midthirties, tall, thin, with blond hair she wore in a blunt cut, and as office managers went, she was a good one.

She gestured to the mountain of file folders surrounding her and said, "I was behind before I walked in."

"Been there," I agreed, and we both laughed.

Immediately upon entering the workforce right out of high school—what I referred to as my parade of jeez-I-thought-that-would-have-worked-out-better jobs—I'd forged a credo, of sorts, the first tenet of which was my strict don't-volunteer-for-anything policy. I knew I was going against everything I believed in—and everything that had served me so well—by taking over Suzie's events, but I had my eye on a big prize: *I could quit my job at Holt's.*

I decided to come right to the point. I mean, jeez, I didn't have all day to stand around. Precious time was slipping past and I hadn't even updated my Facebook page or made lunch plans yet.

"I want to take over for Suzie," I said.

Priscilla sat back in her chair, stunned. "You what?"

"I want to take over for Suzie," I said again.

"Everything?" Priscilla asked.

"Yes."

"Everything?" she asked again as her eyes bugged out.

Wow, I'd really made her day.

"*All* of her duties?" Priscilla asked.

I'd totally overwhelmed her with my generous offer, obviously.

"Of course," I told her.

"Oh, Haley." Priscilla slumped onto her desk. "You're a lifesaver."

I smiled my yes-I-know-I'm-great smile, confident that now Priscilla knew I was great, too.

"Suzie's leaving two weeks early created a real problem for me," she said, and heaved a big sigh. "This is wonderful."

"I'm glad I can help," I told her, still smiling.

"No, really, it's fantastic." Priscilla plastered her palms over her eyes for a few seconds, then shook herself. "I didn't know how I was going to handle everything."

She's totally impressed with me now, I thought.

"I knew it would be a nightmare," Priscilla went on.

I'm her favorite employee—*ever*, no doubt, I told myself.

"You've saved the day," she said. "Thank you, Haley. Thank you so much."

My yes-I-know-I'm-great smile was starting to wilt, so I left and headed back to my office.

Yes, this was a fantastic way to start my day and my campaign to secure permanent, full-time employment status. And surely it wouldn't be difficult. I mean, really, how many events could Suzie—almost nine months pregnant—be handling?

My future flashed in front of my eyes. After I proved myself with the flawless and exceptional execution of not only my events but Suzie's, too, I'd be a shoe-in for permanent, full-time employee status.

And I could quit my job at Holt's.

CHAPTER 2

Meetings were, of course, the bane of every office employee's existence—especially when combined with a PowerPoint presentation guaranteed to dull the senses and numb the butt. I'd suffered through countless meetings in my long, arduous journey toward finding the perfect job, and had learned to survive by drawing on the skill-set I'd perfected in high school and college—looking as if I were paying attention while thinking about something fun.

Of course, cakes and cookies helped, too. I loaded my plate from the assortment on the refreshment table as everyone filed into L.A. Affairs' conference room. This was one of the many benefits I would continue to enjoy once I attained permanent, full-time status.

Vendors from our approved list provided us with scrumptious treats for our meetings at no charge, to keep reminding us how tasty their goods were so we'd keep booking them for events. While this wasn't illegal, it probably wasn't all that ethical—but, really, what did we care?

I helped myself to coffee from the refreshment table and headed for the chairs, which were set up theater style. At the front of the room was the podium. The video screen hadn't been pulled down from the ceiling, so there was still hope we could eat our snacks and get out fast, before this meeting cut into our lunch hour.

"Let's all be seated," Priscilla called, as she stepped up to the podium. "We have a great deal to cover today."

Priscilla didn't look as overwhelmed as when I'd stopped by her office earlier this morning. Obviously, my taking over Suzie's events in true superhero fashion had saved the day for her.

Damn. Wish I'd thought to wear a cape.

While my hard and fast rule on attending meetings was to sit in the back row—preferably behind a tall or large person where I could doze off as needed—I cut in front of two other girls and claimed the seat next to Eve, another of my L.A. Affairs' besties.

Eve knew all the office gossip—I mean, really, *all* of the office gossip—which made her my first choice in meeting buddies. Kayla sat down on the other side of me.

Everyone settled into a seat and the chatter died down. Priscilla started talking about some new vendors that had been added to our approved list. I popped a chocolate chip cookie into my mouth, and just as everything was starting to turn into blah-blah-blah, Kayla nudged me.

"This didn't take long," she whispered.

At the front of the room, Vanessa took over the podium. She was a little shorter than me and had black hair. Everything about Vanessa's appearance was perfect—her hair, her nails, her figure, her clothing, her styling—which was really irritating; if this were high school, I'd start rumors about her. Though she claimed she was only twenty-nine, I was willing to bet she'd made the turn into her thirties.

Vanessa began blabbing about her favorite subject—herself. As usual, she'd come up with another idea of how to better handle an event and felt compelled to share it with everyone—just as if we were interested. And, as usual, Vanessa had printed her suggestion on card stock—and included a photo of herself—that Priscilla was forced to hand out.

At this point, I drifted off.

I'd gotten a text from my best-friend-since-as-long-as-I-can-remember, Marcie Hanover, this morning. She'd been completely out of her mind over a new handbag she'd seen online—something I could totally understand.

While Marcie and I were different in appearance—she was blond and petite—we were in complete sync in our crazed devotion to designer handbags. We'd started a business selling knockoffs at purse parties that had brought in serious cash. Both of us were always on alert for the next "it" bag, and Marcie had definitely found one this morning.

I'd clicked on the link she'd sent and there before my eyes appeared the Sassy, the most gorgeous satchel I'd ever seen in to-die-for blue leather. My heart had actually started to beat faster at the sight. I absolutely had to have one—and I knew Marcie felt the same, which was why we were BFFs.

I munched on another chocolate chip cookie and let the Sassy satchel fill my mind as I mentally reviewed my wardrobe. A handbag in that particular shade of blue would look great with—wait. Hang on. The Sassy wouldn't go with anything I already owned. Oh, well. I'd just have to go shopping.

Just as I was visualizing Marcie and me hitting all our favorite stores, Kayla nudged me again.

"Yes, Haley has stepped up," Priscilla said, standing at the podium again, smiling and gesturing toward me.

Damn. She'd just announced how I'd saved the day by taking over Suzie's events and I'd missed my moment.

"Seriously?" Eve asked, as if she couldn't believe it. *"Seriously?"*

I glanced around. Everyone was staring at me. Wow, they all looked as if I was the office hero, all right.

"So," Priscilla continued, "see Haley if you have any questions."

She blabbed on for a few more minutes, then the meeting broke up. Everyone headed for the door.

"Haley?" Priscilla called, making her way toward me. "I'll bring Suzie's files to you as soon as possible."

"Great," I said, and couldn't help but note that all the other employees were eyeing me, envious, probably, that I'd beaten everyone else to Suzie's events.

"You know, Haley," a girl next to me said, "that new brand of pumpkin-flavored coffee creamer we just got is really good."

Okay, that was weird. But some people showed their adulation in odd ways.

"Thanks," I said, and smiled as the crowd funneled out the door of the conference room into the hallway.

I headed for my office—which I loved. It was my private sanctuary filled with neutral furniture and accented with splashes of blue and yellow. The best feature was the big window where I could stand and look out onto the Sepulveda and Ventura intersection, and the Sherman Oaks Galleria across the street.

One of the things I loved most about my office was that I didn't have to stay in it if I didn't want to. L.A. Affairs had no problem—at least not one that had been mentioned to me—with event planners spending vast amounts of time checking out venues, talking with clients, and coordinating with vendors in person. This, of course, made L.A. Affairs the perfect job for me and I saw no reason not to take full advantage of it.

I grabbed one of my event portfolios and my handbag, and left my office.

"Haley?" Mindy called as I passed her desk. "You know, I just love a fine-point pen."

Jeez, was she getting weirder all the time, or what?

"Good to know," I said, as I breezed out the door.

I took the elevator to the parking garage, got into my Honda, and headed east on Ventura Boulevard toward Studio City.

My biggest upcoming event—and my excuse for getting out of the office—was the high-profile fiftieth anniversary gala for Hollywood Haven, a retirement home for entertainers. The star-studded celebration would take place at the iconic Hollywood Roosevelt Hotel on Hollywood Boulevard, complete with a red carpet, dinner, dancing, and a salute to the Golden Age of Hollywood.

I'd been coordinating the event with the home's assistant director, Derrick Ellery, one of the few people in the place under the age of sixty. Luckily, Derrick was much younger than that—probably midthirties—and he'd been a dream to work with.

I drove into the parking lot and found a spot near the entrance. The Hollywood Haven property was huge, a sprawling complex that had been built in the sixties. The one-story building was laid out in a large U shape with a central courtyard and lush gardens, walking trails, and fountains fanning out in all directions. The building's dark wood and towering trees gave it a calm, restful feel.

The residents had all had careers in the entertainment field—singers, dancers, actors, playwrights, songwriters, screenwriters, circus performers, musicians, acrobats—really, just about everything imaginable. People who'd worked in related fields were also allowed to retire at Hollywood

Haven—talent agents, studio personnel, in-house attorneys, and production crew members.

I'd been there a half dozen times or so since I'd started planning the gala. Derrick and the rest of the staff were super nice, courteous, and easygoing. I'd met only a few of the residents, none of whom had much input on the event. Everything was rolling along smoothly with everyone at Hollywood Haven.

Still, something about the place gave me a weird vibe—which I ignored. The gala prep was going well. Derrick had loved everything I suggested. He hadn't fought me on anything or made any outrageous requests. And, really, all that mattered was that the event turned out great, regardless of my vibe antenna.

I gathered my things and walked in through the main entrance. The spacious lobby had thick carpeting, a massive chandelier, and a couple of comfy seating groups. Every area I'd seen so far at Hollywood Haven was immaculate and upscale—probably because the A-list stars whose donations helped keep the place running figured they might end up here one day and wanted it to look nice.

Karen, the receptionist, was at the front desk, a long counter sort of like the ones in a hotel lobby, talking on the phone. She'd seen fifty, easily, but was fighting it with regular visits to the hair salon to cover the gray—can't say that I blamed her. I was supposed to sign in, but since I'd been here so many times, I just smiled and waved. Karen smiled and waved back, and I headed down the hallway where the offices were located.

I had a number of things I needed to finalize with Derrick for the anniversary gala. Since Hollywood Haven was funded, in part, by big name celebrities who would be in attendance the night of the gala, I'd figured Derrick would be worried beyond all reason that there would be problems. Not so. Derrick was really cool about everything.

I paused outside his office door, gave it a quick knock, and pushed it open.

"Hi, Derrick," I said. "I just need to—"

But Derrick wasn't seated at his desk. He was lying on the floor beside it.

Derrick didn't seem so cool right now.

Derrick seemed dead.

Since this was a retirement home, finding someone dead wasn't an unusual occurrence, apparently. Karen had calmly picked up her telephone and started making calls when I'd gone to her and reported what I'd discovered.

But Derrick wasn't simply dead. He'd been murdered.

I hadn't mentioned that fact to Karen because the place was full of old people in precarious states of health, and I didn't want to be responsible for shocking any of them into a premature heart attack.

When I'd seen Derrick sprawled on the floor beside his desk, there was no missing the huge bloodstain that had soaked the front of his white shirt and saturated the beige carpet beneath him. I'd taken a quick look around his office, then pulled the door closed—careful not to touch the knob—and headed for Karen's reception desk in the lobby.

No way did I want to hang around while the police and the crime scene techs went about their jobs, so I headed outside. I had some quick thinking to do—which was so much easier if I had a Starbucks mocha Frappuccino, my favorite drink in the entire world—yet I had no choice but to push on with my brain cells functioning in as-is condition.

I followed one of the paths that led through the gardens at the front of the building and wound my way through the grounds. Behind me, the parking lot was crowded with official police vehicles. So far, I hadn't seen any of the residents hanging around to get a look at what was going on.

But, jeez, everybody here was old. Guess they'd already seen it all.

Under different circumstances, I'd use this opportunity to hunker down and spend some quality time doing an Internet search for the Sassy satchel that Marcie and I absolutely had to have, but all I could think about was my future.

This look-at-me-I'm-responsible thing was really weird.

What if—yikes!—somebody at L.A. Affairs learned that Derrick Ellery had been murdered, thereby possibly putting Hollywood Haven's fiftieth anniversary gala in jeopardy— along with my permanent, full-time employee status?

My life flashed in front of me—Priscilla downgrading my job performance, being told I'd have to wait months to be reevaluated, having to continue working at Holt's.

Oh my God. *Oh my God.* What would I do?

I drew in a breath to calm myself.

If word somehow reached L.A. Affairs, I'd have to downplay Derrick's role in the gala prep. That would be a total lie, of course, but what else could I do? Whatever it took, I was going to quit my job at Holt's.

My cell phone rang. I whipped it out of my handbag hoping it was Marcie—she's really good at calming me down—but I saw Karen's name on the caller ID screen instead.

"The detectives are looking for you," she said when I answered.

Wow, she sounded super calm. I figured this was the

same voice she used when ordering Chinese takeout. This whole finding-a-dead-body thing must be really routine for her.

I wondered if that was a category on her job performance evaluation. If so, she'd aced it.

"They want to talk to you," Karen said.

I was in no mood.

No way did I want to talk to homicide detectives right now. I'd done that in the past and they'd always had a way of rattling me with their suggestions that I'd done something wrong just because I'd found the victim. They'd pushed and prodded, made nasty remarks, turned on their cop we-think-you-did-it X-ray vision, and accused me of all kinds of things.

Still, I couldn't avoid talking to them. I had to do it. But nobody said I had to make it easy for them.

"I'll be right there," I said, and hung up.

I headed back through the gardens, mentally rehearsing how I'd deal with these detectives. One-word answers, for sure. Absolutely no volunteering information. I'd have to keep this interview short and to the point—no matter what they said or how they treated me.

As I approached the building's front entrance, two gray-haired, average-looking men dressed in can-I-keep-wearing-these-until-I-retire coats and ties stepped outside. Detectives, for sure. They spotted me and came down the steps.

"Miss Randolph?" one of them said.

"Yes," I said, and steeled myself for the verbal throwdown that was about to happen.

"I'm Detective Walker. This is my partner, Detective Teague," he said, and nodded to the man beside him. "You walked in on a bad scene, Miss Randolph. Are you all right?"

"Would you like to go inside?" Detective Teague asked. "Would you like to sit down?"

"Can we get you something to drink?" Detective Walker asked.

Okay, these two looked and acted like two sweet old grandpas, but no way was I falling for their tricks.

"No, thank you," I said.

"I understand you found the victim?" Detective Walker asked.

"Yes," I said.

He shook his head. "I'm so sorry you had to see that."

Detective Teague pulled a little notebook from his pocket. "If you don't mind, could I get your contact information?"

I gave it to him and he wrote it down.

"Now, can you tell us what happened?" he asked. "Do you feel up to it?"

Wow, these two were good. Attempting to lull me into a false sense of security, no doubt. But they weren't fooling me. I saw through their charade.

"When I arrived, Derrick's office door was ajar," I said. "I knocked, pushed it open, stepped inside, and saw him lying on the floor beside his desk. There was no one else in the room, no one climbing out the window. I backed out of the room and alerted the receptionist."

Detective Teague jotted down the info, then said, "Well, I guess that's it."

That's—what?

"We appreciate your help, Miss Randolph," Detective Walker said.

Wait. What was going on?

"Thank you for your cooperation," Detective Teague said.

That's all they were going to ask me? What the heck kind of detectives were they?

"I doubt we'll need anything more, Miss Randolph," he said, "but you never know."

"We'll contact you if we need to," Detective Walker said.

I mean, jeez, come on. I found the body. I was their prime witness. There were a zillion other things they could have asked me. But they were just going to let me leave? What kind of investigation were they running?

"Have a nice day," Detective Teague said.

Detective Walker nodded politely and they walked away.

I stood there feeling slightly miffed. Didn't these two realize how important I was? How could they have thrown me a few softball questions, then let the whole thing drop?

Of course, I'd held my own and not given them much of a chance to ask anything, but still. Maybe I was finally getting the hang of this whole cop-interview thing.

Since there was no use in going inside Hollywood Haven again, I decided to leave. My steps felt quicker and lighter as I headed for my car. Obviously, I'd have to make contact with someone else at Hollywood Haven regarding their anniversary gala, but for now there was nothing I could do.

Except, I realized, stop by Macy's—one of my all-time favorite stores—and see if they had a Sassy satchel in stock.

Oh, yeah, my day just got a lot better.

As I crossed the parking lot toward my car, my cell phone chimed. I pulled it from my handbag and saw that I had a text message from Shuman, an LAPD detective I'd known for a while now.

We'd been through a lot of stuff together—strictly professional, of course. Well, it was mostly professional.

Nothing romantic, though we'd seemed to share a come-hither attraction in the past that neither of us had acted on, except for that one time—long story.

I hadn't seen Shuman in a while, so I wondered why he was texting me. I accessed his message and read, **If you are contacted by homicide detectives DO NOT talk to them.**

Oh, crap.

CHAPTER 3

"This is b.s.," Bella said. "Serious b.s."

"Seriously?" I mumbled.

We were standing in line for the time clock in the break-room of Holt's Department Store along with several other employees, all of us waiting for our this-day-will-never-end shift to begin. Nearby were other employees helping themselves to snacks from the vending machines, heating up their dinner in the microwave, or staring blankly into space wondering where it had all gone so wrong.

Or maybe that was just me.

Had I really been snookered by those two old homicide detectives at Hollywood Haven today? I'd thought I was being so smart, controlling the interview, limiting myself to short, factual responses. But I realized that, after receiving Shuman's text message, apparently I'd been outmaneuvered.

What I still couldn't figure out was how he'd learned so quickly that I was involved in the murder of Derrick Ellery. I was glad he'd texted me, telling me not to talk to the cops, but it sure as heck would have been nice if his warning had gotten to me a few minutes sooner.

I'd texted Shuman back immediately—I'm not big on

suspense—and asked him what was going on. I hadn't heard from him yet.

Someone jostled me from behind and I realized the line was moving forward. I punched in my employee number and pressed my fingertip on the reader of the high-tech time clock, then followed Bella out of the breakroom.

Bella, chocolate to my vanilla, had been one of my Holt's BFFs since I started working here. She didn't like it here any better than I did—thus our BFF status.

Honestly, I wasn't cut out for customer service—unless I was the customer being serviced, of course. The Holt's merchandise was beyond hideous, even for a midrange department store, the customers actually wanted to be waited on, and the store management had certain standards they constantly pushed the salesclerks to maintain—for a lousy nine bucks an hour.

Bella had hung in there at Holt's for a good reason though—the pursuit of her dream career. She was saving for beauty school with the intention of one day becoming the hairdresser to the stars. In the meantime, she practiced different looks with her own hair.

I sensed that Bella was feeling restless, perhaps longing to somehow escape daily life, because tonight she'd sculpted her hair into the shape of a hot air balloon atop her head.

"Seriously," Bella grumbled. "That is seriously some serious b.s."

I'd been so consumed with my own thoughts I hadn't really been listening to Bella—which was bad of me, I know—but she didn't seem to notice.

"Suspicious activity," she said. "That's what they told me. But there's nothing suspicious about it. Somebody was out-and-out trying to charge stuff on my Visa account."

"Oh my God," I said. "Somebody hacked your account?"

"Tried to," Bella said. "But the Visa people didn't let the

charge go through. They blocked it, then called me and said somebody in Peru was trying to charge ten pairs of Levi's jeans on my card."

"That's suspicious, all right," I agreed.

"That's b.s.," she replied. "That's what it is—b.s."

"How did they get your Visa account number?" I asked.

"Beats me," Bella said. "And I had just paid that thing off. I don't want nothing else charged on it."

Bella had recently come into a large sum of money and had used it to pay off some bills, help out her nana, and add to her beauty school savings.

"Hey, where are you going?" Bella asked.

I stopped and realized that the other employees who'd clocked in with us weren't heading out to the sales floor.

"We got a meeting," Bella said. "Didn't you see the sign by the time clock?"

Two meetings in one day?

Now that was some serious b.s.

I moved along with the crowd through the hallway, past the store managers' offices, and into the training room. Rows of chairs were set up theater style. As per my personal policy, I headed for the back row. Luckily, that big guy who worked in menswear was already there, so I sat down behind him. Bella dropped into the chair beside me.

The main differences between the meetings at Holt's and those at L.A. Affairs were that at Holt's there were no tasty snacks to enjoy and, by comparison, everybody here dressed like crap—starting with Jeanette, the store manager.

She was already at the front of the room, peering over half-glasses at the index cards she'd prepared. Jeanette was well into her fifties. She'd been the store manager here for a long time, which meant that she made a huge salary—plus bonuses and other perks—and could afford to dress in really nice clothing. Instead, she always wore outfits straight off Holt's racks.

The clothing was dreadful, and Jeanette's cylinder-shaped body didn't do it any favors. Tonight she had on a neon pink dress.

She looked like the horizon at sundown—the entire horizon.

"First of all," Jeanette said, smiling and favoring us with a raise-the-roof hand wave. "Let's start off with some good news!"

All the employees froze—understandably so. Management's idea of good news was usually far different from that of the employees.

"I'm very excited to announce that the Holt's Department Store chain is acquiring another chain of stores!" Jeanette said.

I was pretty sure the same thoughts flashed in everyone's head: does that mean some of us are going to get transferred; will those employees be replaced in our store; will we all end up doing more work?

Jeanette might have answered some of those questions. I don't know. I drifted off.

Ty Cameron popped into my head. He was my ex-official boyfriend. He also ran the Holt's chain of stores, the fifth generation of his family to be obsessed with and consumed by running the business to the exclusion of all else. He was the latest in a long line of Camerons unable, apparently, to break the curse.

He was also incredibly handsome, I-don't-have-to-cheat-to-pass-tests smart, generous, considerate, loyal, and a terrific dresser. The only thing Ty wasn't good at was dating *me*.

Not that I'm difficult to get along with. I can roll with almost anything. But I do believe that a boyfriend should remember our dates, show up on time, and not spend the entire evening texting and phoning other people about problems at work.

We'd tried to iron out the wrinkles in our relationship, but in the end Ty had admitted he couldn't be the kind of boyfriend I wanted, so we broke up. I didn't fight him on it. I let it happen.

I've wondered since if that was my best move.

Ty and I had seen each other a few times since our breakup. It hadn't gone well. Neither of us seemed ready to move on to the let's-be-friends-now phase of a relationship. We were stuck in some weird kind of no-man's-land that we couldn't find our way out of.

I'd spoken with Ty's personal assistant, Amber, not long ago and she'd told me Ty had been working almost nonstop on acquiring another chain of stores to add to the Holt's retail empire. He'd already opened Wallace, plus Holt's International.

"More b.s.," Bella grumbled.

I realized then that everyone was rising from their chairs. Somehow, I'd missed the entire meeting. Maybe my evening was improving.

"Who ever heard of a Nuovo?" Bella asked.

My senses jumped to high alert. Oh my God. Something interesting had happened in a meeting and I'd missed it?

"What about Nuovo?" I asked, as we moved with the crowd out of the training room.

"That's the chain of stores Holt's is buying," Bella said, and shook her head. "I never heard of them."

"They're really upscale shops that carry designer fashions," I said.

"Figures," Bella said. "I can't afford anything there, even with our employee discount."

"Discount?" I asked. "We're getting an employee discount?"

Maybe I should start paying attention in meetings.

"Yeah, that's what Jeanette said," Bella told me.

Oh my God, I had to call Marcie immediately. We both loved those stores and—oh my God—they probably had Sassy satchels in stock and—oh my God—I could get one at a discount.

Now, absolutely nothing awful could happen to ruin my evening.

"Haley?" Jeanette called.

Obviously, it could.

Bella gave me an I'm-out-of-here eyebrow bob and took off.

I started walking faster—my mother was a former beauty queen and thank goodness I have her long pageant legs—and put real distance between Jeanette and me. I intended to lose her in the lingerie department, but a line of customers in the aisle at the checkout registers slowed my pace.

"Haley?" Jeanette called again. "Haley!"

I could have outmaneuvered her—I bobbed and weaved through a pack of customers with ease while never making eye contact—but it occurred to me that I might benefit from talking with Jeanette. I stopped and allowed her to catch up.

She was slightly out of breath, so I pushed ahead.

"That Nuovo acquisition sounds great," I said. "How much was our employee discount?"

Now her cheeks matched her bright pink dress. It wasn't a good look on her.

"Ten percent," Jeanette said, huffing and puffing.

At an average store, ten percent wouldn't be worth the gas to drive there. But at Nuovo, where designer clothing, shoes, and handbags ran into the hundreds and thousands of dollars, it meant a sizable savings—which could then be spent on other items in the store, of course.

"When will the acquisition be finalized so we can use our discount?" I asked.

"Soon," Jeanette managed to say between great heaving breaths.

"Great," I said, and turned to leave again.

"Haley," Jeanette said, using her store manager voice this time.

Jeanette knew that Ty and I had dated. Though she'd never said anything to me about it, she'd been compelled to cut me extra slack to ensure her own job security. I didn't, however, know whether word had reached her that Ty and I had broken up, so I didn't feel totally comfortable about how much I could get away with now.

Besides, I had two great reasons not to rock the Holt's employment boat: keeping my medical coverage for a few more weeks, and buying a Sassy satchel from Nuovo with my employee discount.

"I want you to take on new responsibilities," Jeanette told me.

I'd already blown my say-no-to-everything policy this morning at L.A. Affairs, and while that had worked out great, I wasn't about to push my luck.

"Sorry, Jeanette," I said. "I can't do that."

"The new duties will allow you to be off the sales floor for most of your shift," Jeanette said.

Okay, she had my attention.

"We're staffing up for the holidays. Thanksgiving is just weeks away and Christmas will be here before we know it," Jeanette said. "I want you to take on the new-employee orientation."

I'd suffered a paralyzing bout of brain-function zone-out during my own orientation, so I couldn't remember what had been covered. I wasn't really clear on all of the Holt's policies. I'd never done anything like this before, and I wasn't sure I was the best person for brand new employees to meet.

So what could I say but, "Sure, I'll do it."

"You'll be working with Lani," Jeanette said, and walked away before I had a chance to say anything, which was probably wise of her.

I headed toward housewares, the somebody-please-kill-me-now department I was assigned to tonight, thinking that doing the orientation might be fun. Maybe I could liven things up a bit for the new employees.

As I wound through the displays of vacuum cleaners, luggage, and small appliances, my cell phone in my pocket vibrated. We weren't supposed to have our phones on the sales floor, but oh, well. I ducked behind a rack of hanging pots and pans and checked my ID screen. It was Detective Shuman calling.

"About time," I said when I answered.

"Miss me?" he asked, and I heard playfulness in his voice.

"I texted you hours ago."

"And you've been thinking about me all this time?" Shuman asked.

"I've been annoyed with you all this time," I told him.

"Not what I was hoping for," he said, and chuckled, "but I'll take it."

I laughed, too. Shuman had that effect on me.

"So, are you psychic? Or did the Bat Signal flash a giant H in the sky over police headquarters today?" I asked. "How did you find out so fast that I was involved with another murder?"

"You're involved in a murder?" Shuman asked.

The playfulness was gone from his voice, which gave me a weird feeling.

"Your text message," I reminded him. "I shouldn't talk to homicide detectives. Remember?"

"What murder are you talking about?" he asked.

Since Shuman was a homicide detective he'd probably been through a really long, tough day investigating the worst sort of crimes imaginable—possibly several of them, since he was calling so late. I decided I could cut him some slack.

"That guy at Hollywood Haven," I explained. "Derrick Ellery. I was planning an event with him for the retirement home, and I found his body in his office today. He'd been murdered."

Shuman didn't say anything.

I didn't like the sound of the silence. All sorts of horrible thoughts jammed my head.

"That's what you texted me about, wasn't it?" I asked.

"No," Shuman said. "It was about your ex."

"*Ty?*"

A zillion horrible scenarios collided in my brain.

Oh my God. *Oh my God.* Something had happened to Ty. Something horrible. He'd been injured. Maimed. Disfigured. He was in a coma, on life support, clinging to life by a frayed thread. Or—oh my God—had Ty been murdered?

Ty might be dead? Dead? Gone? *Forever?*

And all this time we could have been together, enjoying our lives, having fun, and now he might be dead? All because I'd gone along with his stupid idea to break up?

My heart pounded. I felt light headed.

"What *happened*?"

"Take it easy," Shuman said.

"*Tell me!*"

"Ty's okay," Shuman said. "He's not injured or ill. It's nothing like that."

I gulped in big breaths. I had to calm down.

I don't really like being calm.

But, I reminded myself, this kind of thing had happened once before, not long ago. I'd gotten a call from the hospital in Palmdale with the news that Ty had been involved in a car accident. I'd panicked and rushed to the emergency room only to find him sitting in the waiting room with a scratch on his cheek.

I drew in another breath and let it out slowly. "Then what's this about?" I asked.

Shuman was quiet for a few seconds, then said, "Ty is a person of interest in a case I heard about."

A different sort of fear washed over me.

"What—what kind of case?"

"Homicide," Shuman said. "Ty might have murdered someone."

CHAPTER 4

"Are you ready to party?" Mindy shouted as I walked into the office.

I stopped in front of her desk. This morning I had on a totally awesome gray business suit that I'd paired with an equally awesome red Coach satchel. I could see how my fabulous taste in clothing might distract Mindy but, jeez, she should know I'm an employee and not a vendor or client.

Maybe we needed a security camera with facial recognition software for Mindy.

Or maybe some eyeglasses would do the trick.

"Morning, Mindy," I said. "It's me. Haley."

"Oh, Haley, it's you." Mindy giggled, then pursed her lips thoughtfully. "You know, a nice fine-tipped pen would really make my day fly by. I thought you should know."

I thought the tip of Mindy's pen was the least of her problems.

I forced a smile and headed for the breakroom.

When I walked in I saw three large pink boxes on the counter filled with a delightful selection of doughnuts, cinnamon rolls, and muffins—a please-keep-hiring-us gift from a vendor, no doubt. The room smelled like baked goodies and freshly brewed coffee. Everyone was crowded around the microwave, chatting and heating up the delicious looking bakery treats. What a great way to begin the day.

"We're almost out of paper plates, Haley," somebody called.

Everyone here was so nice, so considerate. Was this a great place to work, or what?

"No problem," I said. "I'll eat mine off a napkin."

I made my way to the coffeepot, prepared a cup—extra sugar and French vanilla flavoring to go along with the mega sweet theme of the morning—grabbed a doughnut from the box—chocolate, of course—and left.

Really, how can a day go badly when it started with a chocolate doughnut?

I found out when I walked into my office.

A tall stack of event portfolios sat in the middle of my desk. Where the heck had they come from?

I flipped open the one on top and saw that it was a birthday party Suzie had been handling. Then I remembered that Priscilla had said yesterday that she'd bring them to my office.

I stepped back and eyed the stack. Wow, I hadn't realized Suzie was juggling so many events. This was a lot—really a lot. Way more than I'd expected. How had she managed such a heavy workload while pregnant? Why had she even taken on so much? She must have been totally overwhelmed.

Suzie had probably forced herself into early labor just to get out of doing all these events.

I stowed my handbag and sipped my coffee. I'd have to hunker down, go through the portfolios, and get up to speed on every event—and I would, as soon as I attended to my more pressing matters.

As I moved Suzie's portfolios to my credenza, I noticed

a number of file folders at the bottom of the stack. Had Priscilla brought me those also?

I had no idea what they were all about, but I didn't have time to check them out now. I had a lot to do today.

I sat down at my desk and got started by checking Facebook, booking a pedi, and reading my horoscope while I ate my doughnut and finished my coffee. I was moving ahead with lunch plans and a possible shopping trip after work tonight with Marcie when my cell phone rang. My preprogramed **DO NOT ANSWER** flashed on the caller ID screen.

Yikes! My mom was calling.

I picked up my phone with two fingers and tossed it into my handbag.

My morning seemed to have taken an unpleasant turn. There was only one thing I could do.

I grabbed my handbag and an event portfolio and left.

A run of piano notes followed by voices raised in song greeted me as I walked through Hollywood Haven's front door and into the lobby. The music came from the hallway that led to the residents' wing of the facility. I'd been in that section of the building once, when I'd taken a wrong turn, and knew there was a large dayroom with a grand piano. Since the majority of the residents had been entertainers back in the day, it got a lot of use.

Karen stood behind the front desk and favored me with a big smile. "Good morning, Haley. Welcome! It's a great day, isn't it?"

Not exactly the greeting I expected, given that the assistant director had been murdered here only yesterday. But maybe she was trying to keep it light so as not to upset the elderly residents.

Probably not a bad idea.

I switched into I'm-pretending-to-be-concerned-about-you mode. "How is everybody holding up?" I asked.

"Great!" Karen said. She gestured toward the hallway leading to the residents' wing. "Can't you tell?"

I listened and realized that the residents were singing "Ding Dong! The Witch Is Dead."

I didn't need a weatherman to see which way the wind was blowing.

"I guess nobody is upset about Derrick's death," I said.

"Hardly." Karen rolled her eyes.

Sensing major gossip, I eased closer and said, "What's going on?"

Karen glanced around, then leaned in, confirmation that major gossip was in play.

"To put it mildly," she said, "Derrick Ellery was not well liked around here. Not at all."

This surprised me because Derrick had been terrific to work with the entire time I'd been planning the gala with him. Friendly, easygoing, agreeable, always pleasant. I'd never seen him in a bad mood.

"He seemed like such a nice guy," I said.

"Oh, no," Karen insisted. "In fact—"

She stopped and pulled back. "I really shouldn't say anything."

Damn. I hate it when somebody starts a big, juicy story, then quits. It's like being teased with a fabulous handbag in a department store display case only to be told they're out of stock.

Still, I wasn't willing to let this opportunity to hear some dirt pass me by, not without attempting a work-around.

"Have you heard anything from the police?" I asked. "Do they know what happened to Derrick, exactly?"

"Just that he was shot," Karen said.

I'd figured as much, after seeing the bloodstain on the front of his shirt yesterday.

"Do they have any suspects?" I asked.

"Not that I've heard. Those detectives took our security surveillance tapes," Karen said. "They took my sign-in log, too."

She hadn't been diligent about having all visitors sign in—myself being a prime example—so I doubted the detectives would glean much useful info from it; someone bent on murder wouldn't likely identify themselves on the log, anyway. But maybe the surveillance tape would reveal something.

"How about motive?" I asked.

Karen glanced around, then leaned in again and whispered, "As I said, Derrick Ellery wasn't liked around here. By anyone."

Wow. Karen thought someone here at Hollywood Haven had murdered Derrick? One of the elderly residents? That was hard to imagine.

But what about another staff member?

I was about to ease into this new line of gossip when Karen's phone rang. She reached for it and said to me, "You'll have to talk to Mr. Stewart, Derrick's boss, about the gala."

Mr. Stewart was the Hollywood Haven director. Derrick had mentioned him, but we'd never met.

I gave her a little wave as she answered the phone, then I headed down the hallway toward the offices. Only one office door in the hallway was closed and that was Derrick's, sealed shut with crime scene tape. Snippets of conversations drifted out of the other offices as I walked past. Business as usual, it seemed.

A little nameplate identified the office at the end of the

hallway as that of Mr. Stewart. The door stood open. I peered inside.

It was a roomy office with a large walnut desk fronted by two chairs, a seating area, and the usual cabinets and credenzas. Two huge windows offered a view of the lush grounds and let in lots of sunlight.

An old guy with a gray comb-over and bushy mustache sat behind the desk. He could have been mistaken for one of the residents if it weren't for the dapper three-piece suit he wore. Still, he kind of looked like he'd recently been brought back to life by a jolt of electricity.

"Mr. Stewart?" I called as I stepped inside. "I'm Haley Randolph from L.A. Affairs."

He waved me off with both hands. "This isn't a good time, miss," he said, shaking his head. "I'm not interested in buying anything today."

"I'm your event planner," I said, and held up the portfolio with the L.A. Affairs logo on the front. "I've been working with Derrick on the gala."

"Well, Derrick is no longer available," he said.

Obviously, this guy didn't know I'd found the body. I guess he was a little out of the loop.

"I know," I said. "I need to find out from you who I'll be working with now."

"On what?"

"The gala," I said.

"What gala?"

Okay, maybe he was *way* out of the loop.

"The fiftieth anniversary gala," I said.

Mr. Stewart huffed. "We'll have to cancel that."

Cancel? *Cancel?* No way. I couldn't let the gala be canceled. Not with my job performance review almost here. I had to get full-time, permanent employee status *now*. I was turning twenty-five soon. That meant my life was half over. I couldn't wait any longer.

Besides, I was *this close* to quitting my job at Holt's.

"The gala can't be canceled," I told him.

"I have no time to deal with a gala. I'm swamped here," Mr. Stewart said, gesturing around him.

Nothing but office equipment was on his desk—absolutely nothing. No lines were lit up on his phone. No one was in the office with him. His computer wasn't even turned on.

"There's simply too much going on," he insisted.

I was ready to go over the desk after him like an Olympic gymnast, but I forced myself to sit in one of the chairs instead.

"Actually, everything for the gala is already set," I said.

"It is?" he asked.

"Sure," I said.

Okay, that was a lie, but only a partial lie. What else could I say?

"And we have to think about the Hollywood Haven supporters. The celebrities, the directors, the producers," I pointed out. "They've all arranged their schedules to attend the gala. We don't want to offend them by canceling, especially at this late date."

Mr. Stewart sank into thought. His shoulders slouched, his chin dropped, his face crumpled. He looked like a partially inflated Mylar balloon.

After several minutes he shook his head and said, "But how is it going to look? A gala after a murder on the premises?"

"That won't be an issue," I told him.

Another lie, of course, this one a total lie. But I had a lot at stake here.

"The murder will be solved and forgotten long before

the night of the gala," I said, dismissing the issue with a flick of my wrist. "The detectives will have it wrapped up in no time."

His frown lessened a bit. "Do you think so?" he asked.

"From what I hear it's practically an open-and-shut case," I said.

This wasn't completely untrue. Karen had seemed confident that the murderer was someone who lived or worked right here at Hollywood Haven. That was close to open-and-shut, right?

"Well, it might be acceptable to go ahead with the gala if you think the police can conclude this case quickly," Mr. Stewart said.

"I'm sure they can," I told him.

He ruminated another minute, then said, "If that's true, if they really can get this thing over and done with, then we'll go ahead."

"No problem," I said.

And this was no lie. Because if the cops couldn't discover who the murderer was, I'd do it myself.

CHAPTER 5

This whole thing about Ty being a person of interest in a murder case had been stuck in the back of my brain like a clearance tag on a house-brand handbag ever since I talked to Shuman last night. He'd refused to go into detail—I hate it when someone does that—and had insisted we speak in person.

I'd had no choice but to agree.

I hate that, too.

Even though I should have gone back to the L.A. Affairs office after leaving Hollywood Haven—it was almost noon and I didn't want to miss my lunch hour—I left my car in the parking garage, crossed Ventura Boulevard, and climbed the stairs to the fountain plaza at the Sherman Oaks Galleria.

The Galleria was an open-air shopping center that boasted lots of restaurants, entertainment, stores, and office space. It also had my all-time favorite place, Starbucks.

I spotted Shuman standing near one of their outdoor tables along restaurant row. We'd never been romantically involved—officially or unofficially—but there was something between us, something beyond friendship.

Seeing Shuman always sent that little jolt of *something*

through me. He was several years older than me, a little taller with dark hair, handsome in a guy-next-door kind of way. He had on his usual detective attire, a slightly mismatched sport coat, shirt, and tie.

His cell phone was at his ear and he was pacing back and forth. At first I thought he was in serious-cop mode, then he turned my way and I saw a big goofy grin on his face.

I knew what that meant.

Shuman spotted me, then whipped around and spoke into his phone. He ended the call and turned toward me again.

"Who is she?" I asked.

He tried to swallow his grin, but it got goofier instead. "Brittany," he said. "We've been seeing each other."

"Cool," I said, and I really meant it.

Shuman had been through a great deal of emotional turmoil and I was glad he was seeing someone and his life was getting back to normal.

"Tell me about her," I said.

"You'll meet her," Shuman promised.

I was feeling a little possessive of Shuman all of a sudden. Who, exactly, was this Brittany chick? I needed to check her out. No way was I going to stand by and let Shuman be hurt by her.

"I'd better," I told him.

He pulled out a chair for me at the table. My all-time favorite drink in the entire universe was waiting for me, a mocha Frappuccino. Shuman had gotten a coffee for himself. We sat down.

I took a long sip of my Frappie to fortify my brain cells.

"Ty didn't murder anyone," I said. "He wouldn't do that. I know him. He absolutely would not kill someone."

Shuman didn't respond. I'm sure he'd heard those same

words from countless friends and family members, many of whom turned out to be wrong about an accused murderer.

"Circumstances get the best of people, at times," Shuman said. "Under the right amount of pressure, uncontrollable rage or fear, a lot of people would do the unthinkable."

I couldn't argue with that, though I still couldn't imagine Ty being one of those people.

"What's this all about?" I asked.

"Are you on your lunch hour?" Shuman asked.

"Taking care of company business," I explained.

I could see my office building from here. That counted, didn't it?

Then I wondered if something else was going on.

What about Shuman? Was this strictly a social call? A heads-up between friends? Or something more.

He seemed to read my thoughts. "It's not my case," he said.

That made me feel a little better. Still, I knew I had to be careful about what I said. Shuman was, after all, a homicide detective. I didn't want this to be an occasion where our friendship ended and his official duties began.

"What do you know about Ty's involvement with someone living in Palmdale?" Shuman asked.

Palmdale was a city in the Antelope Valley, about an hour north of L.A. in the high desert. It was a great family community, big on aerospace and green industries. I'd gone there to the air show at Edwards Air Force Base with my dad, an engineer, several times growing up.

"Nothing," I said. "Ty never mentioned knowing anyone who lived there. If he had a friend in that area, I wasn't aware of it."

"Ty was involved in a traffic accident en route to Palmdale not long ago," Shuman said. "Did he tell you about it?"

"Someone in the ER phoned me after it happened," I said. "Ty wanted me to pick him up."

"Did he tell you why he was headed there?"

"He was thinking of opening a Holt's store in the area," I said.

"Did you believe him?"

No, not for a minute.

"Ty's always opening new stores," I said, which was true but didn't answer the question.

Shuman paused. I could tell by his expression that he was mentally debating where to go next with this conversation. It was a cop move, and it made me suspicious of his motives again.

"Did you know Ty rented a car for the drive to Palmdale?" Shuman asked.

I frowned my I'm-trying-to-remember frown, but the details of that day and those that followed were imbedded in my brain.

"I think it was mentioned later," I said. "Something to do with the insurance claim."

"He owns a Porsche. Why did he drive a rental?" Shuman asked.

I'd wondered the same thing.

"He was scouting store locations. Maybe he didn't want to attract attention," I said.

Shuman didn't look convinced.

I couldn't blame him. I hadn't been either.

"Did Ty seem odd after the accident?" Shuman asked. "You know, different somehow?"

Everything about Ty had been different after that. But no way was I getting into all of it with Shuman.

"He took a few days off work, which was unusual for him," I said.

This conversation was getting uncomfortable for me. I decided I needed to move it in another direction.

"So what's this all about?" I asked. "Who was murdered, and why is Ty supposedly involved?"

Shuman hesitated. As with most every detective, he didn't like giving up information. But we'd helped each other out with cases in the past—plus, no way would he think I'd have shared this info about Ty without getting something in return—so I knew he wouldn't hold out on me.

I sipped my Frappie and waited.

"Kelvin Davis. Remember him?" Shuman finally said. "White-collar criminal."

"That hotshot financial guy here in L.A. who bilked his investors out of millions of dollars," I said. "It was all over the news for ages. I remember my parents talking about him."

Actually, my folks had railed on and on about Kelvin Davis for weeks. His investment firm had promised—and delivered, for a while, anyway—huge profits in what turned out to be a multimillion-dollar pyramid scheme. When the whole thing collapsed, hundreds of people ended up losing tons of money, some of them their life savings. Fortunately, my parents hadn't invested with Kelvin Davis, but a number of their friends had.

"That was, what, seven or eight years ago?" I asked.

"Davis was arrested, then skipped out on his bail. Left the country, supposedly. Nobody could find him," Shuman said. "Until a couple of days ago, that is. He turned up dead in an abandoned house in Palmdale. Shot multiple times. His body had been there for weeks before it was discovered."

"There must be a zillion people who lost money because of him and wanted him dead," I said. "What's Ty got to do with this?"

"Ty's name and phone number were found on a slip of paper at the crime scene," Shuman said.

"So? That doesn't mean—"

"It was clutched in Davis's hand."

"Okay, but—"

"The note had Ty's fingerprints on it."

Oh, crap.

My office phone rang. I saw Mindy's name on the ID screen and braced myself.

"Yes, Mindy?" I said when I picked up.

"Haley? Hello? Hello?"

"It's Haley," I said.

"Haley? Is that you?" Mindy asked.

"What is it?" I asked.

"What's what?"

"Do you need something?" I asked, and made sure to say it slowly.

"How did you know? Oh, Haley, you're so smart," Mindy said, and chuckled.

"You called me," I said.

"Oh! Oh, yes, of course," she said. "Let me look. I know I have that here somewhere. One of your clients just arrived. Her name is . . . huh, I know I wrote that down. Oh, yes, here it is. Her name is Ralonda. No. It's Lamonda. Oh, that's not right. It's—"

There's only so much I can take.

"Which room is she in?" I asked.

"Oh, yes. She's in interview room four—no, three. I put her in three. Yes, it's three. Only . . . no, I think it's four. Or maybe it's—"

I hung up.

I wasn't working on an event for anyone named anything remotely similar to Ralonda or Lamonda, so I went to the

stack of Suzie's event portfolios and found one under the
name Laronda Bain. I grabbed it and headed down the
hallway.

As I passed the ladies' restroom Heidi, one of the senior
planners, walked out.

"A light has burned out in there, Haley," she said.

Like I cared?

Honestly, I wasn't in the best of moods after my meeting
with Shuman earlier today.

"Thanks," I managed, and turned down the hallway
where the interview rooms were located.

All of L.A. Affairs' interview rooms were set up with a
desk and two visitor chairs; conference rooms were available for large groups. The furnishings were upscale, chic,
and sophisticated—as were our clients.

Only one of the interview rooms was occupied—room
number two.

"Ms. Bain?" I said, as I walked in and introduced myself.

"Hello," she responded.

Laronda Bain was somewhere in her thirties, I figured. She
had blond hair—with a Beverly Hills blowout, obviously—
had on a YSL dress, Louboutin pumps, and carried a Birkin
satchel. She weighed about one hundred pounds—fifteen of
which seemed to be in her Botox-filled face.

Figure skaters could hold their US Nationals on her
forehead.

That whole thing with Ty and Kelvin Davis's murder in
Palmdale weighed heavily on my mind. But since I desperately needed to ace my upcoming job performance review,
I forced it aside and put on my best look-at-me-I'm-super-
competent expression, which I executed perfectly without
the benefit of Botox.

"I'm handling your event," I said, and sat down behind

the desk. "Suzie took maternity leave a little sooner than anticipated."

"I realize that," Laronda told me

She might have been anywhere from upset to angry to horrified to panicked. Since her face wouldn't move, I couldn't be sure.

"When I phoned the office and learned the news, I rushed over," Laronda said. "I absolutely must have your assurance that a change in planners isn't going to adversely affect my son's birthday party. Are you aware of all the details of the event?"

"Of course," I told her.

Okay, really, I hadn't looked through her portfolio yet. But, jeez, it was a kid's birthday party. How complicated could it be?

Just to show her that I was on top of everything, I opened the portfolio and did a quick scan of the plans for the party.

"You're doing a Harry Potter theme," I said.

I wasn't sure if Laronda smiled, but she definitely nodded.

I flipped through the file and studied several random pages to demonstrate my attentiveness to her event while hoping my eyes wouldn't glaze over. Eight thousand bucks to entertain kids in the backyard of a mansion in Calabasas for an afternoon. Just your typical party for an eight-year-old.

"I've decided to add a feature," Laronda said. "Hogwarts Academy. Life size, so the children can play in it."

She considered this a *feature*? Everything was all set and she springs this on me *now*?

How the heck was I going to pull this off—in time for the party?

I gave her my nothing-rattles-us-here-at-L.A.-Affairs smile—I'm pretty sure there's a box for that on the employee job performance review—and said, "No problem."

"Very good," she said, and left.

I went back to my office and phoned Lyle, the guy who did construction projects for our events. He said he'd have to see what he could work out. It didn't sound promising.

The rest of the afternoon passed in a blur of attempting to review Suzie's events. My mom called twice—I didn't answer either time—then one of the other assistant planners sent me a really annoying e-mail about her printer paper, and Marcie texted to say she hadn't been able to locate Sassy satchels for us.

Five o'clock finally rolled around. I got my handbag and left. Thankfully, I wasn't scheduled for a shift at Holt's tonight.

As if I hadn't dealt with enough problems already today, I absolutely could not stop thinking about Ty.

No way would he have killed someone—despite what Shuman had said about snapping under duress. It wasn't something Ty would do.

Still, he'd lied to me about some of the things that had happened the day of, and following, his car accident.

That wasn't like him either.

So was it possible—remotely possible—that Ty had murdered Kelvin Davis at that abandoned house in Palmdale?

The idea played around in my head.

Technically, most anything was possible. But I didn't like being caught in a possibly-maybe-hypothetical mental loop. I needed facts—even if I didn't like what I'd have to do to get them.

Chapter 6

Even though I'd assured Mr. Stewart that everything for Hollywood Haven's fiftieth anniversary gala had been handled, that wasn't the complete truth.

The planning for an event, especially one of this magnitude, started months in advance. The big items were secured first—venue, caterer, florist, that sort of thing—while others were arranged and accomplished as the planning went forward and the event drew nearer.

There were always things to take care of, even on the day of the event, which was why I was at Hollywood Haven the next morning. I needed Mr. Stewart's input on a few things and his okay to move ahead with them.

Karen wasn't at the front desk when I walked in—no sign of a sign-in log to replace the one Detectives Walker and Teague took into evidence—so I headed down the hallway where the offices were located. Crime scene tape was still stretched over Derrick Ellery's door, and I wondered how much progress the detectives had made in the case.

Voices drifted out of Mr. Stewart's office at the end of the hallway as I approached. I stopped in the doorway and saw him seated at his desk. Two men and a woman, all of them probably on the upswing to sixty and dressed in business attire, were standing over him, talking at once.

This was no pleasant chitchat among friends.

The woman spotted me. "Yes?" she demanded, loud enough to get everyone's attention.

The others quieted and glared at me.

Mr. Stewart looked frazzled and slightly disheveled. Unlike yesterday, his desk was piled high with file folders, printouts, and binders.

Had I picked a bad time to show up, or what?

"Miss Randolph," Mr. Stewart said, and looked relieved that I'd broken the momentum of the group. He glanced at the others and said, "She's handling our anniversary gala."

"Hello," I said, and held up my L.A. Affairs portfolio.

They mumbled a greeting.

"If this is a bad time, I can come back later," I said.

I almost wished he'd ask me to leave. There was a majorly bad vibe in the room.

"No, no," Mr. Stewart said, and shot out of his chair. He cupped my elbow and moved us into the hallway.

"Tough crowd?" I asked, and nodded toward his office.

Mr. Stewart drew himself up and straightened his shoulders.

"Our transition is understandably bumpy, as you can imagine," he said. "Derrick handled so very many aspects of the running of our care facility. All of us—the entire staff, in fact—are now juggling responsibilities and sharing duties until his replacement can be named."

"Who should I speak with about the gala?" I asked, and mentally crossed my fingers that my contact person wouldn't be anyone I'd just seen inside his office.

"I've turned that entire matter over to Rosalind Fletcher. She's our acting assistant director," Mr. Stewart said.

"Is she inside your office?" I asked.

"No. No, she's not," he said.

I was relieved I'd dodged that potential problem. But I couldn't help but wonder if this Rosalind Fletcher's temp promotion had something to do with the fracas I'd walked in on.

"As I've already mentioned, dealing with the anniversary gala isn't high on anyone's priority list, and there's concern about how it will look if we go ahead with it," Mr. Stewart said. "If it's too much for Rosalind to handle, given her additional workload, we'll have to cancel."

"It won't be," I said. "I'll make sure of it."

Mr. Stewart frowned and said, "Well, we'll have to see about that. Now, if you'll excuse me?"

He stepped back into his office and the contentious conversation started up again.

This was the second time Mr. Stewart had threatened to cancel the gala. Obviously, I was going to have to take matters into my own hands.

Karen had told me she strongly suspected Derrick's murderer was someone who worked or lived at Hollywood Haven. That meant I needed to find a person who could give me the inside info on everything that was going on here.

I'd worked for enough corporations to know where the heart of any organization lay, so I headed back down the hallway to an office I'd noticed earlier, the one with the little plaque that read, VIDA WEBSTER, HUMAN RESOURCES, on the wall beside the door. I stepped inside.

This was a two-person setup, with a receptionist desk near the door—which was empty at the moment—and an inner office that was larger. A woman was seated at the desk.

"Vida?" I called as I walked to the doorway of her office. I glanced at her nameplate and saw that I'd guessed correctly.

She looked up from the file folder she was reading and gazed at me over the top of her half glasses. "Can I help you?" she asked.

Even seated I could see that Vida Webster was short and a little on the full-figured side. She wore her black hair sculpted into the shape of a football helmet. The buttons on her peach-colored business suit pulled a little, and I knew without looking that she was wearing sensible pumps.

I introduced myself and held up my L.A. Affairs portfolio—which I was starting to think of as my Captain America shield—and dropped into the chair in front of her desk at her invitation.

"I was just in Mr. Stewart's office discussing the fiftieth anniversary gala," I said, "and, honestly, I have some concerns about going ahead with the event in light of Derrick Ellery's death."

Okay, that was a total lie, but I was in a tight spot. Something drastic had to happen if I was going to solve this murder and keep the gala moving forward.

I leaned in a little and said, "I know that in your position as head of Human Resources you're aware of what's really going on with the employees. So I'd like to get your thoughts on the gala."

Vida stared at me, her eyes wide, her lips pursed. She didn't move. For a moment, I thought all her joints had locked up, or something.

"I mean, who would know better than you?" I added, thinking that an extra dose of flattery might thaw her a little.

After another long moment, Vida snapped out of her stupor.

"Yes, of course you'd come to me. And I appreciate your

consulting me on this issue," she said. "I see no reason to cancel the gala because of Derrick Ellery, of all people."

Okay, now we were getting somewhere.

"I understand he wasn't well liked here," I said.

"Not well liked, indeed," Vida said, shaking her head.

Everyone who worked in HR had to take some sort of oath of silence, or something, and promise to keep everything they learned about employees to themselves. No gossiping was allowed, which, to me, made this a totally boring department to work in. But since Derrick Ellery was dead now, I figured Vida had freed herself from this commitment and was ready to dish the dirt.

"Derrick overstepped himself," Vida told me. "He didn't follow established policy and had no regard for proper procedures."

Since I'm not big on following policy or proper procedures, I didn't think I'd stumbled over a motive for murder. Still, Vida was definitely wound up about the whole thing, and I'd found that this was the best time to get information from someone—strictly in the line of duty, of course.

"In all my twenty years working here I've never had to deal with anyone like him," Vida declared. "Why, the way he carried on. The things he did. The way he treated people."

She was on a roll now. I got the feeling she'd been holding all of this in for a long time. I didn't interrupt her.

"His conduct was disgraceful. Indiscriminately firing people for the most minor of infractions," Vida said.

My maybe-this-is-a-clue senses jumped to high alert.

"Derrick fired people for little or no reason?" I asked. "Who?"

"Karen, of all people," Vida muttered. "It was outrageous."

Okay, now I was confused.

"Derrick fired Karen? Karen, the receptionist?" I asked.

"He wanted to," Vida told me. "She was on his list—in fact, she was next on his list. He told me so."

"What had Karen done?"

"He was arrogant and insolent. Overbearing," she said. "This is what happens when proper procedures aren't followed. I know. I've worked here for years. But Mr. Stewart was anxious to fill the position."

"Why did he want to fire Karen—"

"It's never good to rush in to making a decision of that magnitude. Never. I tried to explain that to Mr. Stewart, but I was overruled," Vida said. "And look, just look at what it's led to."

"So, back to Karen—"

"I've worked here for years—*years*. I know what can happen."

First, I couldn't get Vida to talk. Now, I couldn't get her to shut up.

"Did Karen know Derrick wanted to fire her?" I asked.

Vida sat with her eyes narrowed and her lips pinched, lost in thought for another minute, then said, "Someone must have told her. I have no idea who it might have been. Word always gets out, no matter how hard we try to keep personnel issues confidential."

At this point, I'd had all of Vida I could take. But she'd given me my first murder suspect.

I thanked her and left her office, remembering when I'd arrived at Hollywood Haven the day of Derrick's murder. Karen had been at the front desk. But I had no way of knowing how long she'd been at her post. She could have slipped down the hall, into Derrick's office, and murdered him minutes before I arrived.

Karen hadn't been upset when I'd told her I'd discovered the body. In fact, she acted as if it were a routine matter. Did she already know he was dead? Had she shot him in his office because she'd found out he wanted to fire her?

The prospect of losing your job wasn't the greatest motive for murder, but I could see it happening.

Of course, I only had Vida's word that Derrick had planned to get rid of Karen and she'd seemed really eager to throw Karen out as a suspect. Too eager?

It made me wonder if something else was going on.

CHAPTER 7

I really could have used a mocha Frappuccino right now, but I had to push through. I headed back down the hallway checking out the nameplates until I spotted one that read ROSALIND FLETCHER, OFFICE MANAGER.

Inside, I saw another two-office arrangement. A tiny gray-haired lady who looked as if she were a resident who'd wandered in sat at the receptionist's desk.

Jeez, I really hoped that wasn't Rosalind. No way would the gala go forward if she was in charge.

"I'm looking for Rosalind," I said.

"Outside, dearie. On the patio off the dayroom. You'll see her there," she said, and pointed in the completely wrong direction.

I had no idea what Rosalind looked like and since most everybody I'd seen here at Hollywood Haven looked pretty much the same, I didn't bother to ask.

I hoofed it back through the hallway to the lobby—Karen wasn't there—and turned down the corridor that led to the residents' wing.

I stopped at the entrance to the dayroom, a huge space filled with several comfortable seating groups, televisions, card tables, and a grand piano. There was a table with a half-finished jigsaw puzzle, a large shelving unit full of books, and a bulletin board with fliers pinned to it. One wall was all glass, providing a gorgeous view of the spacious patio and the beautifully landscaped grounds.

About a dozen elderly residents sat around the dayroom, some playing cards, others watching TV or reading, a few sitting alone. A stoop-shouldered man was at the piano playing a song I didn't recognize.

Three women standing nearby must have seen the I'm-kind-of-lost look on my face, because they walked over. They were all thin, easily approaching seventy. But they were still rocking the fashions. Their hair was done—except for one who wore a turban—and two of them wore citrus-colored capris and tops, the other a caftan. They'd loaded themselves down with jewelry.

"What do you need, honey, what do you need?" The lady in the caftan and turban fluttered her fingers against her neck. "I'm Delores, honey. Tell me what you need."

"I'm looking for Rosalind—"

"Who?" another of them asked.

"That's Trudy," Delores explained.

"Rosalind," the third one repeated in a loud voice. "She says she's looking for Rosalind."

"And that's Shana," Delores said.

"I can't hear anything with all that racket," Trudy said, and made a rude gesture at the pianist. "He thinks he's Billy Barnes."

"He's no Billy Barnes," Shana agreed.

"Billy was a genius," Trudy said. "A genius."

"So what do you need Rosalind for?" Delores asked.

"I'm the event planner for the anniversary gala," I said, and introduced myself.

"Oh, the gala," Shana declared. "We're so excited about the gala."

"I can't decide what to wear," Trudy said.

"Everybody's excited about the gala," Delores told me. "So what do you need Rosalind for, honey? What's she got to do with the gala?"

"She's the acting assistant director now that Derrick is . . . gone," I said.

"And good riddance," Trudy declared.

"Amen to that," Shana agreed.

Delores edged closer and glanced at the event portfolio I was clutching.

"So what is it, honey?" she asked. "You need something? You need help with the planning? We can help."

"We're good at this sort of thing," Shana said. "We all worked production for years. All the major studios. You need help with a project? We're your gals."

This was the most enthusiastic bunch I'd met here at Hollywood Haven since Derrick's murder. The ladies seemed to be in pretty good physical shape and were thinking clearly. I didn't want to turn something over to them, but I didn't want to hurt their feelings either.

"Swag bags," I said, picking the easiest thing I could think of. "I need ideas for swag bags for the presenters at the gala."

Shana flung out both arms. "We got this," she announced.

The other two nodded in agreement.

"Don't give it another thought," Trudy said. "We'll put our heads together and come up with a great list."

I just hoped that list wouldn't include Beta VCRs and Bartles & Jaymes Orange Sunset wine coolers.

"Let's go, girls. We've got a lot of work to do," Delores said, and they hurried away.

I got a weird feeling as I watched them disappear down the hallway that led to the residents' living quarters. Sort of happy and sad at the same time.

I crossed the dayroom and went outside onto the patio. Wrought iron and wicker tables and chairs were set up, surrounded by shrubs, potted palms, and planters of blooming flowers. Several of the residents sat enjoying the mild November sun, more made their way along the walking trails that spread across the grounds.

I didn't spot anyone who looked as if she might be Rosalind. I was debating whether to ask someone to point her out to me or to just leave—I mean, jeez, I'd already spent a huge chunk of my morning doing actual work—when an elderly man ambled over.

"Greetings," he said, with a wide, easy smile.

"Hello," I said, and couldn't help smiling back.

He'd probably been a little taller than me decades ago, but now he was shrunken, a little stoop shouldered. He was thin, frail, with what was left of his dark hair combed over his shiny bald spot. He had on a slightly rumpled shirt and a sport coat.

"It's a beautiful day, and your presence has made it more beautiful," he announced. "A beautiful girl should have beautiful things."

With a flourish, he presented me with a small arrangement of artificial flowers that seemed to magically appear—except that I'd seen him pull it from the sleeve of his jacket.

"Thank you," I said, taking the flowers. "They're lovely."

"As are you, my dear," he said, and bowed slightly. "A gift for you from Alden the Great."

A woman joined us. She was fortyish, tall and thin with dark hair, and dressed in casual pants and a sweater.

"He's a magician," she said.

"She knows, sweetie," he said. "Everybody knows who I am. I'm opening tonight at the Stardust. It's all over town."

"Yes, Dad, it is," she said, and patted his arm. She turned to me. "I'm Emily Kerwin."

I introduced myself.

"You've seen me on the billboards, haven't you?" Alden asked.

Emily forced a brave smile. My heart broke a little.

"Yes," I said. "And on the big sign out front."

Alden beamed. "It's going to be a hell of a show."

"I'm sure it is," I said.

"You bet. Oh, hey, is that Dean and Sammy over there? Excuse me, girls." Alden headed toward a table at the edge of the patio where two men sat.

Emily watched him go, then sighed and turned to me.

"Thank you," she said. "The doctors told me to just go along with whatever he's saying, unless it's harmful, of course. Otherwise, he gets more confused, more upset."

My heart went out to her. It couldn't be easy dealing with someone in his condition, and even more difficult if it was your father.

"Was he really a magician?" I asked.

"Alden the Great." Emily smiled with pride. "He played all the big clubs. Vegas, New York, Chicago, Miami. The magic is the one thing he can still remember."

"Must be tough on you," I said.

Emily nodded. "They take good care of him here. Are you visiting someone?"

"I'm the event planner for the anniversary gala," I said.

"Do you work here?" she asked.

"No, I'm with L.A. Affairs," I explained.

"You're not here every day?" she asked.

"I stop by when something comes up about the gala."

Emily was quiet for a while, then asked, "They're still having it? They're not canceling because of Derrick's murder, are they?"

"It's going forward," I assured her.

"So you'll come back often?" she asked.

"As often as it takes," I said.

Emily seemed anxious to talk, so I decided this might be a good time to get some info on the murder.

"Did you know Derrick?" I asked.

"Everybody knew Derrick. He was very friendly with the residents," Emily said, then added, "Too friendly, if you ask me."

"How so?"

"I guess he thought he was being helpful, but he seemed more nosy than anything." She sighed. "Some of the residents don't have family who visit regularly and watch out for them. You know, there's no one to take care of their doctor appointments, their personal business, or brighten up the holidays."

I glanced around at the residents who were seated alone and wondered how long it had been since someone visited them.

Not a great feeling.

"It's worrisome to see how—"

Emily stopped as her gaze zeroed in on her dad trundling down one of the garden paths alone.

"Excuse me, Haley," she said, and hurried after him.

The future flashed in my head. Would my mom and dad end up in a place like this? Would I?

Yikes! No way did I want to think about that.

In fact, I didn't want to think about the gala anymore either. I headed back inside.

I still had to find Rosalind and finalize a few things, but I'd do that later. There was still time.

I crossed the dayroom and was headed down the hallway toward the lobby when I spotted a very frail-looking elderly lady with white hair, wearing a floral print mumu and seated in a wheelchair. Pushing it was a woman in her late forties, dressed in jeans and a T-shirt. I could see a family resemblance. Mother-daughter, I figured.

The mom sat stoically, staring off at nothing. The daughter bent over her shoulder, complaining about something.

I guess not all family visits were good ones.

Yeah, I'd definitely had enough of Hollywood Haven for one day.

But at least I'd discovered one possible murder suspect, plus a few I-wonder-who-they-are others.

Vida Webster had been quick to point out Karen's impending firing. She'd also mentioned other workers whom Derrick had let go for minor rule infractions. I didn't know who those people were, but I knew someone who might be able to tell me.

I passed the reception desk—still no Karen—and left the building. I jumped in my car and headed down Ventura Boulevard, then swung into the first Starbucks drive-through I came to.

I ordered a mocha Frappuccino—I definitely needed a *venti* right now—and took care of my most unpleasant task while I waited in line.

My mom had tried to reach me several times but I hadn't answered her calls. Really, there was no rush. If there'd been an actual family emergency someone other than Mom would have called me.

Mom's a former beauty queen. Really. She's not great in a crisis. Believe me, she's the last person you'd want to depend on if something major went down.

I couldn't put off contacting her any longer—yet I knew how to do it without actually talking to her. Right now, at this very moment, was Mom's standing appointment with her hairdresser. No way would she answer—even if it was a real family emergency.

I pulled out my cell phone and called her. When her voicemail picked up I left a quick message.

I inched forward in line and called Detective Shuman. I figured that if anybody could root out the names of the Hollywood Haven employees that Vida had mentioned, whom Derrick had fired for minor rule infractions—making them possible murder suspects, something I could use more of—it would be Shuman. He hadn't caught the case but surely he could contact Detectives Walker and Teague and find out what was going on with the investigation.

Shuman didn't pick up, so I left a message explaining what I needed.

The line moved forward. I pulled up to the window, paid, grabbed my mocha Frappuccino, and took a long sip. I desperately needed the boost because now I had to call Ty.

CHAPTER 8

Ty had a large corporation to run on two continents, thousands of employees, millions of dollars at stake, and four generations of ancestors breathing down his neck. He was busy, super busy. He made no secret that his commitment to Holt's Department Stores came first.

So as I pulled away from the Starbucks with my frosty cup of I-desperately-need-the-boost mocha Frappuccino in hand and activated my Bluetooth, it didn't occur to me that Ty would answer my call. Before the second ring finished, he picked up.

"Haley?"

I nearly ran up on the curb.

His voice sent a shiver through me, reminding me of all the times he'd whispered my name in our most private moments, when he'd called to me because he wanted to share something he thought interesting, when he'd laughed at an outlandish thing I'd done.

And when he'd said good-bye to me that last time when we'd broken up.

We'd seen each other twice since that day. Once was when we'd run into each other on the street.

Let's just say I hadn't handled it well.

The second time was at a wedding we'd both ended up attending—long story.

From the voices I heard in the background on Ty's end of the call I knew he was in his office in downtown L.A. with subordinates crowded around his desk, or he was in a meeting. I'd heard that racket often when we were dating and I'd tried to talk to him about something.

Surprisingly, a few seconds after Ty answered my call the chatter ceased abruptly and I heard a door close.

"Haley . . . I'm . . . I'm glad you called. Really glad," he said. "How . . . how are you?"

"I'm—"

I didn't know how to answer. I'd had a tough time immediately after things ended between us, stuck in breakup zombie land for a long time. But now I was better. I was good. Great, really.

Or so I'd thought until I heard Ty's voice.

I swung into a parking lot and pulled crossways across four spaces.

"I'm good," I forced myself to say, but really my heart was racing and my palms were sweating, and I didn't know how I felt at the moment.

A long silence stretched between us. I couldn't seem to think of anything to say, and neither could he.

I guess I should have planned this call better.

Maybe I should have planned a lot of things better.

"So, uh, what's up?" Ty finally asked.

Time was precious to Ty. He always had a tight schedule and he hated being late for anything. I couldn't bear the thought that he'd tell me he had to go.

"I heard about the thing with Kelvin Davis," I said.

Ty didn't respond. In my head I pictured him frowning slightly and mentally calculating where this conversation might go. Ty was always several steps ahead of everything and everybody.

"I know you're a person of interest in the murder investigation," I said. "I just wanted to make sure you were doing okay."

"Yes. Of course. I'm fine," he said.

I picked up a note of concern in his voice, which made my heart beat faster for a different reason.

"Everything is all right?" I asked. "No problems?"

"None," he said.

I wasn't sure I believed him. But I didn't know if he was trying to protect me from something, or if he simply thought this was none of my business.

"Great," I said. "So, well, I guess that's it then."

"Haley?"

"Yes?"

He didn't say anything, and I couldn't seem to put together a coherent sentence. Apparently, he couldn't either.

Another few seconds passed, and it hit me that this conversation had become totally awkward and uncomfortable. Plus, I didn't want to be left hanging on the line when Ty announced—as he'd done a zillion times when we were dating—that he had to go and attend to something more important than me.

"Look, I've got to run," I said.

"Oh. Okay," Ty said. "Well, uh, thanks for calling."

"Bye."

I ended the call and fell back against the seat, exhausted.

After I left L.A. Affairs for the day—I'd hardly gotten anything accomplished, thanks to my conversation with Ty—I drove to my parents' house in La Cañada Flintridge, an upscale area in the foothills that overlooked the Los Angeles Basin.

Visiting Mom in person was sometimes quicker than having a telephone conversation with her. At her house, she'd often get distracted by her own reflection in a mirror—she was, after all, a former beauty queen—and I could slip away unnoticed.

I exited the 210 freeway, wound my way through the streets, and pulled into the circular driveway outside my folks' home. The house—actually, it was a small mansion—had been left to my mom along with a trust fund, by her grandmother. No one in the family knew—or was willing to say—just how all of that came about.

Not that Mom cared, of course. She'd taken what she considered her rightful place among the wealthy of Los Angeles, a place she truly belonged. She'd dragged my dad along with her, as well as me and my two siblings.

My older brother flew F-16s for the US Air Force, and my younger sister attended college and did some modeling. Dad was an aerospace engineer. The only loose cannon in our family was, of course, Mom.

I parked my car, and by the time I reached the front door, it opened. Juanita, Mom's housekeeper for as long as I could remember, smiled as I walked inside. For me, Juanita had always been a soft spot to land during my childhood when Mom was—well, when Mom was being Mom.

"She's in her study," Juanita said.

I headed through the house to the room Mom had deemed her study, where the only thing she actually studied were the issues of *Elle, Vogue, Harper's Bazaar*, and *Cosmo* she received each month. No way would Mom allow a new fashion trend to slip past her unnoticed.

Now that I was here, I was concerned about why Mom had been repeatedly trying to reach me. Past experience told me, however, that it was something that would benefit her, not me.

"Hi, Mom," I said, as I stepped into her study.

She was seated on a chaise, flipping through a magazine, dressed in a Zac Posen sheath and Louboutin stilettos. Her dark hair was perfectly coiffed. Her nails and makeup were flawless.

Just your average housewife wiling away a quiet evening at home.

"There you are," she declared, and rose from the chaise. "I've been trying to reach you. I've had the most brilliant idea."

I was afraid of that.

Mom often had brilliant ideas. She'd started—and abandoned—numerous businesses and hobbies over the years, most with disastrous results.

"I've been dying to tell you," she said.

I braced myself.

Mom drew herself up into her pageant stance—chin up, shoulders back—and announced, "I'm going to get a job."

Oh my God, where had she come up with that idea? No way had she thought it up on her own. Had she read an article in *Elle*, maybe?

"I read an article in *Vogue*," Mom said.

Close enough.

"It's time," Mom told me. "Time for me to step up and help the world."

Mom hadn't worked for the entire time I was growing up—I'm not sure she'd ever held a job.

"I'm not clear on how you finding a job is going to help the world," I said.

It was the nicest thing I could think of.

"I'm going to focus on my career now," Mom said. "I want to work for a truly worthwhile cause at a foundation or a large charitable organization. Possibly adopting pets.

Saving the planet, perhaps. Maybe feeding hungry children in—Africa, Syria? Where are children starving?"

"Everywhere, Mom."

"Well, then that just proves that I must find a position quickly," she told me. "I need your help."

Oh, crap.

"I want you to write my résumé for me," Mom said.

How was I going to write a résumé for someone who hadn't actually worked anywhere?

"You found that fabulous job working for that big company downtown," Mom pointed out.

I'd never gotten around to telling Mom I'd left that job a while ago because the company had gone out of business and that I was working someplace new.

This was definitely not the time to mention it.

"I know you'll do a fabulous job on a résumé for me," Mom said, "and I'll secure a position where I can make a real difference in the world."

As far as I knew, Mom's greatest accomplishments were walking comfortably in five-inch heels and readily recognizing the subtle difference between the shades of ecru and eggshell.

Not even David Copperfield could make a résumé appear that would get her a job. Still, I couldn't fight her on it.

"Sure, Mom, I'll get started on it," I told her.

"Call me if you have any questions," she said.

I saw no point in asking my how-the-heck-did-I-get-involved-in-this question, so I left.

"Aren't you supposed to be helping with the new employee orientation?" Sandy asked.

I'd successfully blocked out my new assignment—though my visit with my mom earlier this evening was still rattling around in my head—but it all came crashing back thanks to that gentle reminder from Sandy, one of my Holt's BFFs. We were in the housewares department packing throw pillows and small rugs into boxes and loading them onto U-boat carts.

Sandy was a little younger than me, with hair that varied in color depending on her mood. Today it was red.

Sandy didn't seem to have a plan for the rest of her life—or the immediate future—beyond working for Holt's and continuing to date her tattoo artist boyfriend, who treated her awful and who I often wished would be abducted by aliens.

"Jeanette asked me to help out with the orientation," I said. "Is that tonight?"

I paused, a brown-print throw pillow in each hand, wondering if I'd overlooked the announcement in the breakroom beside the time clock.

That happened a lot.

"Am I supposed to be doing the orientation now?" I asked.

"No," Sandy said, rolling up a rug. "I was just wondering if you'd met Lani, the girl who does them."

I vaguely remembered Jeanette saying someone by that name was the person I'd be working with.

"She's, you know, kind of weird," Sandy said.

"Who's weird?" Bella asked, as she walked over from the bath department across the aisle.

"Lani. The orientation girl," Sandy said.

Bella shuddered. "That's one weird chick, all right."

"What's wrong with her?" I asked.

"She's quiet, kind of keeps to herself," Sandy said.

"Yeah, weird," Bella said. "Why are you packing all this stuff up?"

"A new line of merchandise is going in," Sandy explained.

"You want to hear some crap?" Bella asked.

I always wanted to hear some crap.

"I had a date with a new guy last night," Bella said. "He fell asleep on my sofa watching television."

"Oh my God," Sandy said. "What did you do?"

"Went through his wallet," she said.

"So, did he have much money?" Sandy asked.

"He was loaded," Bella said.

"What does he do?" Sandy asked.

"I don't know. He can be a drug dealer for all I care. I'm dating him again," Bella said.

We've all got our priorities.

"Maybe you two will get married," Sandy said. "Hey, Haley, that reminds me. Have you picked out your wedding colors yet?"

I cringed. "I'm not getting married."

"But you caught the bouquet," she said.

We'd been at a wedding not long ago and I'd caught the bouquet. Sandy kept insisting a marriage proposal was in my future.

I guess the toughest part of that whole ordeal was that Ty had showed up at the wedding. We'd acknowledged each other with a glance and a nod, which was totally awkward, but we hadn't spoken.

Thank goodness he hadn't brought a date.

"What about you?" Bella asked Sandy, and I was grateful she'd run interference on my behalf. "What happened with that guy you met on vacay?"

"Sebastian?" Sandy sighed and her expression took on a dreamy air. "He's really cute."

"Damn right," Bella agreed.

"But I already have a boyfriend," Sandy said, looking a little sad.

"You should dump that loser," I told her, for at least the zillionth time.

"Or date both of them," Bella suggested.

"That wouldn't be right," Sandy insisted.

"When did you become Saint Sandy?" Bella asked.

"My boyfriend is an artist," she said.

"He does tattoos," I pointed out.

"It's art, Haley," she said. "And I wouldn't think of disturbing his bliss by causing a problem in our relationship. He says I'm his muse."

Bella shook her head. "I'm out of here."

She went back across the aisle to the bath department. Sandy and I managed to stretch out loading the merchandise until closing time so we wouldn't have to wait on actual customers. I got my handbag—a Dooney & Bourke barrel that always lifted my spirits—from my locker in the breakroom and was headed for the front doors when I spotted Jeanette at the customer service booth.

I knew she was counting on me to help out with the new-employee orientation and carry a full work schedule when swarms of crazed shoppers descended during the upcoming holiday shopping rush. But I wouldn't be here. As quick as Priscilla at L.A. Affairs got the words "full-time-permanent-employee" out of her mouth, I was going to quit Holt's

It hit me that the decent thing to do was to forewarn Jeanette so she could either work on her the-entire-Holt's-chain-will-collapse-without-you speech, or practice her backflip because I was leaving.

Really, I was pretty sure I knew which she'd do.

Of course, the timing of my resignation had taken on an additional dimension now that Holt's was in the process of acquiring the upscale, trendy Nuovo stores. I still needed to find a Sassy satchel, and if I could get the ten-percent employee discount, that would be great. However, I didn't know when that might happen.

Ty flew into my head. If we were still dating, I could just ask him when the acquisition would be finalized.

That couldn't happen now, of course.

I considered phoning Amber, his personal assistant. She and I were cool with each other—even after the breakup—and I knew she'd tell me. She'd probably offer to go shopping with me.

Both of those things seemed like more than I could take on at the moment. But then something else hit me—I could ask Jeanette.

"Hey, Jeanette," I said, stopping next to her. "How soon before the Nuovo acquisition will be completed?"

"Anxious to use your employee discount there?" Jeanette asked, looking very pleased with herself for some reason.

A twinge of guilt zapped me. With my resignation from Holt's looming on the horizon, I'd probably use the employee discount once or twice before I officially quit.

I guess something showed in my expression—I'm usually way cooler than that—because Jeanette looked concerned.

"You are planning to use the discount often, aren't you?" she asked. "It is one of your favorite stores, isn't it?"

"Well, sure. Of course," I said.

Jeanette looked at me for a few seconds, like she suspected something else was going on—jeez, I'm usually a lot cooler than this—then said, "Not all of the details have been finalized, but we should know something definite in a few days."

"Great. Thanks," I said.

I made my way through the store and out the door. It

had been a weird day and I was anxious to get home—before anything else weird happened.

I crossed the darkened parking lot with the other employees. As I approached my car, I saw someone standing next to it.

It was Ty.

CHAPTER 9

"Hi."

"Hi."

Ty and I gazed at each other, neither of us saying anything else. We were caught in some sort of mutual tractor beam that we couldn't pull away from but wouldn't allow either of us to think up a sentence.

It had been a weird day. Now, it was a weird night. I didn't know what was going on. Maybe there was a full moon.

I didn't want to take my eyes off Ty long enough to look.

The lighting in the parking lot was awesome—diminished to reduce the store's carbon footprint, supposedly, but I figured what they really wanted to diminish was the electric bill—and Ty looked great. Tall, handsome, well-groomed, wearing an obscenely expensive suit, while I looked as if I'd worked two jobs today, one of which was as a minimum wage grunt who'd spent the last four hours hauling crappy merchandise around.

We'd broken up. I shouldn't care how I looked. Right?

"You sounded . . . worried . . . on the phone today," Ty said. "I wanted to make sure you were okay."

That was a lame reason for him to drive all the way up here from his office downtown. Was it just an excuse to see me?

I shouldn't even consider the possibility. Right?

"So are you . . . okay?" he asked.

"I'm concerned," I said, "about the situation with Kelvin Davis."

Had my reason for contacting him earlier today been lame? Had I used it as an excuse to hear his voice? Maybe see him?

"But I guess the whole thing has been cleared up by now," I said.

"Very nearly," Ty said.

"When you talked to the detectives on the case, explained everything, they knew you weren't involved, didn't they?" I said.

"I, uh, I haven't spoken with the detectives yet."

Ty shifted his weight and leaned his head left, then right, stretching his neck.

I knew what that meant.

I noticed then that Ty's shirt collar was open and his tie was loose. His hair fell across his forehead. For him, this was the equivalent of being a total wreck.

"Why haven't you been interviewed by the detectives yet?" I asked.

"My attorneys advised against it." Ty tried for a you-know-how-they-are grin, but couldn't quite pull it off.

I realized that lines were etched around his eyes and mouth that I'd never noticed before. Was he not sleeping well? Was he worried more than he admitted? Or maybe both?

"Attorneys know best," I said. "Things like this can get out of control, if you're not careful."

Ty came from an old-money Los Angeles family that

had been around for generations. They were prominent and wealthy. Kelvin Davis had been a media sensation. His death could turn into a circus, with Ty in the center ring.

"That won't happen . . . I don't think," Ty said, and tried again to smile.

The parking lot lights dimmed further. I looked around and saw that we were the only ones still there.

"I'd better let you go," Ty said.

Would he ask me to go have coffee?

I shouldn't want that. Right?

"Yeah, I'd better go," I said.

I pulled my car keys from my handbag and clicked the locks. Ty opened the door for me.

I walked closer. The heat, the scent that was uniquely his, nearly overwhelmed me.

"Well, good night," he said.

I lingered for a moment, close to him, smelling him, feeling his warmth, wanting him—

I dropped into the driver's seat.

"Good night," I said.

I started my car and drove away.

Before, I'd been concerned. Now I was worried.

I pulled out of the Holt's parking lot and headed for my apartment, my conversation with Ty—and the feelings I'd had for him—zinging around in my head.

No way could Ty kill anybody. It simply couldn't happen. I didn't doubt it for a minute. Yet, why had his attorneys advised him not to talk to the detectives working the Kelvin Davis murder investigation?

Was there evidence I didn't know about? Something Shuman hadn't learned or passed on to me?

Then another thought hit me—could Ty be hiding something?

I stopped in the line of traffic at a red light, feeling kind of icky inside. I forced myself to think back to the day when I'd been in my office and someone from the emergency room at the Palmdale hospital had called with the news that Ty had been in a car accident. I'd rushed to pick him up, relieved that he wasn't injured.

The car behind me blew the horn. I realized the light had changed. I drove forward.

Ty had asked to stay at my place. Amber had brought over clothes for him, along with gifts and cards his friends and employees had sent, and his belongings she'd retrieved from his wrecked car. She'd mentioned that Ty had suddenly canceled his appointments for that afternoon and had rented a car for the drive to Palmdale. I'd found a receipt in his pocket from a convenience store where he'd stopped and bought a soda—and where he'd changed out of his Tom Ford suit into jeans and a polo shirt.

All of that could have been explained away—except that Ty didn't explain it. And when he did answer some of my questions, I'd gotten the strong feeling that he was lying to me. Nothing about that day, or his trip to Palmdale, made any sense—especially the fact that he'd acted super strange during his stay at my place.

I hung a left at the entrance to my apartment complex and wound my way to my building. I sat in my car. My chest felt heavy and my head had started to hurt.

I didn't want to get out.

I didn't want to go up to my apartment.

Finally, I forced myself out of my Honda and up the stairs. I let myself in. I didn't put my keys or handbag down, just kept going while I could make my feet move.

When Ty had stayed here with me, Amber had brought over some of his things. We'd broken up shortly after that. Ty hadn't known that a small duffel bag of his was in the closet of my second bedroom, so he hadn't taken it with him. I'd found it later, but things were too awkward between us for me to attempt to return it. I hadn't even been able to pick it up, let alone open it.

I walked into my second bedroom, switched the light, and opened the closet door. I pulled out the duffel bag and unzipped it.

Inside were bundles of cash and a handgun.

It was a Gucci day. Definitely a Gucci day.

I settled into my office, juggling the I-can-delay-starting-work-a-little-longer cup of coffee and doughnut I'd just gotten from the breakroom and the fabulous Gucci tote I'd treated myself to a couple of weeks ago. It really popped against the navy blue business suit I'd also treated myself to during the same shopping trip.

Still, as fantastic as my ensemble looked, I couldn't shake the worry and the icky feeling that had weighed me down since last night.

Fifty grand. In cash. Stuffed into a duffel bag, along with a nine-millimeter handgun.

"Ty, what did you do?" I murmured as I placed my handbag in my lower desk drawer.

I sat back in my chair and sipped my coffee.

In my heart, I knew Ty couldn't have murdered anyone. But after finding the gun and the cash—I couldn't resist counting it; who could?—I hadn't been able to shake the notion that he'd been involved with Kelvin Davis's death somehow. What else could I think?

And what the heck was I supposed to do about what I'd discovered?

I reached for my doughnut—I definitely needed massive quantities of chocolate to figure this out—and noticed a yellow sticky note on my computer. It read, "My plants are dying," and was signed by somebody whose name I didn't recognize and festooned with a sad face in each corner.

Somebody's plants weren't doing well? And whoever it was thought I wanted to know about it?

Jeez, what was going on in this office lately?

I yanked the sticky note off my computer and tossed it in my trash can.

With my coffee and doughnut in hand, I walked to my window that overlooked the busy Sepulveda and Ventura intersection. I always liked being in high places. It seemed to give a different perspective to things and make me think better—of course, the chocolate, sugar, and caffeine helped, too.

I could go to Detective Shuman with what I'd found. I could confide in him. We shared a massive secret—long story—that was so huge we instinctively knew that neither of us could ever mention it, even to each other. Sort of like an unspoken pact.

I knew that if I told Shuman what I'd found in the duffel bag and asked him not to tell anyone, he would respect my wishes.

But did I really want to put him in that position?

I thought about it for a few seconds—my reasoning powers spurred on by another bite of my chocolate doughnut—and decided I couldn't do that to him. If the situation should blow up and it became known that Shuman possessed that knowledge, it could seriously hurt his career.

Of course, I could always confront Ty. Maybe there was a simple explanation totally unrelated to the Kelvin Davis murder.

I finished off my doughnut and thought about talking to Ty. In less than three seconds I decided that I couldn't do it. Our relationship—or whatever it was—was in a weird place. I didn't want to make it weirder by trying to discuss what I'd found. He'd probably assume I thought he was guilty of Kelvin Davis's murder, and I didn't want a rift between us.

Besides, the fewer people who knew I was withholding possible evidence in a murder investigation, the better.

There was, of course, nothing else I could do but investigate Ty's involvement with Kelvin Davis myself.

I returned to my desk, got my cell phone out of my handbag, and called Amber. I expected to leave a message—she's super busy taking care of most everything in Ty's life—but she answered right away.

"Don't mention my name," I told her before she could say anything.

"It's cool. He's not here," Amber said. "How are you doing?"

"Not that great, really," I said.

"You heard?"

"I think I'm more worried about it than Ty is," I said.

"I doubt that," Amber said. "The whole thing is ridiculous. Ty had absolutely no involvement with Kelvin Davis. He never invested with that creep. None of Ty's family invested with him. Neither Ty nor anybody close to him lost a cent because of Davis's scam. There's no connection between them. If there were, believe me, I would know about it."

Apparently, Amber didn't know that Ty's name, contact info, and fingerprints had been on a slip of paper clutched in Kelvin Davis's dead hand. I sure as heck wasn't going to tell her.

Still, I was glad to hear there was no other link between Ty—or his family—and Davis. That should go a long way toward keeping the cops at bay.

Yet something had caused Ty to take a sudden, covert

trip to Palmdale that day. Was it mere coincidence that it was around the time Kelvin Davis was murdered?

"Remember Ty's traffic accident?" I said.

"That whole thing was odd," Amber agreed. She paused for a few seconds. "You don't think Ty was somehow involve—"

"No. No way. Absolutely not," I told her. "But has he started prepping for opening a store Palmdale?"

"He's been working almost nonstop on the Nuovo acquisition," Amber said.

"I heard about that," I said.

"This has been a tough one. A total nightmare. The Nuovo people are asking for the moon—and he's giving it to them, for some reason."

"He is? That doesn't sound like Ty."

"I don't get it either," Amber said. "But he's determined to see this thing go through."

"So nothing's going on in Palmdale?" I asked.

"He doesn't even know anybody there," Amber said.

Because she was a fabulous personal assistant, Amber kept a list of names, addresses, phone numbers, and e-mail addresses of Ty's personal and business contacts. She kept his calendar so she most always knew where he was, who he was with, and why he was there. Amber also reviewed the monthly statements for his credit cards and cell phone, monitoring them for fraudulent charges and overbillings. So if Amber said Ty didn't know anybody in Palmdale, I believed her.

We were both quiet for a minute, then Amber said, "You two should get back together."

The notion zapped me speechless.

"He's been working himself like crazy since you broke up," Amber said. "Besides, anybody can see you two belong together. You know, Haley, Ty would do anything for you."

I knew Amber meant well. Plus, she wasn't the first person who'd said Ty and I should be together.

"Let me know if you hear anything," I said. "Will you?"

"Of course," Amber said, then added, "Ty hasn't been the same since you two ended things. Just think about it, okay?"

Thoughts of Ty had been seeping into my mind during parts of every day since we'd broken up. And now, with this whole murder investigation thing hanging over us like a black cloud, how could I think about anything but him?

CHAPTER 10

"Haley? Haley? Hello? Haley?" Mindy said when I answered my office phone.

I'd just hung up with Amber and I was in no mood.

"Yes, Mindy?"

"Oh, Haley! There you are!" She giggled. "One of your clients is here. Her name is . . . oh, now let me see, where—"

I hung up.

Okay, I know that was bad. But, jeez, there's only so much I can take.

Since I had no idea which of my clients had shown up without an appointment, I left my office and cruised past the interview rooms until I spotted Laronda Bain. She was seated in front of the desk, dressed in head to toe Michael Kors. Since her face was still in Botox deep-freeze, I had no idea what kind of mood she was in.

Not that I really cared.

Still, I managed to put on an I-need-to-keep-this-job smile and walked into the interview room. I dropped into the chair behind the desk and before I could say anything, she started in.

"I haven't heard from you," Laronda declared. "Is there a problem?"

It took me a few seconds to remember that she was the mom putting on the extravagant, you've-got-to-be-kidding-me Harry Potter birthday party for her eight-year-old son. Since I hadn't looked at her event since the last time she was here and had requested Hogwarts School be constructed in her backyard, I had no idea what was going on with it.

So what could I say but, "If there had been a problem, I would have handled it."

Laronda might have been pleased with my response. I couldn't tell.

"I've decided to gift the party guests with a costume," Laronda declared. "Each child will pick a uniform from one of the four Hogwarts houses, though I imagine Gryffindor and Slytherin will be the most popular."

She wanted custom made costumes? For twenty children? Now? At this late date?

I wished my face was full of Botox so Laronda couldn't read my expression.

Then my employee job performance review bloomed in my head, followed quickly by the vision of walking out of Holt's for the very last time—a great motivator.

"No problem," I said.

"Contact my assistant. She'll give you the costume sizes for the children," Laronda said, then left.

I left, too, and went back to my office.

This whole thing with Ty was consuming my thoughts and sapping my energy. I needed to make some progress on finding out exactly what he'd been up to in Palmdale. Luckily, I had two sources to turn to for info.

I grabbed my cell phone off my desk and walked to the window. Traffic was heavy on the streets below, as always, and people were coming and going from the nearby office buildings and the Galleria. I called Detective Shuman. His voicemail picked up, so I left a message. Next I tried Jack Bishop.

Jack was a private investigator who managed to be totally hot and totally cool at the same time. He was gorgeous, smart, and beyond competent. We'd worked together many times and seeing him, or hearing his voice, or even thinking about him always made my heart beat a little faster. Nothing romantic had ever happened between us, but we'd had a couple of close calls.

Jack was wired in to most everything that happened in L.A. If anybody could uncover info on the Kelvin Davis murder investigation and Ty's possible connection, it was him.

My hand trembled a little as I punched in Jack's number on my cell phone. His voicemail answered—jeez, he had the sexiest voice *ever*—so I left what I hoped would come across as an oh-so-clever message.

Just as I turned toward my desk, my cell phone rang. My heart jumped. Wow, Jack had called back already.

"Hey there," I said when I answered, using my I-can-be-as-cool-as-you-are voice.

"How is it coming?" my mom asked.

Mom? Oh my God, I thought I was talking to Jack and it was Mom? Damn. That's what I get for not checking the ID screen.

"Haley? How's it coming?" she asked again.

I had no idea what she was talking about.

"Fine," I said.

"You're finished with my résumé already?" she asked.

Oh, yeah, her résumé. I'd forgotten about it because, really, I figured Mom would have forgotten about it.

"I've been thinking, and I've decided we should focus on a particular area," she said.

Note: Mom said "we" when I was the one doing all the work.

"Sure, Mom, that would be great," I said, as I collapsed into my desk chair.

"I'd like an outdoor job," she said.

I looked down at my cell phone, then pressed it to my ear again.

"Did you say you wanted to work outdoors?" I asked. "As in, not inside? Actual outside?"

Okay, this was really weird because Mom's idea of being in nature was walking the grounds of the Beverly Hilton.

"Alexander McQueen just previewed a line of the most fabulous casual wear," Mom said.

Now it made sense.

"You know, Mom, if you're outside there will be a lot of bugs," I pointed out. "Spiders, too."

Mom gasped in horror.

I understood how she felt. I was wary of anything that had more legs than I had.

"Perhaps the outdoors isn't really my milieu," Mom said.

"Let me know. Bye," I said, and hung up.

I sprang out of my desk chair. I'd really been in the office too long already today.

I grabbed my things and left.

When I walked into the reception area at Hollywood Haven, the first thing I noticed was that Karen wasn't at the front counter. She hadn't been there the last time I was here, either. I wondered if she was out sick.

Or had she been fired?

Vida in HR had told me Karen was on Derrick's hit list of employees to get rid of. But Derrick was gone now.

Maybe he wasn't the only one who wanted Karen out of there.

I'd come to the retirement home to talk to Rosalind, the gal who'd taken over for Derrick. I needed her input on a number of things for the anniversary gala. But now I had to find out what was going on with Karen.

I walked down the corridor past the offices and saw that crime scene tape was still stretched across Derrick's door. Not a good sign. Apparently, Detectives Walker and Teague hadn't closed the case yet.

I really needed to talk to Shuman and find out what was up with the investigation. I glanced at my cell phone, hoping he'd returned my call. He hadn't. This didn't suit me, of course, but what could I do?

The door to Rosalind Fletcher's office was open, so I stepped inside. The same elderly woman sat at the reception desk. Her chin rested on her chest and her eyes were closed.

Great. Just what I needed. Somebody who was, literally, asleep on the job.

"Excuse me?" I said.

The woman didn't move, didn't respond. I rapped my knuckles on the door frame. No change. Wow, she must be a really deep sleeper.

"Excuse me?" I said, a little louder.

Still nothing.

Maybe she was hard of hearing, I decided. Maybe if—

Yikes! Was she dead?

I went into semi panic mode.

Was she really dead? Sitting up at her desk? While I was standing here looking like an idiot trying to talk to her?

I was about to bolt from the office when she suddenly roused, plastered on a smile, and gazed up at me.

"Can I help you?"

Oh my God. Why did thinking that this lady was dead bother me so much? It's not like I'd never seen a dead body.

Maybe it was because I'd never seen one sitting up before.

No two ways about it. I was never taking on another event at a retirement home, and I intended to make that clear to everyone who'd listen at L.A. Affairs—after my job performance review, of course.

"I need to talk with Rosalind," I said.

She smiled sweetly. "She's in a meeting."

"When will she available?" I asked.

"Not long."

This was a retirement home where elderly residents wiled away years and years of their lives. "Not long" could mean anything.

Plus, Rosalind's receptionist had been asleep and she was really old. I wasn't sure she knew who Rosalind was, let alone where to find her.

"Thanks," I said, and left.

I figured I'd give Mr. Stewart a try and see if he knew where I could find Rosalind. I walked down the hallway and saw that the door to his office was closed. I glanced around, didn't see anyone, and leaned closer, listening. No raised voices this time.

Rosalind could have been inside meeting with Mr. Stewart, since he'd closed the door. Or maybe he was napping. Or maybe he was dead.

No way was I going in there.

I headed back, crossed the lobby—still no Karen—and went into the hallway that led to the residents' wing. Someone was at the piano playing a tune that was kind of familiar. When I reached the dayroom I saw four women crowded around the pianist, singing along. Alden the Great was in the far corner presenting a bouquet of flowers that he'd pulled from his jacket sleeve to an elderly woman. His daughter Emily was beside him. She saw me and waved. I waved back.

Emily seemed to be here a lot, so I decided I'd ask her if she'd seen Rosalind. I headed that way.

"Haley? Haley, dear," someone called.

I spotted Delores, Shana, and Trudy hurrying toward me. All of them sported updos and bright orange nail polish, like they'd had a sleepover and done each other's hair and nails. If so, the party was definitely over, because they all looked troubled.

"We heard," Delores declared.

"Say it's not so," Shana implored.

"It can't be true," Trudy insisted. "It simply cannot be true."

"Tell us, honey," Delores said. "Come on now, be straight with us. We can take it."

All three of them gazed wide eyed at me. I had no idea what they were talking about.

"The gala," Trudy said. "We heard it might be canceled because that horrible Derrick went and got himself murdered."

I wasn't sure how they'd found out the home's upper management had doubts about going ahead with the gala. Maybe Mr. Stewart had said something, or perhaps it was another staff member. I didn't like this kind of rumor circulating. I had too much at stake—oh, and it would be nice for the residents to attend the gala, of course.

"I'm sure the gala will proceed as planned," I said. "Some of the staff members were a little concerned that it might look bad to go ahead with it unless the murderer is caught."

"It was that Mr. Stewart, wasn't it?" Delores said. She

shook her head. "He's such a wimp. That's what he gets for letting everybody else run the place all this time. He's forgotten how to make a decision."

"And besides," Trudy said, "everybody knows it's that Vida who had it in for Derrick."

"Those two," Delores agreed. "Like oil and water. That's what they were. Oil and water."

If I'd had this-might-be-a-clue antennae, they would have stood straight up and wiggled.

"Vida Webster?" I asked. "The head of HR?"

"Her and that hair of hers," Trudy said, and sniffed distastefully. "A bad dye job, if you ask me."

"Thinks she's Liza Minnelli," Shana said, rolling her eyes.

"She's no Liza Minnelli," Trudy said. "We heard them arguing."

The other two ladies nodded.

"Honey, you should have heard the things those two said to each other," Delores told me.

"Vida and Derrick?" I asked, just to be sure.

"It got ugly, honey," Delores said. "Let me tell you, it got very ugly."

"She told him he wasn't fit to walk through the front door of this place," Trudy said, "let alone be the assistant director."

"That's exactly what she said," Shana agreed.

"And then Derrick threatened Vida," Trudy said.

"Derrick told her she'd better watch her step," Shana said, "or he'd see to it that she got thrown out of here."

"Ugly," Delores said. "Like I said, ugly."

"We heard it all," Trudy said. "Word for word."

"Every word," Shana added, and pointed toward the patio. "Right out there. Right next to the fountain."

Vida had told me that Derrick had intended to fire Karen. Now, it seems, Vida was also on Derrick's hit list.

I couldn't help but think this was a heck of a coincidence. I wondered if Vida had been lying to me about Karen. Had she told me about Karen's impending termination to throw suspicion off herself?

I didn't know. But at least now I had two murder suspects.

Chapter 11

When I left the dayroom and headed down the hallway, I spotted Karen standing behind the front desk. Finally. Where the heck had she been?

No wonder Derrick wanted to fire her if she was never at her post.

I mean that in the nicest way, of course.

"Hi, Haley," Karen said when I walked up.

"I didn't see you earlier," I said, using my I-hope-it-sounds-as-if-I'm-genuinely-concerned-and-not-just-fishing-for-info voice. "I was afraid you were out sick, or something."

"Busy, busy," Karen said. "Just trying to keep up with everything."

I caught a glimpse of a lighter and a pack of cigarettes sticking out of her jacket pocket and figured she'd been on a smoke break. This was a nonsmoking campus, so I imagined she'd found a secluded spot outside where nobody would see her—especially since the place had dozens of oxygen tanks that might blow up.

I'm pretty sure something like that would be mentioned in a future employee job performance review.

Karen leaned toward me. "This place has turned into a complete zoo lately. Everybody is doing somebody else's job, taking up the slack since Derrick's . . . not here any-more."

"I guess he's really missed?" I asked.

Karen made a really unattractive snickering sound.

"Believe me, nobody misses Derrick," she said. "Except Mr. Stewart, of course."

I was glad Karen had jumped right in on the topic of Derrick's murder and everything that was going on here at Hollywood Haven, because that was exactly what I wanted to talk to her about.

"Rosalind got bumped up to acting assistant director," Karen said. "She's going crazy trying to untangle the mess Derrick made."

I gave her an oh-my-god eyebrow bob and said, "You're kidding."

"It's true. In fact"—Karen glanced around, then leaned closer and lowered her voice—"I heard that Rosalind is thinking about going to the board and complaining."

"About Derrick?"

"About Mr. Stewart," Karen said.

Oh, wow. This was some good stuff. I had to keep Karen talking.

She, however, needed no promoting.

"There are . . . shall we say *questions* . . . about Derrick's qualifications for the assistant director position," Karen said. "Derrick smooth talked Mr. Stewart into giving him the job. That was Derrick. All he could do was talk."

I remembered then that somebody had told me Derrick's chattiness had offended some of the residents.

I leaned closer, matching Karen's now-we're-seriously-gossiping posture and tone.

"I heard Derrick got a little too nosy with some of the residents," I said.

"There were complaints from the families," Karen said. She shook her head. "Nothing ever came of it, of course. Mr. Stewart wasn't about to reprimand Derrick. He doesn't like to rock the boat, if you get my meaning. He just wants to sit in his office and draw his paycheck until he retires."

"There was no push-back from the families?" I asked.

"More complaints, but nothing ever became of them—at least, not that I've heard," Karen said. "Everybody was wary of Derrick."

That was great for the residents who had family members visiting regularly. But what about the others? The ones who were, essentially, left here to fend for themselves?

"And let me tell you something else," Karen said, leaning even closer. "Rosalind isn't going to let Mr. Stewart get by with anything. She'll—"

Raised voices drew Karen's attention. I turned and saw a very frail white-haired woman in a wheelchair being pushed by a younger woman. The elderly lady faced forward, a stoic expression on her face as the other woman railed on about something. I realized I'd seen the two of them before.

"Ida Verdell," Karen whispered. "And that's her daughter Sylvia."

Sylvia was probably midforties, tall with dark hair, dressed in jeans and a knit top that I was pretty darn sure she'd bought off the clearance rack at Holt's.

"Sylvia visits her mother almost every day," Karen whispered.

Judging by Ida's expression, I didn't know if she was enjoying her daughter's visit or enduring it.

"Really? Almost every day?"

"Don't ask me why," Karen said. "Sylvia isn't happy about the visits, and she makes sure nobody else is happy either."

"She's a complainer?" I asked.

"She's made a nuisance of herself with the whole staff," Karen said.

I wondered if that included Derrick.

Karen must have somehow read my mind.

"She and Derrick," Karen said. "There was bad blood between the two of them."

Bad enough for Sylvia to murder him? I wondered.

"Why? What happened?" I asked.

Karen shook her head. "I never heard the details. But it was something huge. I heard Sylvia yelling—screaming, actually—at Derrick in his office one day."

"When?" I asked.

"Last week sometime," Karen said.

The possibility that I'd come across yet another murder suspect zapped my brain. If Sylvia had been arguing with Derrick last week, perhaps Sylvia had stewed over it all weekend, growing angrier and angrier until she barged into Derrick's office and murdered him.

Of course, whatever they were arguing about could have been nothing significant. After working with customers and clients at Holt's and L.A. Affairs, I'd learned that people could lose their minds over the smallest thing. For all I knew, Sylvia could have been complaining to Derrick about something as non-murder-worthy as the amount of garlic in the spaghetti sauce.

"And poor Ida," Karen said. "Sylvia's always giving her a hard time about something."

We both watched as Sylvia swung the wheelchair round and headed back toward the residents' wing, leaning over Ida's shoulder, yammering on.

Karen kept watching the two of them.

"It's the saddest thing," she said, shaking her head. "Ida had a good career going for herself. She was an actress.

This was years ago, of course. She was beautiful. All the major studios wanted her. She could have been a huge star."

I caught one last look at Ida as Sylvia pushed her wheelchair around the corner.

That tiny, frail woman had been a young, vibrant, sought-after actress, destined to become a huge star? It was hard to fit both of those images into my head.

"Too bad she fell in love," Karen said. "It ruined everything."

Ty flashed in my mind, along with the days I'd spent in breakup zombie land after we'd ended things.

"What happened?" I asked.

"He was a musician and a songwriter making quite a name for himself in Hollywood," Karen said. "Arthur Zamora. You've heard of him, I'm sure. No, maybe not. You're too young. He was before your time but his songs are still being played today. He was a timeless composer—at least, that's what everybody says about him."

"So what happened with him and Ida?" I asked.

"You've never heard this story? Everybody talks about it," Karen said. "Well, anyway, they fell deeply in love. They were in all the celebrity gossip columns. Their pictures were plastered in all the newspapers and magazines. One of those fairy-tale romances, you know? Then he dumped her."

"Oh my God."

"Just like that," Karen said, and snapped her fingers. "He took up with some other actress right away. It devastated Ida. She plunged into depression. Couldn't work. It ruined her career."

"She must have really loved him," I said.

"And it gets worse," Karen said.

How could it get any worse?

"He's here. Right here. In this facility," Karen said, and waved her hand around. "But he still won't talk to her."

The image of Ida seeing Arthur, knowing he was close, still feeling that love for him, bloomed in my head. It must have been crushing for her. My heart hurt thinking about it. No wonder she looked so sad all the time.

"After all these years?" I asked. "Why won't he talk to her?"

"Beats me," Karen said. "His health is poor. A mild stroke, not long ago."

"That's really sad," I said.

"Arthur gave all that music to the world, but has nothing for himself," Karen said. "He never had any kids. Ida eventually got married, so at least she has Sylvia. She's not the greatest daughter, but Ida's not alone. She has someone who visits and cares about her."

There must have been similar stories about the residents here. Most of them had been successful, well-known performers. They'd given so much. Had they gotten an equal amount back in return?

All the more reason for the anniversary gala to go forward, I decided. The residents at Hollywood Haven deserved their night in the spotlight.

"Have you heard anything new about the investigation into Derrick's death?" I asked.

Karen seemed annoyed and said, "Those detectives. Back here again, asking more questions, looking at things."

"Like what?" I asked.

"They're making a nuisance of themselves," Karen said. "I don't know why they continue—"

The phone on Karen's desk rang. Just as she lifted the receiver, two couples in their fifties walked through the entrance. They all had sad, forlorn expressions, an easy give-away that they were in need of a good spot to place an elderly parent.

I'd had about all of Hollywood Haven I could take. I waved to Karen and left.

My day definitely needed a boost, I decided as I got into my car. And what better boost could there be than talking to a hot private detective with a toe-curling Barry White voice?

I activated my Bluetooth as I pulled out onto Ventura Boulevard and called Jack Bishop.

"Meet me tonight," Jack said, when he answered. His voice was low and tense.

Oh my God, I'd caught him in the middle of some awesome private investigator thing. A stakeout, a takedown, a surveillance operation.

This was so hot.

Oh my God. He was probably carrying a gun.

Even hotter.

If I only knew what he was wearing.

"Text me," I said.

Jack disconnected and I'm pretty sure I made a little mewling sound—how could I not? His life was totally awesome.

How come my life wasn't totally awesome?

I definitely needed to work on that—right after I hit Starbucks.

A few blocks down the street I spotted my favorite place in the entire world, cruised through the drive-through, and bought myself a mocha Frappuccino. Since I couldn't come up with a good reason to do anything else, I went to L.A. Affairs.

The Frappie had my brain cells hopping pretty good when I got into my office, so I decided to take advantage of the mental boost and straighten up a bit. The event portfolios that Priscilla had brought me when I'd taken over for Suzie were stacked on my credenza, an unsightly reminder that I had actual work to do.

I picked them up and was deciding which file cabinet drawer to dump them in when I spotted the folders Priscilla had also brought in. I glanced through them and saw that they were vendor files. I checked the two on top. One was for an office supply store, the other a restaurant equipment company.

Okay, that was weird. Why would Priscilla have given them to me?

It was a mistake, I decided, as I dropped the vendor files onto my desk. At the time, she'd been overwhelmed with all the work heaped on her by Suzie's early departure—and overwhelmed, too, no doubt, by my generous offer to relieve her of that burden. I'd take them back to her later.

Rearranging the portfolios was all the straightening up I could manage for one day, so I moved on. I had a ton of things to do.

Marcie and I were still on the hunt for a Sassy satchel. I'd hoped I could buy one at Nuovo using my ten-percent employee discount, but no way could I count on the acquisition going through while the Sassy was still the hottest bag of the moment. If it meant I'd have to forgo my discount to get the bag, I'd do it.

I can make the hard decisions when I have to.

Sipping my Frappie, I sat down at my desk and logged on to the Internet. Searching all the upscale stores in L.A. was the best way to find a major must-have like the Sassy. It wasn't always successful, however. That, of course, meant the search would go to the next level—boutiques and specialty shops. And if that failed, I could draw on my extensive experience with color coding and grid patterns for stores of every variety in other major cities.

I'd just finished perusing the Neiman Marcus site—honestly, I'd gotten sidelined by their awesome wallet selection—when Priscilla marched into my office and up to my desk.

"Haley, what is going on?" she demanded.

At moments such as this, I've found it best not to say anything.

"You're supposed to be managing things," she told me.

I'm supposed to be—what?

"The responsibilities of the facilities manager are yours now," she said.

The facilities—what?

"We're experiencing massive problems," she told me. "Because of you."

Me? I'd caused massive problems? What the heck was she talking about?

I had a major flashback to my last job—well, really, a lot of my previous jobs.

Not a great feeling.

Priscilla sighed, exasperated, and said, "You volunteered to take over for Suzie, did you not?"

Okay, that much I understood.

"Yes," I said.

"All of her responsibilities," Priscilla said. "All of them. That's what you told me. Right?"

"Yes," I said.

"Everything. Correct?"

Wow, she was making it really hard for me to blame whatever was wrong on somebody else.

Hard, but not impossible.

"Let's move this along, Priscilla," I said. "What, exactly, is the problem?"

She drew in a breath to calm herself and said, "Suzie was our facilities manager, a duty you assumed, which means

you are in charge of seeing to it that our office has everything it needs to run smoothly."

Oh, crap.

"Now, I'm hearing complaints," Priscilla said. "A light
is out in the ladies' room, the breakroom is out of necessi-
ties, the plants are dying, office supplies are running short.
There's no pumpkin-flavored coffee creamer. What is
going on?"

Thankfully, I'd consumed nearly all of my Frappie and
my brain cells were hopping pretty darn good.

"I'm glad you came to me, Priscilla, because I had intended to schedule a meeting with you first thing in the
morning," I said, using my I-sound-like-I-know-what-I'm-
talking-about voice, and gestured to the vendor file folders
I'd—thank God—placed on the corner of my desk. "I've
been going through these contracts and, frankly, I have
some serious concerns."

Priscilla gave me a double blink, the beginning stage of
back-down mode.

"You do?" she asked.

"I wouldn't dream of taking over the position of facilities manager without first doing a complete audit of the
vendors," I told her. "It would be totally irresponsible on
my part."

"Oh." She was in total back-down mode now.

"The prices we're being charged for the services we're
receiving are questionable," I told her.

Priscilla glanced at the vendor folders. "Really?"

"I urge you not to blame Suzie," I said. "After all, she
had a great deal on her mind and I'm sure she was doing
the best she could."

"Well, yes, I suppose you're right," she said.

"And don't be hard on yourself either, Priscilla. I'm sure
you trusted Suzie and used your very best judgment in giv-

ing her this responsibility," I said. "But don't worry. I'll handle everything."

"Oh, well, yes. Thank you, Haley," she said.

"We can keep this between the two of us, if you'd rather," I offered, as if I was doing her a big favor.

"Oh, dear. Yes, that would be a good idea. Thank you, Haley," Priscilla said. "Let me know what you uncover when you complete your audit."

"Of course."

Priscilla left the office and I collapsed in my chair.

No two ways about it, I'd had enough of L.A. Affairs today. I grabbed my things and headed out.

I was meeting Jack Bishop.

CHAPTER 12

Jack had sent me a text message earlier in the day, asking me to meet him at a restaurant in Sherman Oaks after I got off work. I was scheduled for a shift tonight at Holt's, but oh, well, I would just go in late. No way was I passing up the opportunity to get the info I needed from Jack—and it was merely a coincidence that he was totally hot.

I took Ventura Boulevard, found the restaurant, left my car with the valet, and walked inside. The place had an industrial vibe to it with concrete floors, exposed pipes, and lots of metal—like the decorator thought maybe you'd want to weld something while you waited for your drink order.

"Haley."

Jack's breath brushed my right cheek and his voice activated my toe-curling-gooey-stomach gene.

I turned and oh, wow, he looked great. Jeans, a charcoal sport coat, and a black crew neck sweater that accentuated his dark hair and gorgeous eyes. Tall, handsome in a rugged, I-could-model-for-J-Crew kind of way.

"Jack."

I'd meant to sound sexy and cool, but I'm pretty sure I didn't pull it off. Understandable under the circumstances.

"I have a table for us," he said.

We wound through the bar to a spot in the corner. The place wasn't particularly crowded yet, and the music was low. A perfect spot for talking.

When we reached the table Jack had staked out for us, I saw a beer at one place, a soda at the other. Jack knew my policy about drinking and driving—one of the things I was a real stickler about.

"Is this a social call?" Jack asked, as we sat down.

"I need you," I said.

"Happy to accommodate you," Jack said, and grinned.

Jack had a seriously toe-curling grin. Still, I thought it was better to stick to business.

"I want some phone records," I said.

"Not exactly the need I was hoping to fill," Jack said, turning up the amperage on his grin. "Whose records?"

"Ty's," I said.

Jack's expression shifted, as if he was definitely not willing to accommodate me with phone records—or with anything else.

There had always been some heat between Jack and me, but he'd kept his distance because I had an official boyfriend—something else I was a real stickler about. After Ty and I broke up, Jack had still held back, telling me he didn't think things were over between Ty and me. I guess now he figured he'd been right—and he wasn't all that happy about it.

Jack sipped his beer. "Are you stalking your ex?"

"It's that thing with Kelvin Davis."

"I know he's involved," Jack said. "What's that got to do with you?"

I wasn't surprised Jack already knew that Ty was a person of interest in the homicide investigation. Jack knew everything. It was way cool.

"Stay out of it," Jack said. "It's high profile. It could turn into a media feeding frenzy in a heartbeat."

"I can't stay out of it."

"You don't owe him anything," Jack told me.

"I know but . . ."

Jack's expression changed again and I knew he realized I was holding something back—and he wasn't happy about it.

I probably should have told him about the cash and gun in Ty's duffel bag that I'd discovered in my bedroom closet, but I couldn't trust the info with anyone—not even Jack. Besides, I didn't want to involve him any deeper.

Jack pushed to his feet, grabbed his wallet, and slapped a twenty down on the table.

"Ty Cameron doesn't deserve you," Jack said. "He never deserved you."

He walked out.

I pulled into the Holt's parking lot and found a spot near the door. I glanced at my wristwatch. My shift had started forty-five minutes ago. I'd run into my apartment and changed into jeans and a T-shirt after leaving the restaurant where I'd met Jack, further delaying my arrival, but there was no need to waste the mental energy coming up with a good excuse for being tardy.

Not when something else way more important was on my mind.

My meeting with Jack hadn't gone exactly as I'd hoped. Not only had I not gotten the phone records I asked for, I'd made him so mad he'd stalked out.

I felt really icky about it. Jack and I had always helped each other out with cases in the past, so I wasn't sure why my request for Ty's phone records had crossed some sort of line with him, even though I knew he'd never especially liked Ty. I didn't want to lose Jack as a friend—or whatever it was we were to each other.

Still, I needed those phone records. I hadn't been able to find any connection between Ty and Kelvin Davis that involved the financial scams that had devastated so many people. That could only mean one thing—whatever had gone on between Ty and Kelvin was personal.

I glanced at my wristwatch again. Now I was fifty minutes late.

Ty's personal assistant had access to his phone bill, which might have a list of the numbers he'd called, depending on the carrier, but I didn't really want to involve Amber. I didn't want her to know what I was up to. She was cool about Ty and me, but I didn't want to put her in the middle of something.

I sat there for a while trying to figure another way to get the records, or another course of action I could take, but nothing came to me. Maybe I should have hit Starbucks and gotten another mocha Frappuccino on the way here.

I checked my watch and saw that now I was fifty-six minutes late. I grabbed my things and went into the store.

The place was quiet, as usual for this time of night. The customers seemed to be holding back, getting ready for the big after-Thanksgiving sale coming up soon.

I spotted Bella and Sandy, and two other girls who worked here whose names I couldn't remember. I waved as I went by—sort of like being in a parade.

The breakroom was empty when I walked in, but I knew it wouldn't be that way for long. By the time I stowed my handbag in my locker the door flew open and in stormed Rita.

I hate her.

Rita was the cashiers' supervisor. If she dressed in Holt's

clothing it would be an upgrade. Tonight she wore her usual stretch pants and a knit top with a farm animal on it.

Somebody ought to report her to PETA.

"You're late," she told me.

Rita lived for someone to be late for a shift—especially me.

She hates me too.

Holt's we-never-got-out-of-fourth-grade attendance policy stated that if an employee was late for a shift, their name was written on the whiteboard by the fridge. Five tardies in one month and you got fired.

"I'm not late. I'm early," I told her, and pointed to the time clock. "Two minutes early."

"You were supposed to be here an hour ago," she said.

"I was?" I gasped—yes, I actually did that—and said, "I must have read the schedule wrong."

"Don't give me that," Rita said. "You're late and you know it."

"If I was late, would I be *exactly* one hour late?" I asked.

Rita glared at me but didn't say anything. I mean, really, what could she say?

I punched my employee number into the time clock, pressed my finger to the reader, and headed out of the breakroom. Rita gave me major stink-eye as I glided past, but she didn't write my name on the whiteboard.

I win.

My day had been kind of crappy, so what better way to end it than working in a crappy store in a crappier than crappy department. I headed for the area I'd been assigned to these last few days, where I'd been moving the current stock to another location to make room for what would surely be yet another brilliant campaign courtesy of Holt's marketing department.

"Hey, Haley," someone called.

I spotted Grace in the customer service booth. She had the place to herself for the moment—no annoying customers—so I walked over.

Grace was in her early twenties, going to college and working at Holt's so she could—well, I didn't remember, which was bad of me, I know. She was petite, and she always did the coolest things with her hair. Lately she'd been wearing it super short with blond spikes. She really pulled it off.

"Are you working with me tonight?" she asked.

I'd served my time in the customer service booth—really, they should issue orange jumpsuits for that department—and was glad I'd been released.

"I'm in the new section," I said.

"Can you believe what marketing is doing this time?" Grace asked, and rolled her eyes.

I couldn't—because I had no idea what she was talking about. Somebody had probably told me at some point, but I'd drifted off.

That happens a lot.

"The guys from the display department hung the sign today," Grace said. "Check it out."

I didn't really need yet another reason to wish I was elsewhere tonight, but I pushed through and headed toward my assigned department. I mean, really, how bad could it be?

I turned the corner and saw just how bad it was.

Suspended from the ceiling over six empty shelving units was a huge blue and gold sign that read, PAPER-PALOOZA.

Really.

"Hi, Haley," someone called.

Colleen popped up from behind one of the shelving units, smiling and waving for no apparent reason.

"We're working together tonight. You and me. To-gether," she called. "Isn't that the coolest thing?"

No. It wasn't even mildly cool.

Colleen was young and she'd worked here since before I started. I liked to be generous in my thoughts about her, but it was impossible. Either there was something wrong with her mentally, or she was the nicest person on the planet. I didn't know which. It took all the patience I could muster to deal with her—which wasn't much even on a good night.

"We've got this whole new department to stock," Colleen said, still smiling. "Isn't that cool?"

"Not really," I said.

"And it's all paper." She pointed to the sign. "That's what the sign means. Paper-Palooza. That's what's on the sign."

"Yeah, okay."

"The stockroom is full of it. The paper. Like all kinds of paper," she said. "Like the sign says."

"Yeah, I figured."

"You know, like paper plates, paper towels, paper nap-kins—"

"I got it," I told her.

"—copy paper, toilet paper, tissue paper—"

"I understand, Colleen. Really."

"—paper cups, paper—"

I walked off.

The housewares, bath, and kitchen departments were a blur, and of course, so were the customers, as I hurried toward—well, I didn't know where I was headed. I just had to get away from Colleen.

No, I realized, it wasn't just Colleen I wanted to escape. It was the ridiculous Paper-Palooza, the endless stocking, the hideous merchandise—everything about working at Holt's.

I stopped beside the shoe department as a totally fantastic idea flew into my thoughts.

Maybe I could quit now.

Like now. Right now. Tonight. I could march into Jeanette's office, resign, and leave the store doing a series of high-kicks worthy of the Rockettes in the Macy's Thanksgiving Day parade.

I heard myself sigh as the idea oozed through my head, sinking into every brain cell and lighting up each of them as if I'd just found a Louis Vuitton satchel on a clearance table.

Then the image of a different handbag rose to the top of my thoughts—the Sassy satchel. I really wanted to find one and I really wanted to buy it at a discount—something that wouldn't be possible if I quit before the Nuovo acquisition went through.

I thought about it for a while. A ten-percent discount. Was it worth continuing to work here?

Maybe, maybe not. But my medical insurance was worth it.

Damn. When did I get so responsible? It was seriously ruining my mojo.

I tried to calm myself—something I'm not particularly good at—and drew in a big breath. I only had a short while to go before my job performance review at L.A. Affairs would free me of this place. I could hang in there. I could do it.

With no other choice, I headed back to the Paper-Palooza—but I took the long way around, of course. As I circled the store and passed the accessories department, I spotted Detective Shuman.

Oh my God, what was Shuman doing here? He hadn't mentioned coming by the store.

My thoughts raced ahead—sort of like the big rush at the first moment of a sample sale.

Did he have some info about Derrick Ellery's murder? Good news? Like maybe the killer had been caught and the case was solved, meaning there was no chance the Hollywood Haven gala would be canceled and that my standing as fabulous event planner wouldn't be jeopardized so I could ace my job performance review, get full benefits, and quit my job at Holt's?

Was I overreaching here?

I headed toward Shuman and—what the heck?

A girl was with him.

CHAPTER 13

I used one of my stealth moves—something I'd perfected here at Holt's to avoid actually waiting on customers—to sneak up on Shuman and the girl he was with. He had on his usual slightly mismatched coat-shirt-tie combo, so I figured he'd just come from work. She was tall with high-school-length blond hair, and had on jeans and a sweater.

They were standing in the accessories department, in front of a display of scarfs, hats, and gloves. She was giggling and making a big show of handling the merchandise, and Shuman looked completely enthralled, as if he'd never seen a knit hat in his entire life.

Then it hit me.

Oh my God, was this the girl Shuman had been talking to on the phone the day I'd met him outside Starbucks at the Galleria when he'd seemed positively giddy? Was this Shuman's new girlfriend?

I froze—completely abandoning my stealth approach—and looked harder at her. She was young—I mean, really young, like maybe not even twenty yet.

Shuman caught sight of me and turned, and I saw the same big goofy grin on his face I'd seen at the Galleria.

"Hi, Haley," he said. He took her elbow and turned her toward me. "This is Brittany."

"Hey, girl," she said, and grabbed a scarf off the shelf. "Would you look at this thing? It's so ugly it's awesome! I love it!"

Shuman's grin got bigger, as if she'd just explained Einstein's theory of relativity—in German.

"Oh my God, I've got to try this thing on!" she said, and dashed to the closest mirror.

Shuman watched for a few seconds as she draped the scarf around her neck, then turned to me, still smiling.

"How old is she?" I asked.

"She's legal," he said.

"Barely."

Shuman chuckled, as if that were the cutest thing he'd ever heard.

"We're on a date," he explained.

"Where are you headed, the pony rides?"

Shuman laughed harder. "Dinner."

"You realize you'll have to get her drunk in the parking lot first," I said.

Shuman snickered, and I was glad. He'd been through a lot lately. I hadn't seen him smile so much in a long time.

"So what brings you to Holt's?" I asked.

He watched Brittany for a while longer as she posed in front of the mirror with the scarf tied in a huge knot under her chin, then gave himself a little shake and turned to me again.

"You called," he said.

It took me a few seconds to remember that I had, indeed, called him, and a few more to remember why. I'd gotten distracted by Brittany, too. Now she'd added a hat to her look.

"Derrick Ellery's murder," I said. "Those two detectives

assigned to the case haven't contacted me again for more info. What's up with that? I'm the one who found him dead. Anyway, I know they're not going to give me any information. Have you heard something?"

Shuman tore his gaze from Brittany and shifted into cop mode.

"I thought you were going to ask me about the Kelvin Davis murder investigation," he said.

I hadn't intended to do that, but I saw no reason not to get any info Shuman might have.

He seemed to read my thoughts and said, "Ty Cameron hasn't gone in for an interview."

"I heard," I said.

"It arouses suspicion," Shuman told me.

"His attorney advised against it," I said.

"Which makes him look guilty," Shuman pointed out.

I couldn't disagree, so I decided this was an excellent moment to change the subject.

"What about Derrick's murder? Have you heard anything?" I asked.

"It's not my case," Shuman said.

"Yeah, I know."

We just looked at each other for a few seconds. Both of us knew where this was going, but it was a little dance we had to go through quite often. Shuman was an LAPD homicide detective and, naturally, didn't like to share info on an ongoing investigation. That was all well and good and perfectly understandable—for anyone other than me, of course.

Shuman hesitated for another few seconds—a power move, which was totally hot, of course.

"I've asked around, heard a few things," Shuman said. "Walker and Teague aren't making much progress in the case."

"Was there anything useful on the surveillance tape at Hollywood Haven?" I asked.

"The residents and visitors, the employees. Delivery and service people," Shuman said. "Nobody unusual."

We both glanced at Brittany, still in front of the mirror. Now she had on a different hat and two scarfs.

"What about Derrick's personal life?" I asked.

"He had a lot of girlfriends. Models, actresses, business executives," Shuman said. "I'm not sure how he afforded to date those kinds of women. I didn't think a retirement home paid that well."

I wouldn't have thought so either.

"Derrick was popular with the ladies, huh?" I said. "Odd. From what I heard at Hollywood Haven, almost nobody there liked him."

"How so?" Shuman was in full cop mode now.

"He'd fired a number of employees for little or no reason," I told him. "Did you hear anything about them from Teague and Walker? Their names, maybe?"

Shuman shook his head. "No, and it's not likely that I could get detailed info on the case without a good reason."

"A lot of the residents thought Derrick was nosing into their business and asking too many personal questions," I said.

Brittany dashed across the department, jumped in front of us, and struck a pose worthy of a *Vogue* cover. She had on yet another hat, two different scarfs, and had double layered two pairs of gloves.

"Do I look fabulous?" she asked, in a sultry voice, preening and exaggerating her pose. "Or do I look fabulous?"

Shuman sighed deeply. "You look fabulous."

Brittany burst out laughing and threw herself against Shuman. He embraced her and laughed.

"Do you want those?" Shuman asked.

Brittany jumped away and pulled off the hat, scarfs, and gloves.

"No way. These things are hideous," she declared, still laughing. She gave me a little isn't-he-silly eye roll.

I could see why Shuman liked her. I liked her, too.

"We'd better go," he said.

Brittany fluffed her hair into place again and said, "Yeah, Haley, let's get together sometime. We can go shopping, or something. It will be fun."

"Sounds great," I said.

"I'll let you know if I hear anything new," Shuman said to me. "Sorry I wasn't much help."

I waved as they walked away.

Shuman must have been really taken with Brittany because, obviously, he hadn't realized he'd been a great deal of help, even if he didn't have easy access to the names of the employees Derrick had fired.

If Derrick Ellery had been dating multiple women, that meant he had a lot of money, probably more money than he earned from his salary at Hollywood Haven. I needed to find the source. Follow the money—that's what all the crime shows on TV advised, anyway.

Shuman had also helped me out with something else.

If there were no unidentified or suspicious people on the surveillance tape, that meant only one thing—someone who lived, worked, or routinely visited Hollywood Haven was a murderer.

Was there a worse way to start out a day at the office than by doing actual work?

If so, I couldn't imagine what it was.

I arrived at L.A. Affairs and went straight to my office, a Starbucks mocha Frappuccino in hand. No way was I going to the breakroom for coffee, not with all the other employees in there, some of them sure to give me stink-eye because the supplies were running low.

I still couldn't believe I'd volunteered to take Suzie's position as facilities manager.

Maybe I should start paying better attention.

As I sipped my Frappie and settled in at my desk, I made a list of all the complaints I'd heard—the ones I could remember, anyway—and dug out the vendor files. I'd told Priscilla I intended to do an audit of each one, but since that had been nothing but a big, fat, I'm-desperate-to-save-my-job lie, I logged on to each vendor site and ordered the supplies the office needed and completely disregarded each company's stated price. I requested rush deliveries on everything because, apparently, no one in the office could function without pumpkin-flavored coffee creamer.

Since the office plants were dying, I figured there was some sort of problem with our plant service, so I looked up their phone number and called them. After I made my way through the always annoying maze of prompts, I finally got a real person on the line.

"Let me check on that," she said, after I identified myself. A few minutes of always annoying music played, and she returned to the line. "Our service was canceled by your office last week."

Suzie must have done that before she left L.A. Affairs. Couldn't she have followed up on it and gotten a new service? Just because she went into labor, was that a reason to shirk her duty? She could have done it from the hospital. The first few hours of labor weren't all that difficult, so I'd heard, anyway.

"Why did we cancel your service?" I asked.

"Your representative indicated you were looking for a lower priced service," she said.

"You can have the job back if you can get somebody out here this morning," I told her.

I could have negotiated with her and gotten a better price, but plants were dying and I had a ton of other things to do. I mean, jeez, I hadn't even checked my Facebook page yet today.

"I'll have someone there by ten," she said. "I'll send you a new contract."

"Great," I said, and hung up.

Falling back into my chair, I drank the last of my Frappie, relieved that all my annoying jobs were completed. Then my cell phone rang. It was Mom.

Crap.

I could have let her call go to voicemail, but since my other what-did-I-do-to-deserve-this tasks had gone smoothly, I decided to answer.

"I've had a brilliant idea," Mom announced.

Jeez, what was I thinking?

"I want to work abroad," Mom said. "I want to help disadvantaged people in third-world countries."

I couldn't see Mom pulling that off. Her idea of roughing it was driving her Mercedes without the seat warmer on.

"You know, Mom, things are pretty primitive in those places," I said.

"Yes, I know," she said. "That's why they need me. I can help the women with their hair and makeup. I can demonstrate the importance of facial cleansers, toners, and moisturizers, and advise them on other crucial beauty issues."

I was pretty sure the women in Mom's target audience wouldn't appreciate a presentation on fat clothes, eyelash curlers, and cutting your hair to make it grow.

"I don't think that's the kind of help they need, Mom," I said. "Most of them don't even have clean running water."

"What? No running water? I've never heard of anything so outlandish," Mom said. "It's ridiculous. What are people thinking, living in those conditions? What kind of people would do that?"

"Poor people."

"Still, they should have some sort of standards," Mom insisted.

Really, there was nothing I could say to that.

Finally, Mom said, "It's obvious my help isn't needed under those circumstances. I'll keep thinking."

"Sounds great, Mom."

I hung up before she could formulate another brilliant idea, which wasn't all that nice of me, but oh, well.

What had my life turned into? I'd been forced to do actual work first thing in the morning *and* deal with my mom.

I definitely needed to amp up my cool factor.

It seemed I could do that best by leaving the office. I grabbed my things and headed out.

CHAPTER 14

Since my past attempts to connect with Rosalind Fletcher at Hollywood Haven hadn't worked out, I called and made an appointment with her as I drove out of the parking garage. Of course, showing up unannounced and hoping to catch her was an excellent reason to leave the office and avoid other duties, but go-time for the gala was approaching and I had to get on with the final preparations.

I drove to the retirement home and parked, and as I headed toward the entrance I spotted Alden the Great and his daughter strolling along one of the garden walkways. I smiled and waved. Emily waved back.

Karen wasn't at the front desk when I walked through the reception area—she was probably out back having a smoke—which was starting to seem the norm, rather than the exception. I spotted sweet old Ida Verdell in her wheelchair, staring ahead with an empty gaze. Her daughter Sylvia was pushing and railing on about something.

Sylvia, it seemed, was always in a cranky mood. Karen had mentioned that she was always complaining to the staff about something. She'd had a major argument with Derrick a few days before his murder.

There wasn't much to go on but I couldn't rule Sylvia

out as a suspect. Of course, I had no motive or evidence. It was just a feeling.

I also had a feeling about Ida—sorrow. After hearing about her tragic love affair with that musician and composer, seeing her made me sad.

Ty popped into my head. Would I end up like Ida one day, sitting and thinking about him and our love affair that had ended?

I gave myself a mental shake.

Better to focus on the gala, I decided. Besides, today was Friday. No sad thoughts should be allowed on a Friday.

I headed down the hallway to Rosalind's office. The door stood open and I heard voices inside.

Even though I was on time for my appointment, obviously someone was in with her. I paused in the hallway and listened—just to see if I could determine whether or not their conversation was winding down, of course. But from the tone of things and the raised voices, I could tell that wasn't likely to happen soon. So what could I do but walk inside?

The receptionist's desk was empty. Rosalind's office was crowded with three older women—residents, most likely—who were upset about something and giving the woman I took to be Rosalind a hard time. Everyone was on their feet; arms waved, voices were loud.

Rosalind spotted me. The three women stopped talking and turned, and I realized they were the gals who'd volunteered to help me with the swag bags for the gala.

I didn't know how I failed to recognize them—even from behind—since they were all wearing neon bike shorts, visors, and tons of jewelry.

"Haley, thank God you're here," Shana declared.

"We got problems, honey," Delores told me. "Let me tell you, we've got major problems here."

I hoped those problems didn't include canceling the gala or the swag bags I still needed.

Not to sound selfish, of course.

"Can I help you with something?" Rosalind asked me.

She was probably over the hump into sixty, judging from her heavy jowls and eyelids, but her hair showed no gray and she had on a sharp-looking business suit that she'd accessorized well. She had a competent, capable, I-can-handle-anything air about her, even though she looked slightly annoyed—whether it was with me or the gals, I didn't know.

I introduced myself as I held up my L.A. Affairs portfolio, and said, "I called you earlier."

She gave me an I'm-in-the-middle-of-something-but-I-know-I-have-to-do-this nod, and said, "I'll be with you shortly."

That should have been my cue to back out of the office, but no way was I moving until I found out if the gala—thus my job performance review and my opportunity to quit my job at Holt's—was in jeopardy.

Luckily, I didn't have to ask what was going on.

"Again," Delores said. "Again, it's happened. This time to Shana."

"It's disgraceful," Trudy said. "A place like this, and we have to deal with this sort of thing."

"And nothing is being done about it," Delores said.

Okay, I was completely lost.

Trudy must have realized this, because she said, "Shana's earrings were stolen. Right out of her room."

"I was going to wear them to the gala," Shana said. "And now I don't know what I'm going to do."

"Personal possessions are disappearing right and left. Right and left," Delores said. She picked up a sheet of paper from Rosalind's desk and waved it. "And what's being done? I'll tell you what's being done. We're filling out forms. That's it. Filling out forms."

"Forms," Trudy muttered. "Are words on a paper going to get Shana's earrings back? I ask you. Are they? No, of course not."

"We know who took them," Shana said. "It's common knowledge. We know who took everything."

Wow, I was really glad I'd stayed.

"Who?" I asked.

"Nothing has been proved," Rosalind insisted. "I won't sully the reputation of one of our employees by accusing—"

"It was Derrick," Shana said.

Rosalind heaved a frustrated sigh.

"He was always coming in our rooms, uninvited," Shana said. "Completely uninvited."

"Pretending he was interested in us, claiming he wanted to help," Trudy said. "Help us. Can you imagine?"

"And all the while stealing our things," Shana said.

"This should put an end to that rumor once and for all," Rosalind declared. "Derrick Ellery certainly could not have taken your earrings since he's . . . no longer with us."

"Of course he could have," Shana said.

"Listen, honey," Delores said. "Shana wasn't wearing those diamond and ruby earrings every day. They're not the kind of thing you prance around in like they were some cheap knockoffs. They could have been taken weeks ago and she wouldn't have known."

"Derrick could have taken them," Trudy said.

"And I'm sure he did," Shana said.

"The homicide detectives must have searched Derrick's home," I said. "If they found your earrings they'd have to return them."

Trudy brightened. "I hadn't thought of that."

"Haley, honey, you're a genius, an absolute genius," Delores said. "Isn't she a genius?"

"A genius," Shana said.

"If you fill out the form, I'm sure Rosalind will give it to the police," I said.

"Along with all the other forms the other residents have filled out, I hope," Delores said, giving Rosalind semi-major stink-eye.

"Yes, of course," Rosalind said.

"Okay, then. Let's go, girls," Delores said.

The three of them gave me a little finger wave and left the office.

Shana leaned back inside and said, "And don't you worry about those swag bags, Haley. We're working on them. We've got a list—a big list, and we're narrowing it down. They're going to be fabulous. You'll see. Fabulous. So don't worry. We're handling everything."

"Thanks," I said.

Shana disappeared out the door.

Rosalind drew in one of those thank-God-that's-over breaths and dropped into her desk chair. I got the idea she wasn't happy about taking on the extra duty of notifying the police about the thefts, but very glad the gals were mollified and out the door.

"Please, sit down," she said, and gestured to the visitor's chair in front of her desk.

Her office was neat and organized, though stacked high with all sorts of folders, binders, and printouts. I wondered if Mr. Stewart had taken all the crap off his desk and dumped it here for Rosalind to take care of.

That's what I would have done.

"I appreciate your taking the time to see me," I said as I sat down. "I know you're short staffed and very busy since you've taken over Derrick's position as assistant director."

"I'm playing catch-up on a great number of things," Rosalind said. "My work ethic is decidedly different than his was."

She, along with most everyone else I'd talked to here at Hollywood Haven, made no secret of her dislike for Derrick. I wondered if Rosalind had more reason than the others, like maybe she'd been passed over for the assistant director job that Mr. Stewart had given to Derrick. If so, she was bound to resent it.

Enough to murder him?

Maybe.

I was mentally composing a clever way to ease into that topic, but Rosalind put a stop to it.

"What, exactly, can I do for you?" she asked, in a no-nonsense junior-high-teacher voice.

I hate that voice.

I'd hated junior high, too.

"The menu for the gala. I need the final okay for the caterer." I opened the portfolio and handed her the list of appetizers, beverages, meal, and dessert selections Derrick and I had agreed on. "If you're happy with everything, I need your signature at the bottom."

Usually, at this point I'd go over any items I felt might need a second look, but Rosalind didn't seem interested. She gave the list a quick once-over, then signed and passed it back.

"Everything is being handled and is on schedule," I told her.

Usually when I said that to a client I got a big smile, or at least an I'm-relieved sigh. But Rosalind did neither.

"I'll need your final approval on a few things," I said. "I'll let you know as they come up."

"That will be fine," Rosalind said. "Thank you."

I left her office, sure she was glad I was gone, and also sure I was the easiest situation she'd dealt with today.

As I headed down the hallway I spotted Alden the Great and Emily ambling across the lobby. From the residents' wing piano music drifted out of the dayroom and I recognized Frank Sinatra's "Fly Me to the Moon"—though it was definitely not Ol' Blue Eyes voicing the lyrics.

"Hi, Haley," Emily called.

She stopped. Alden tottered ahead, his pace a little slower than usual, I noticed.

"You're here again?" Emily asked, and walked over.

"Just finalizing a few details for the gala," I said. "How's your dad?"

"This isn't one of his best days," she said with a sad smile. "So you'll be coming back again?"

"Several more times," I said.

"Great. So—" Emily glanced at her dad. He was headed down the hallway to the business offices.

"Oh, dear."

She waved as she hurried to catch up with him. I saw her take his arm gently, speak softly to him, then steer him back the other way.

I noticed then that Sylvia was seated on one of the sofas in the lobby and had parked Ida and her wheelchair next to her. As usual, Sylvia was frowning and yammering on about something.

Too bad Ida's love affair with Arthur Zamora hadn't worked out. If they'd married she might have ended up with a daughter as kind and caring as Alden the Great was blessed with. He'd won the daughter lottery for sure.

My brain did a flash-forward to one day in the future when I might have to come and visit my mom or dad at a place like this. Yikes! Definitely not something I wanted to contemplate now—or ever, really.

I spotted Karen at the front desk, finally. Jeez, if things didn't work out for me at L.A. Affairs, maybe I could get hired here. Karen was almost never at her post—my kind of job.

But she didn't look the least bit happy when I walked up. She was wringing her hands and frowning, and looked completely stressed out. I was sure she was desperate for a cigarette break.

I didn't bother with niceties.

"What's wrong?" I asked.

When Karen looked up at me, I saw tight lines around her mouth and dark circles under her eyes.

"I might be in trouble with the police," she said.

My maybe-she-did-it senses jumped completely off the scale.

I'd been told that Derrick had wanted to fire Karen, and I wondered if she'd found out and had ended the situation by murdering him. Had Detectives Walker and Teague wondered the same thing?

"What happened?" I asked, and achieved, I think, the perfect mix of outrage and concern crucial to push this sort of conversation forward.

"The police, they came back and started asking me questions again," Karen said. "They think I saw something the day Derrick was murdered."

"Like what?" I asked.

Karen nodded toward the hallway that led to the business offices. "I can see Derrick's office from here."

I turned and saw that, sure enough, Derrick's office door was clearly visible from Karen's position at the front desk.

"They said the security cameras don't cover the hallway or any of the interior, some sort of privacy issue," Karen said. "So they think I must have seen the murderer go into Derrick's office."

Oh my God. This was some good stuff.

"What did you tell them?" I asked.

"People are always coming and going—all the time. Staff, residents, visitors," Karen said.

"And?"

"It's all routine. So that's what I told them," Karen said. "I didn't see anything that day that stuck out in my mind."

"But?"

"Well, after I got home, I was thinking about it," Karen said.

"Yes?"

"Well, I realized that I'd seen something kind of unusual."

"What was it?"

"I remember because it happened just a few minutes before you arrived," Karen said.

Jeez, if this conversation got any slower I was going to have to get out and push.

"Yeah, okay, so what was it?" I asked.

Karen gulped. "Well, just a few minutes before you got here and went into Derrick's office, I saw Mr. Stewart coming out."

"Was that unusual?" I asked.

"Mr. Stewart never went to Derrick's office. Derrick always went to his," Karen said. "I don't know why I didn't remember it before."

Oh my God. Had that old gray-haired guy shot and killed Derrick?

The thought flashed in my head that Mr. Stewart had been the one who hired Derrick before his background check was completed, only to learn later that he wasn't qualified for the position. Had something happened between the two of them that caused Mr. Stewart to think he could be in major trouble if that fact became known? Had he murdered Derrick to try and cover things up?

"My God, I actually saw who killed Derrick! And I didn't tell the police!" Karen wailed. "Am I going to get in trouble for, you know, withholding information? Are they going to arrest me? I can't go to jail—I can't!"

Karen was on the verge of an all-out snit-fit, right here in the lobby. I glanced around. People were staring. I had to calm her down.

I'm not good at calming anyone down.

Luckily, I saw an easy fix to this situation.

"Here's what you should do," I told her. "Make a list of everyone you saw near Derrick's office that day and—"

"Including your name?"

Oh, crap.

"Technically I wasn't there until later," I pointed out. "Make the list, then call the detectives and explain that you thought about it further, so you wrote down the names of everyone you could remember being in the hallway outside Derrick's office the day he was killed."

Karen took a few seconds to mull this over, then nodded slowly. "That way I'll look as if I'm helping."

"Exactly," I said. "Then let the police take it from there."

"Great. This is perfect. I'll work on the list today and call the detectives—no, I'll wait until Monday to call them so I'll have plenty of time to think about it over the weekend," Karen said, and gave me a bright smile. "Monday. Yes, I'll call them on Monday. Thank you, Haley. Thank you so much."

I headed toward the front door. Emily and Alden the Great were still puttering across the lobby. Mr. Stewart nodded to them as he walked past. Sylvia wasn't talking, for a change, a welcome relief to everyone within earshot.

Delores and Trudy sat huddled close to Shana as she filled out the form Rosalind had given her. Vida and Rosalind were a few yards ahead of me, heading for lunch, I supposed. The gals gave them stink-eye as they went past.

Outside, I made my way across the parking lot to my car, still thinking about what Karen had said—or what she hadn't said.

She hadn't mentioned seeing any former employees whom Derrick had fired going into his office the day of his murder. Karen would have noticed that right away, I figured, so I could pretty much mark any of them off my mental suspect list.

Still, Karen's sudden revelation that she'd seen Mr. Stewart go into Derrick's office seemed odd to me.

Was it true?

Or was she ratting out someone like most everyone else I'd spoken with at Hollywood Haven?

CHAPTER 15

I rolled out of bed Saturday morning, ran through the shower, dried my hair while I pulled on my clothes, put on my makeup as I drove, and whipped into the Holt's parking lot with a full ninety seconds to spare before my shift started. The lot was crowded, which was strange for so early in the day, and a large group of people was gathered by the front entrance, which was even more strange. Customers didn't usually line up awaiting the official start of business except during our Black Friday, Christmas, or blow-out sales.

But as I raced toward the door, I realized these weren't customers. About a dozen people formed a loose line across the entrance. They held up homemade signs fastened to sticks with PAPER-PALOOZA POISONS THE PLANET scrawled across them in big green letters, and were chanting the same phrase.

Oh my God. Protesters.

Leave it to corporate.

I swerved around them and dashed toward the door.

Jeanette was standing inside.

Today she had on a tan tent dress embellished with orange, brown, and gold geometric symbols and patterns around the hem.

She looked like a human tepee.

Jeanette watched my approach, then turned the key and let me in, frowning and looking more than slightly worried—though I'm sure it was her monthly bonus that concerned her, not the safety and well-being of the store employees, should the situation with the protesters turn ugly.

I slipped inside—forcing my gaze onto the floor so as not to sustain permanent retina damage from Jeanette's I'll-wear-anything-if-I-get-it-at-a-discount dress—and she locked the door behind me. I dashed to the breakroom and clocked in four seconds ahead of time—a personal best for me.

Everyone else who'd already clocked in was headed out the door to the sales floor. I spotted Bella standing in front of one of the vending machines, finishing up a soda. She waited while I stowed my handbag—a gorgeous Prada satchel—in my locker.

Bella's apparent desire to escape was reflected in her hairstyle again today. She'd sculpted her hair into what seemed to be a biplane atop her head.

"What the hell is wrong with all those people out front holding up those signs?" Bella asked. "It's Saturday morning. They ought to be sleeping in."

"Or shopping—someplace other than Holt's," I said, as we walked out of the breakroom. "Where are you working today?"

"They got me in the sewing department," Bella grumbled. "I hate that department. That old lady who works there is always showing me pictures of her cats on her cell phone."

"Come work with me in the paper department," I said.

"Colleen's supposed to be there today. Maybe she'll trade with you."

Bella shook her head. "Something's wrong with that girl."

Customers streamed through the aisles as Bella and I headed toward the back of the store and my assigned corner of where-did-it-all-go-so-wrong. I spotted Colleen straightening boxes of tissues in the Paper-Palooza as a dozen shoppers swarmed over the merchandise.

"Hi, Haley. Hi, Bella," Colleen said as she wiggled her way out of the throng of customers. "Wow, would you just look! Everybody loves our department! Isn't it the coolest thing!"

"No, not really," I said. "Listen, Colleen, wouldn't you like to swap with Bella and work in the sewing department today?"

"You're working in sewing today, Bella? Oh, wow, you're so lucky," Colleen said. "That lady who works there has the cutest pictures of her cats. You should ask her to show them to you."

I tried again.

"How about if you work in sewing and Bella works here," I said.

Colleen froze and looked back and forth between Bella and me.

"What?" she asked.

Maybe I should have used smaller words.

"You in sewing," I said. "Bella here."

"You mean work someplace else?" she asked.

I tried fewer words.

"You. Sewing department."

"And not get to work here today?" she asked, and looked horrified. "But this is our department, Haley. It's ours. We, you know, we stocked it and everything. So it's, like, it's ours. Yours and mine. I can't just leave. It wouldn't be right. You know, it wouldn't."

"Those cat pictures are starting to look pretty good," Bella said, and headed down the aisle.

Another wave of customers bore down on us and crowded into the department. Apparently, the Holt's marketing team had managed to reach shoppers, not just protesters. They loaded up with paper products, forcing Colleen and I to do actual work by replenishing the shelves with merchandise from the stockroom, which wasn't so bad because at least I got off the sales floor for a few minutes—well, more than a few.

For some reason, the twenty-roll packs of toilet paper were a favorite item with the shoppers. I went into the stockroom, loaded a U boat, and rolled it to the department. I grabbed a double-armful and was ready to wade into the fray when Jack Bishop walked up.

Oh my God. Jack Bishop.

He looked gorgeous.

I looked like an idiot.

Really, it's impossible to look cool when you're bear-hugging five twenty-roll packs of toilet paper—even if it is ultra soft two-ply.

How humiliating. Of all the times for Jack to see me. Why couldn't he have dropped by L.A. Affairs when I was wearing one of my fully accessorized, everybody-should-see-me-in-this awesome business suit—and all the women who worked there could see him with me and be totally jealous?

Jack's gaze dipped to take in the jeans and red sweater I had on, which fit really great—but that wasn't the point. Oh my God, I couldn't wait to quit Holt's.

"Can you take a break?" Jack asked.

I can always take a break.

I tossed the packs of toilet paper back on the U-boat and led the way down the aisle and through the double doors into the stockroom.

The stockroom was my favorite place in the store—other than the breakroom, of course. There were towering shelving units stuffed with new, fresh, untouched merchandise—and, of course, no customers.

Few employees, too.

The truck team showed up on mornings when there was a shipment to unload, and the ad-set team worked overnight. Sales personnel came back here only to check on something if a customer absolutely insisted, and then sat and rested—or maybe that was just me.

At the moment, Jack and I had the place to ourselves. The store's canned music track played softly in the background. Huge combo packs of bedding filled the shelves around us.

I was surprised to see Jack, after the way we'd parted at the restaurant when I'd asked him to get Ty's phone records. Since he was here he must have had a change of heart—and I wondered why.

He didn't give me a chance to ask, though. He got down to business immediately.

"I found something," Jack said.

He pulled a folded slip of paper from the pocket of his jeans and held it between two fingers.

Several seconds dragged by. I didn't grab for it. Finally, Jack spoke.

"One number," he said. "One call."

Okay, that surprised me. You'd think anything resulting in a clandestine rendezvous, fifty grand in cash, and a handgun would require considerably more prep work.

"That's it?" I asked, and now I was tempted to grab the paper. "One call? You're sure?"

Jack grinned his I'm-too-hot-to-make-a-mistake grin—which was, of course, way hot.

"The call was placed a few days before your ex was involved in that traffic accident on the way to Palmdale," Jack said.

Okay, that didn't look good. That one phone call definitely tied Ty to the location of Kelvin Davis's murder.

"You want to tell me what this is all about?" he asked, and flipped the paper between his fingers.

I hadn't told him about Ty's duffel bag in my closet and I still didn't want to. No way did I want to drag Jack into a police investigation if things went sideways and the cops discovered I'd been withholding evidence in a murder case.

So what could I do but ignore Jack's question—sort of?

"You know that Ty's a person of interest in Kelvin Davis's murder," I said. "I thought there would be more of a connection between Ty and somebody in Palmdale. One call? That's not much to go on."

"There could have been more," Jack pointed out. "He might have wanted to keep the caller's identity a secret so, after the initial contact, he bought a burner."

A disposable, prepaid phone was a possibility—though it was hard to imagine my color-inside-the-lines ex-official-boyfriend knowing about them well enough to purchase one.

"That's possible," I said. "His assistant is involved with his personal finances. He might not have wanted her to know about the call."

"Or he might have foreseen police involvement," Jack said, "and didn't want to leave an electronic trail."

It hit me then that the car accident Ty had been in on his way to Palmdale might not have been his first trip there. For all I knew, he'd gone there many times. Plus, there was the possibility that whomever he'd spoken with on the phone had made the trek to L.A. to see him.

"What else can I do for you?" Jack asked.

Only he didn't ask in his private detective voice. He'd shifted to his Barry White voice.

I'm totally defenseless against Jack's Barry White voice.

He took a step closer. Wow, he smelled great.

"So how about it?" he asked, easing even closer. "Are there any more of your needs I can fill?"

Oh my God. Had somebody turned up the heat in the stockroom?

He braced his arm against the shelving unit behind me and leaned in.

"I behaved badly when we were at the restaurant," he whispered.

I felt his breath on my cheek.

"I shouldn't have done that," he said.

My heart pounded.

"Can you forgive me?" he asked.

My breath came in short little puffs.

"Maybe we should kiss and make up?" he said, and lowered his head.

The stockroom door burst open and banged against the wall.

"Haley! Haley! Haley!" Colleen cried as she rushed down the aisle.

I didn't realize what was happening—can you blame me?—but Jack whipped around and stood in front of me.

"Where's Haley?" Colleen wailed.

I hate her.

"Have you seen Haley?" she asked. "Oh, gosh. I have to find her. She's in charge of toilet paper. We need toilet paper. She's supposed to be getting the toilet paper!"

Jack nodded toward the rear of the stockroom and said, "I saw her back there a few minutes ago."

"Haley!" Colleen yelled, and hurried away.

Jack turned around and gave me a smoking hot grin, then slipped the paper with the phone number on it into the front of my sweater and left the stockroom.

I grabbed the shelving unit to keep from falling.

Oh my God. Jack had almost kissed me. But he hadn't—because of Colleen.

I hate her.

I hate the Paper-Palooza sale.

I hate Holt's.

Now, I even hate toilet paper.

No way was I living like this any longer.

There was no undo button I could hit that would cancel out everything that had just happened, but there was still something I could do about it.

I charged out of the stockroom and forced my way through the throngs of shoppers who had descended on the Paper-Palooza like locusts on an Oklahoma cornfield. I didn't slow down until I reached Jeanette's office.

I charged inside. She sat behind her desk, studying the computer screen and tapping on the keyboard.

"I'm quitting."

I might have said that a little too loud.

She looked up at me, her eyes wide.

"I won't be working here much longer and I won't be here for the holidays."

I'm sure I said that too loud.

"I'm done!"

I stormed out of the office.

CHAPTER 16

My day at Holt's had just ended. I was tired, hungry, and slightly out of sorts, but I couldn't seem to bring myself to start my car and drive out of the parking lot.

I'd pulled an eight-hour shift today, so it was getting dark. The big cursive Holt's sign glowed neon blue atop the building. The store was still open, so the Paper-Palooza protesters continued waving their signs and chanting near the entrance. As the day had gone on it seemed that fewer customers were in the store, so I figured shoppers had left after seeing the commotion out front. I'm sure the management team was worried about profits and public opinion—I was just irritated by the whole thing.

I didn't feel so great about screaming my resignation at Jeanette this morning. I was glad I'd told her I was quitting, but I should have handled it differently. I doubted she'd thought much about it, given the protesters and what could be a sizable drop in store sales and her monthly bonus.

And, of course, there was that moment in the stockroom with Jack.

From the pocket of my jeans I pulled the folded paper that he'd slipped into the front of my sweater. It felt warm to the touch and still carried his scent—or so it seemed, anyway.

I sat there staring down at it.

Of course, Jack hadn't provided just the phone number. There was also an address and a name—a woman's name.

Seeing the words and numbers printed on the slip of paper still made me feel kind of icky, even though I'd read them as soon as I'd blasted out of Jeanette's office this morning. Ty had been in contact with a woman in Palmdale. Once, for sure; maybe—probably—more than that.

And he'd done it while he and I were dating.

I had no real reason to think there was anything romantic going on between her and Ty. This Brianna King could have been anyone—a cousin, an aunt, a mentor, an old friend. Still, I couldn't shake the feeling of betrayal that had been bearing down on me all day.

Why else would Ty not have mentioned her to me?

Why else would he have kept her a secret?

And how could she not be connected to the murder of Kelvin Davis, which Ty had become involved with?

I'm not big on suspense—usually. But right now, at this moment, I wasn't sure I wanted to know exactly who Brianna King was and why Ty had kept her presence in his life hidden from me.

Of course, I could have called my best friend, Marcie, and talked it over with her. She had a way of making me feel better about things—as only a BFF can. But this ache in my chest and around my heart couldn't be eased, soothed, or calmed with a maybe-she's-this-maybe-she's-that conversation.

Still, I had to find out.

I knew my limitations, and only a *venti* mocha Frappuccino with extra whipped cream and double chocolate drizzle would get me through the rest of this evening. I started my car and drove to Starbucks.

The drive-through was quick, so I got my Frappie in record time, parked, and pulled out my cell phone. I figured that if anybody would recognize the name Brianna King it would be Ty's personal assistant. Even though I'd asked Amber if Ty knew anyone in Palmdale and she'd said no, there was a possibility that Amber had heard the name but not made the connection.

It was prime let's-hit-a-club time on a Saturday night, but Amber answered right away. I heard music and voices in the background, so I figured I'd interrupted her evening—which was just the excuse I needed to keep this conversation short.

"Hi, Haley. What's up?"

Amber didn't sound rushed or anxious to get rid of my call, which I appreciated. I came right to the point.

"Does Ty know anyone named Brianna King?" I asked.

"No," she said.

I was always amazed at how well Amber remembered every detail of Ty's life and kept up on absolutely everything.

"Why?" she asked.

I hesitated for a few seconds, then said, "You don't want to know."

"I can live with that," Amber said.

I was also amazed at how she could be so deeply involved in Ty's life, yet separate herself from everything personal.

"She must be someone from back in the day before I started working for him," Amber said.

"Yeah, probably," I said. "Thanks anyway."

"Sure," Amber said. "And did we have this conversation?"

I'd never put her in a tough spot by asking her to keep anything from Ty, but I really didn't want him to know what I was doing.

"No, I'd rather we hadn't," I said, "if you're cool with that."

"No problem," Amber said.

I thanked her again, ended the call, and took a long sip from my Frappie.

Only one person remained whom I could call for info. I scrolled through my contact list and hit the button for Ada, Ty's grandmother.

Ada was a hoot. We'd gone shopping and sightseeing together back when Ty and I were an official couple. I liked her a lot and we'd had a great time together.

I'd run into a friend of hers at a wedding who'd left me with the impression that Ty hadn't told his grandmother we weren't together any longer. I really hoped that situation had been remedied; I didn't want to be the one to break the news to her.

"Haley, dear, how are you?" Ada said, when she answered my call.

She sounded upbeat and cheerful, as always.

"I'm hanging in there," I said. "How about you?"

"Troubled," she said. "I know that you and Ty broke up."

Hearing those words spoken aloud sent an unpleasant jolt through me—still, after all this time.

"Oh, that boy," Ada muttered.

Ty was in his thirties, ran an international corporation on two continents, was responsible for hundreds of millions of dollars and a vast number of employees, and Ada still referred to him as a boy. Oh well, I guess grandmas were allowed.

"I don't know what he's thinking sometimes," she said.

"Typical of the Cameron men. Thinking something completely to death—then doing the wrong thing."

I couldn't help smiling, knowing that Ada was still in my corner.

"Ada, I was wondering if you knew anyone named Brianna King?" I asked.

She was quiet for a few seconds, then said, "That name is vaguely familiar. Let me think for a minute and I'll remember—oh, dear."

Her "oh, dear" made my heart lurch.

This couldn't be good.

I braced myself and asked, "You know her?"

"I *knew* her," Ada pointed out. "I haven't heard her name mentioned in a long time. Years, really."

I started to feel kind of icky.

"Ty met her in Europe the year after he graduated college," Ada said. "She was touring with friends, the same as he was."

Now I felt really icky.

"Turned out, she was from right here in the L.A. area. She came around for a while with his other friends, then . . . well, I don't know what happened, exactly," Ada said. "She just disappeared and Ty never mentioned her again."

Yeah, okay, now I felt super icky.

"Why are you asking about Brianna?" Ada said. "Is Ty involved with her again?"

I mentally scrambled, desperate to come up with a reasonable excuse for asking her about Brianna.

Jeez, I wish I'd thought of that before I called.

Luckily, my tricked-out Frappie had pumped up my brain cells to peak performance levels.

"Ty's assistant called me," I said. "She's organizing a function and she came across Brianna's name for the guest list. She didn't know who Brianna was, and I don't know, so I thought you might."

"What sort of function?" Ada asked.

She sounded a little suspicious now—not that I blamed her.

"Some sort of award," I said. "Ty doesn't know about it yet, so please don't say anything."

Okay, that was an outright lie, but what else could I say?

I didn't want Ada to know the reason I'd asked about Brianna. I wasn't even sure she'd been told that Ty was a person of interest in the Kelvin Davis murder investigation—and no way was I going to be the one who broke that news to her.

"I see," Ada said, in that I'm-not-sure-I-believe-this tone.

I decided it was better to let Ada think I was checking out a possible girlfriend in Ty's life rather than that I was investigating his involvement in a major crime.

"And," I said, "I wondered if she was somebody Ty was dating now."

"I see," Ada said, and it sounded as if this was something she understood.

"But, please, don't say anything," I said. "I don't want Ty to think I'm . . . well, that I'm checking up on him, like some crazy psycho ex-girlfriend."

"I'll keep this to myself," she promised, then shifted topics. "And you and I must go shopping again soon."

"You bet," I said, and was relieved because I really liked Ada. "See you soon."

"Take care, dear," she said, and hung up.

I sat in my car a while longer, thinking as I finished my Frappuccino. My next move was obvious, but difficult to commit to. I wasn't sure I wanted to learn exactly what had happened between Ty and Brianna King in Europe after they'd both graduated college.

I knew what had probably gone on, but I didn't want to think too much about the details.

But I did wonder why, after returning to Los Angeles, Ty had introduced Brianna to his family and brought her around often only to have her suddenly disappear from their lives. Bringing a girl to meet the family wasn't a decision made lightly—and Ty never made a decision in that fashion.

Of course, all of that had happened many years ago—nine or ten years ago, if my math was right. A lot could have changed. Back then, Ty was younger, freer, as of yet not burdened with the running of the Holt's Department Store chain. Maybe he hadn't been taking life so seriously.

And what about Brianna King? What was up with her? Her life must have changed, too, although it didn't escape my notice that Ada had recognized Brianna by her last name, which meant she hadn't married.

Whatever had gone on between Ty and Brianna must have been over and done with a long time ago, given that Ada had to cast her thoughts back nearly a decade to remember who Brianna was. They'd moved on, gone their separate ways, and gotten on with their lives.

Until recently.

What happened, I wondered? What had changed?

I had to find out.

On Sunday morning, I punched Brianna King's home address into my GPS and headed north on the 14 toward Palmdale. The freeway climbed higher and higher and wound through sparsely populated rugged hills and past pockets of houses and businesses until it crested a hill and I descended into the Antelope Valley, the entrance to California's High Desert, home to Palmdale, Lancaster, and dozens of other towns and communities.

I'd come here to pick up Ty from the hospital after his car accident, but that wasn't the only time. My dad was an aerospace engineer so, when we were kids, he'd taken my brother, sister, and me to the annual air show at Edwards Air Force Base, situated at the other side of the valley.

My GPS took me off the freeway at the Rancho Vista Boulevard exit, then west past a shopping mall, restaurants, and lots of other businesses. The streets were crowded—though not as bad as in L.A.—and the area looked prosperous.

After a few miles, I turned left on Resort Way and navigated a maze of residential streets until the GPS announced I'd reached my destination. I drove to the end of the cul-de-sac, flipped a U, and pulled in at the curb in front of a house down the block and across the street from Brianna's.

It was a neighborhood of tract homes probably built within the past few years during the boom, before the housing market—and the economy—collapsed. The houses varied in size—some one story, others larger—and were situated on small lots nicely landscaped with shrubs, green grass, and flower beds. It looked like a warm, welcoming, safe place to live and raise a family.

And this was where Brianna King lived?

It didn't sit right with me, for some reason.

I stayed in my car, unsure of what to do. My first instinct was to ring the doorbell and ask this Brianna King just what the heck was going on. I held back, though, watched the house and waited.

I'm not good at waiting.

Just when my patience reached its end, the garage door on a house down the block opened and a little girl rode out on her two-wheeler. A woman, who must have been her mom, came out after her, set up a folding chair in the driveway, and watched as the girl cruised around the cul-de-sac.

Soon, other garage doors on the street opened and more children came out bringing bikes, three-wheelers, and scooters with them—along with their moms and dads to keep watch. The kids knew each other. They laughed and talked as they rode. The parents waved to their neighbors. Some of them joined up on the sidewalk and chatted.

The garage door on Brianna's house rolled up. A girl on a bicycle rode down the driveway and joined the other kids riding around the cul-de-sac.

My heart started to beat faster.

She was a cute little girl, dressed in yellow pants and T-shirt and wearing a pink sparkly helmet over her light brown hair.

I started to feel sick.

She looked as if she was about eight years old.

Eight. Nine, maybe. Born around the time Brianna had disappeared from the Cameron family. A year, perhaps, after Ty and she had returned from Europe.

An icky, yucky feeling settled over me.

Was that little girl Ty's child?

CHAPTER 17

"Haley? Haley? Haley!"

I stopped, looked back, and saw Jeanette weaving toward me through a cluster of shoppers near the checkout lanes. For once, I really hadn't heard her call my name and deliberately ignored her. I'd been zoned out, my thoughts someplace else.

I'd been that way all day since driving back from Palmdale this morning, so out of it I'd actually waited on customers today—that's how upset I was about the whole Brianna King thing.

My shift was over—I'd never be too whacked out to inadvertently work overtime—but the store was still open, so I stepped out of the aisle and into the area near the front door and waited for Jeanette to catch up.

Today, she had on a circle-skirt dress that had, literally, every imaginable color in its swirl pattern.

She looked like a rainbow that had melted, then been hit by a tornado.

"Haley," Jeanette said, as she stopped next to me, "I want to update you on what's going on—"

The protesters' "Paper-Palooza poisons the planet" chant

drifted in when the doors opened, then cut off abruptly when they closed. Through the glass I saw them—still a dozen or more—waving their homemade signs and walking in a large circle.

Jeanette cringed. "I'm still waiting for corporate to decide how to handle the situation. This has never happened before."

Protesters unhappy about a sale on paper products weren't even on my radar at the moment. Call me selfish, but there it was.

"We're the only store being targeted right now, but that could change at any moment," Jeanette said. "It seems to be a local group of activists looking for publicity. If they get it and their cause gains momentum, this could be a huge, costly public relations nightmare."

"I have to go, Jeanette," I said, and gestured outside. "I'm meeting someone and I don't want to be late."

That was a lie, which, I know, wasn't very nice of me, but I just didn't have the emotional capacity to take on someone else's trouble at the moment.

My excuse to leave could have been true, though. Marcie had texted me earlier and suggested we go shopping. She'd heard from someone who worked with her that the must-have Sassy satchel had been spotted at one of the high-end boutiques on Montana Avenue, a super cool shopping area in Santa Monica. I'd texted back that I wasn't up for it. I hadn't offered an explanation, but Marcie was cool with it, as a BFF would be.

"I received a memo from corporate today," Jeanette said. "The acquisition of the Nuovo shops is still going forward, there's no question about it. But due to the delay and the inconvenience, it's been decided that the employee discount on merchandise will be increased. It will be twenty percent now, rather than the ten percent reported earlier."

Yes, my thoughts had been in a fog most of the day, but this news definitely penetrated.

Oh my God. Corporate had done something nice for the employees? They'd actually upped our discount?

Jeanette seemed to be waiting for me to turn a cartwheel, or something, but I was too stunned to speak, let alone move.

"Well, have a nice evening," Jeanette finally said, and headed toward the rear of the store.

Wow, could this day get any weirder?

I left the store, skirted around the protesters, and headed for my car. It was dark and the feeble we're-desperate-to-save-a-dime security lighting was barely bright enough to illuminate the parking lot. Just as I reached my Honda, a petite blonde jumped out of the car parked next to mine.

"Haley?" she called.

Oh my God. It was Marcie.

"Didn't you get my text?" I asked as she walked over.

"I got it, which is why I'm here," she said. "If you're not up for shopping, something's definitely wrong. What is it?"

Is she the greatest bestie on the planet, or what?

"I don't know where to start," I said.

"Get in the car," Marcie said. "We're going to Starbucks."

Luckily, the nearest one was only a few minutes away in one of the area's many upscale strip malls. We both got our favorite drinks and found a table outside on the patio. The area was lit with twinkle lights in the trees and shrubs, and the weather was Southern California perfect.

Marcie didn't say anything right away, which I appreciated. She knew I had to fortify myself with at least a third of my Frappuccino.

"Okay, what's going on?" she finally asked.

"I think Ty might have been involved with someone while we were dating," I told her.

"Oh my God," she said.

"I think maybe he has a child with her," I said.

"You're kidding."

I explained that I'd learned about Brianna King—I left out the part about Jack giving me her info—and that I'd talked to Ty's grandmother, then gone to her house in Palmdale and seen the little girl. Marcie listened, didn't interrupt or ask any questions until I'd spilled the whole story.

"Did you see the girl's mom? This Brianna King?" she asked.

"She came out of the house and watched the little girl," I said. "She chatted with the neighbors, which made me think she actually lived in the house and wasn't just visiting."

"What did she look like?"

"Tall, dark hair, pretty," I said.

"Sounds like you," Marcie said. "Ty's type."

It was true, but it didn't make me feel any better.

"What was the house like?" Marcie asked.

"Very nice, and in a great neighborhood," I said. "There was a BMW in the garage."

"So you think Ty had a fling with her in Europe, brought her home to meet the family, then it all fell apart when she got pregnant?" Marcie asked.

"It makes sense," I said.

"Not really," Marcie pointed out.

Marcie is almost always right about things.

I hate it when other people are right about things.

"Why not tell his family?" Marcie asked. "Even if Ty and Brianna didn't want to get married, why keep it a secret? Ty has a great family. They would have understood.

This would have been their first grandchild. They would have welcomed Brianna and the baby, wouldn't they?"

"Probably," I said. "But maybe not. Who knows what really went on? Maybe it was Brianna's idea. Maybe she didn't want Ty's family to know."

"So you're thinking that Ty stayed in touch with her all of these years, even while you two were dating?" Marcie asked. "He's been involved with the little girl's life? He's supported the two of them?"

"You think I'm crazy, don't you?" I said.

"I think you need more information," Marcie replied. "Give me her address."

I dug through my handbag for the slip of paper Jack had given me and held it up. Marcie typed the info into her cell phone.

"When I get to work in the morning I'll ask my friend in the mortgage department to do a property search," she said.

Marcie worked at a huge bank downtown. She'd been there for years, had worked in several departments, and had friends throughout the building. She'd done this sort of thing for me before.

"I'll find out who the legal owner of the house is. If it's Ty, then you'll know for sure." Marcie looked up at me. "If you really want to know, that is."

My heart ached as I thought about it, but I knew I had to go through with it. I had to find out.

"I want to know," I said.

What I didn't know was what any of this had to do with the murder of Kelvin Davis.

Maybe nothing.

Maybe everything.

*   *   *

Working at L.A. Affairs had suddenly become a lot like working at Holt's.

What had happened to my life?

I didn't know but it sure as heck wasn't what I wanted to face first thing on a Monday morning.

I stood in the supply room staring at the few remaining office and breakroom supplies on the shelves. Unlike the stockroom at Holt's, this one at L.A. Affairs was small—not any bigger than a walk-in closet—harshly lit and totally devoid of anything that might be remotely fun to try on or try out.

Stacked in the center of the room were the supplies I'd ordered last week, still in their brown shipping boxes. Someone had left them here for me to open and shelve—just like at Holt's except that Bella and Sandy weren't here for me to chat with and make the time go by quicker, and there was no chance that I might get to abandon the chore by hiding from a customer.

Since I'd worked at Holt's for such a long time I was a pro at opening boxes and shelving merchandise, but this morning I managed to stretch it out for an inordinate amount of time. I'd brought the official supply inventory folder with me and checked off each item as I pulled it from its shipping box.

Everything that I'd ordered had arrived, so in theory L.A. Affairs could continue to function now that the pumpkin-flavored coffee creamer was on hand and the paper plates had been replenished.

Maybe Mindy could ace her job as receptionist once she held one of the newly acquired fine-tip pens in her hand. Who knows? Maybe that was all it would take to turn her into an efficient, alert, crackerjack receptionist. And I'd be responsible for the stunning metamorphosis.

Maybe that would be noted in my job performance review.

The plant service had been in and done whatever it was a plant service did, and I'd received a confirmation e-mail from the building maintenance department that the fluorescent lightbulbs I'd requested for the ladies' restroom had been installed.

I finished shelving everything, delivered the supplies to the breakroom, took Mindy a pack of pens, and went to my office, glad that the unpleasantness was over and done with.

Then it hit me—my duties as facilities manager wouldn't end until Susie came back from maternity leave.

Then something else hit me—what if she didn't come back? What if she wanted to stay home with her baby?

I'd kick in for a nanny if I had to.

Just as I was settling in to catch up on everything I'd let slide this morning, my office phone rang. It was Mindy.

"Edie, you have a call—"

"It's Haley."

"That's right," Mindy said, and giggled. "Yes, Haley. That's who you are."

"Is there a phone call for me?" I asked.

"What? Oh. Well, let me see. No, no, there's no phone call for you," Mindy said. "You have a client. Yes, a client. A woman. Her name is . . . let me look. Oh, yes. Here it is. It's a Mrs. Potter. I wrote it down—"

I hung up.

Maybe I could get a refund on the fine-tipped pens.

I didn't have a client named Mrs. Potter, but I had a pretty good idea who had arrived sans appointment to speak with me. I grabbed the portfolio and searched the interview rooms until I spotted Laronda Bain.

Thanks to the Botox that gave her an I-just-came-to-life-in-a-wax-museum look, I didn't know if she was happy or sad, worried or completely relaxed over the prep for her son's Harry Potter-themed birthday party.

"You were on my schedule to call this afternoon," I said as I sat down across the desk from her, which, oddly enough, was the truth. Like I said, I'm really pretty good at this job.

"Everything is being handled and will be ready in plenty of time for the party?" Laronda asked.

"Of course," I said.

"Good, because I've thought of something additional," she said.

Oh, crap.

"I'd like the entrance to the party to be unique and special," Laronda said.

"That's one of the things I'd intended to speak with you about this afternoon," I said.

Okay, that was a lie, but so what.

"I think entry to the party should be through a door marked 'platform nine and three-fourths,' designed after the King's Cross railway station," Laronda said.

Good grief. How much major construction did she want for a kid's eighth birthday party? And how did she think I was supposed to pull this off on such short notice?

I'd heard rumors of an event-planner relocation program. Maybe I should check into it.

"I'll get right on it," I said.

"Thank you," she told me, and I'm sure she was smiling on the inside even though her face couldn't show it.

Laronda left and I went back to my office. As I passed the window and glanced across the street at the Galleria, I was pretty sure I heard Starbucks call my name. I was plotting my escape when my cell phone rang. Marcie's name was on the ID screen.

I knew she was calling about the property search on Brianna King's house that we'd discussed last night.

I got a weird feeling.

"I just received the info," Marcie said when I answered.

My weird feeling got weirder.

"Are you sure you want to know?" she asked.

Oh, crap.

CHAPTER 18

"Hang on," I said, and collapsed into my desk chair. My mind raced. What if Marcie told me the property report revealed that the house Brianna King and her daughter lived in actually belonged to Ty? What if Ty and Brianna had been involved all these years? What if that little girl was his?

What if he'd really kept that secret from me during the time we were dating?

Heaviness settled around my heart, making it a little hard to breathe. Could there be a bigger betrayal?

How could Ty do something like that to me?

Then another thought flew into my head. Really, Ty hadn't done anything—that I knew of with certainty, anyway. This whole thing existed only in my head. I'd made it all up after seeing Brianna's house, neighborhood, and that little girl.

And what did that say about me?

I didn't feel so great about myself. I'd jumped to conclusions. I'd thought the worst of Ty. Now I could find out the truth.

I pressed my cell phone to my ear and said, "Tell me everything."

"I know you didn't ask about this, but I checked on a couple of other things," Marcie said. "Brianna King has checking and savings accounts with about nine grand in them. She's got a few credit cards, all with low balances."

Marcie could get into trouble for accessing this sort of information without the person's permission, but she knew how to game the system so it was very unlikely that anyone would find out that she'd done it. Still, it was a risk and she'd take it for me. Is that a terrific bestie move, or what?

"Sounds as if she has a pretty conservative lifestyle," I said.

"It does," Marcie agreed. She paused, and I heard her draw a breath. "Okay, here's the deal on the property. The house is in Brianna's name. Her name alone. Ty's name appears nowhere on the deed."

A whoop of joy welled inside me, but something about Marcie's tone made me hold back.

"But that's good, isn't it?" I asked. "It means Ty's not involved, right?"

"As I said, he's not on the title to the property," Marcie said. "But get this—there's no mortgage."

"She paid off her house? Already?" I asked.

"No. There was never a mortgage," Marcie said. "It was purchased outright with cash."

My icky, sickly feeling came back with a vengeance.

"Who put up the money?" I asked.

"I don't know. That information isn't available. There's no way I can find out," Marcie said. She was quiet for a few seconds, then said the same thing I'd been thinking. "Nothing I've found in her background indicates she ever had that kind of money, which means—"

"—that somebody who has a lot of money bought the house for her," I said. "Somebody like Ty."

Neither of us said anything for a while, but a zillion

thoughts flew through my mind—and all of them were hurtful, troubling, and disheartening.

"Sorry. I guess this info didn't help anything," Marcie said. "You still don't know what was going on between her and Ty."

"I needed to hear it," I said. "Thanks, Marcie."

I ended the call and just sat there at my desk.

Only a few minutes ago I'd chided myself for thinking the worst about Ty. I didn't want to keep doing that. There could very well be a logical, innocent reason for everything I'd learned that had nothing at all to do with Ty.

But at the moment, I couldn't imagine what it might be—nor could I think of a way to find out.

There seemed to be nothing I could do at the moment but perform actual work.

I hate it when that happens.

The portfolio for Laronda Bain's party sat atop a stack of folders on my desk, so I started there. I phoned Lyle, the guy who owned the construction company L.A. Affairs worked with, and explained about the latest addition to the Harry Potter-themed birthday. Luckily, he was okay with it, said it wouldn't be a problem to build, and promised to send an estimate by the end of the day.

He'd done lots of work for our overindulged clients, so we both knew that Laronda would have her railway platform regardless of the price.

I spent the next few hours calling vendors, venues, and clients, ordering what I needed for upcoming events that I'd been handling, plus those I'd inherited from Suzie. My most pressing event was the Hollywood Haven fiftieth anniversary gala. Everything was coming together on schedule, with the exception of the swag bags.

The gals at the retirement home had promised to come up with a list of suggested items with which to fill the bags, but I hadn't seen anything from them yet. I couldn't wait much longer, so I decided I'd better hurry them along. I grabbed my handbag—a gray and white Burberry that I'd paired with my gray pencil skirt and blazer—and the Hollywood Haven portfolio, and headed for the door.

Just as I stepped into the hallway I spotted Priscilla barreling toward me, her gaze boring into me like twin mascara-fringed laser beams.

Good grief, what now?

I walked back into my office and she followed me.

"What's going on with all these rumors that are circulating?" Priscilla asked in a low, urgent voice. "What's happened? What's going on?"

On occasions such as this I've found it better to say nothing for as long as possible. Believe me, it's better that way.

Priscilla rushed ahead and said, "I've had phone calls, texts, and e-mails from personal assistants, management teams, and production offices."

Oh, crap. This couldn't be good.

"I'm fielding their questions as best I can," Priscilla said. "But is it true? Is Hollywood Haven canceling their gala?"

Oh my God. What was going on? How had that rumor gotten started?

"This is a public relations disaster," Priscilla declared. "A-list stars are expected. Their schedules have been arranged so they can attend this event. Our wealthiest clients will be in attendance. Our every move is being scrutinized by the very people who keep us in business. And now there's talk that the gala will be canceled? Everyone's plans will be unwound? L.A. Affairs will be the talk of Hollywood—and not in a good way? What is going on, Haley?"

"That's exactly what I intend to find out," I told her,

using my I've-got-this voice. I held up the Hollywood Haven portfolio. "I'm on my way over there right now and I intend to get to the bottom of this."

Priscilla looked slightly embarrassed that she'd barged in and delivered this information with I-could-have-a-stroke-at-any-second urgency, but she also looked relieved.

"You'll keep me informed?" she asked.

"Of course," I said.

I left before she could ask anything else.

I didn't know where the rumors had come from that the anniversary gala would be canceled, but I had a pretty good idea. Mr. Stewart had mentioned it and so had Rosalind. They were both worried about how it would look, in light of Derrick Ellery's murder.

I wasn't going to let the event be canceled, of course, so I figured that the best way to make sure the gala went ahead was to solve Derrick's murder—now. Really, I should have been putting more effort into it all along. I'd gotten distracted with other things when I should have stayed focused on what was most important—solving the murder, executing a flawless event, acing my job performance review, and quitting my job at Holt's.

The thought raged in my head as I drove out of the parking garage and turned onto Ventura Boulevard. Likely suspects popped into my thoughts.

Mr. Stewart materialized immediately.

At first glance it seemed that he had no reason to murder Derrick, since Derrick took care of most everything at the home and made Mr. Stewart's job easier. But, as it turned out, that wasn't really true.

Mr. Stewart had hired Derrick as the assistant director even though Vida hadn't completed his background investigation. Then, it was learned that Derrick had lied on his résumé and wasn't qualified for the position. And not only that, but he caused problems with the residents that had generated numerous complaints.

None of this made Mr. Stewart look good in the eyes of the powers that be at Hollywood Haven. In fact, it could have caused him real trouble. Was he in danger of losing his job? Had he killed Derrick to cover up his mistake in hiring him?

I wondered, too, if the complaints from the residents had turned into something bigger. Had lawyers gotten involved? Legal action could devastate the retirement home's reputation, to say nothing of draining their profits.

Karen had told me last week that she'd seen Mr. Stewart coming out of Derrick's office only minutes before I'd gone in and discovered his body. That put him in the right place at the right time, with a solid motive.

Karen had also told me that she would talk to the homicide detectives today and make them aware of what she'd seen. I intended to ask her about it when I got there.

Other than Karen's eyewitness account, no proof and no evidence existed that Mr. Stewart had done the deed. But maybe I could find some.

Jack Bishop popped into my mind—certainly the most pleasant thought I'd had all day. He did consulting work— which was code for digging up dirt—for a number of companies in Los Angeles, including the Pike Warner law firm. I knew there was a database that contained info on every lawsuit that was filed, and that Jack could gain access to it.

I activated my Bluetooth and called him. His voicemail picked up. He was probably busy doing something way cooler than what I was doing at the moment.

Usually, I asked him to call me—just so I could adequately explain things, not because I liked the sound of his voice, of course—but I was short on time so I left a message requesting that he check to see if there were any lawsuits filed that involved Hollywood Haven and Mr. Stewart. Hopefully, he'd get back to me quickly.

The suspects in Derrick's death that Detective Shuman had told me about were a lot harder to pin down. Shuman had reported that Derrick had a number of girlfriends. There wasn't much I could do to follow up on them without specific info.

But Shuman had made a valid point when he'd wondered how Derrick had afforded to date so many different women. I hadn't thought Hollywood Haven paid that well, and neither had Shuman.

At the next traffic light I stopped and dashed off a quick text message to Marcie asking if she could find any bank accounts for Derrick Ellery. I didn't have much of his personal info to give her, but she knew her way around the system and, hopefully, she could come up with something.

The light turned green and I drove forward with the line of traffic.

From the talk I'd heard at Hollywood Haven I'd learned that both Vida and Karen were on Derrick's hit list, both in danger of being fired by him. Had one of them taken the ultimate I'm-keeping-this-job step and done away with Derrick before he could give them the boot?

Neither Vida nor Karen seemed the type, but when it came to losing your job, your income, your benefits, and possibly the roof over your head, people could get desperate and sometimes felt justified in taking drastic steps. I wasn't going to rule out either of them, especially Vida, who had been seen arguing with Derrick.

And what about Sylvia? Karen had told me that she was

a chronic complainer and that there was bad blood between her and Derrick. They'd even gotten into a screaming match in Derrick's office, which seemed like something more than a routine gripe involving conditions at the facility. But what? I'd ask Karen today if she'd overheard anything specific.

By the time I turned into the Hollywood Haven parking lot my mental list of suspects was exhausted and I hadn't come up with anything new or compelling, just a lot of questions. I needed more information and I could think of only one other place to get it, at the moment.

As I whipped into a parking space I scrolled through the contact list on my cell phone and called Detective Shuman. He didn't answer, but I wasn't surprised. His duties as a homicide detective kept him hopping most of the time. I left a message asking if he'd heard anything more about the murder investigation, and ended the call.

I sat there for a few minutes, trying to think of someone else who might have some info I could use, but I didn't come up with anybody, so I gathered my things and headed for the entrance. The day was gorgeous, as always, and a number of the residents were puttering along on the walking paths through the gardens while others sat on benches in the shade.

Just as I reached the front door someone called my name. I turned and spotted Emily hurrying toward me. Alden the Great stood by one of the fountains chatting with several other men.

"Hi, Emily," I said when she reached me.

I expected we'd have our usual short, pleasant conversation, but the troubled look on Emily's face startled me.

"What's wrong?" I asked.

Emily glanced around, then said, "Can I talk to you about something? It's important."

Oh my God. Now I was worried.

"Of course," I said.

"I need your help." Emily glanced around again, then leaned in and whispered, "It's about a . . . well, I guess you could call it a crime."

CHAPTER 19

Immediately I had a vision of—well, nothing. The only serious crime I knew about at Hollywood Haven was the murder of Derrick Ellery, and I couldn't imagine how Emily might be involved. But if she was, somehow, or if she had vital information, it sure as heck would make my life easier.

"Let's go over here," I said, and led the way to one of the wooden benches near the entrance.

Emily sat down next to me, then glanced around and leaned in a little. She was definitely nervous and keyed up. I'd never seen her like this before.

Oh my God, was she about to tell me who'd murdered Derrick? Could I be that lucky?

"Please," Emily said, "promise me you won't tell anybody."

"Of course not," I said, as I immediately made a mental list of everybody I'd tell and in what order.

It's expected, really.

Emily drew a big breath and said, "It's my dad."

I glanced at her sweet elderly father standing slightly unsteadily on his feet as he talked with several men by the fountain. He seemed perfectly harmless, but his thoughts were clouded by dementia. Had he done something without really understanding his own actions? Had he murdered Derrick?

"I was in his room not long ago, straightening out his closet," Emily said. "Dad's a real pack rat and not particularly neat—Mom used to say he could make anything disappear but a mess—so I wanted to be sure he could find his clothing and get to everything easily. And . . . well, I found some things."

A vision of the handgun that had killed Derrick bloomed in my head.

"What kinds of things?" I asked.

"A scarf, women's shoes, a book, some really nice earrings, a hairbrush—all sorts of things," she said.

Oh. Well, so much for solving this murder on the spot.

"None of it belongs to Dad, of course," Emily said. "I'm afraid he took those things from the other residents."

I was a little disappointed that this conversation wasn't about Derrick's death, but it seemed a crime had been solved nonetheless.

"I'd heard some complaints from the residents about things that had been stolen," I said.

"I'm sure Dad didn't really mean to steal them," Emily said. "He's a magician. He thinks he's still doing his magic act. He gets confused."

"I can see that happening," I told her.

"I'm sure he never used any of the items," Emily said. "He just put them in his closet and forgot about them."

"I know all the residents will be relieved to have their belongings returned to them," I said.

"No." Emily shook her head. "No one can find out. If the management staff learns what he's done, they will kick him out of Hollywood Haven immediately. No questions asked."

"Maybe," I said. "But maybe not. This kind of thing must have happened before. I'm sure they'd understand."

"I can't take the chance," Emily said. "Dad loves it here. He gets great care. I'm afraid if I move him to a different facility he'll become more confused in strange surroundings."

Yikes! No way did I want that to happen.

"Plus, Dad's care is almost completely paid for here because of all his years in the entertainment field," Emily said. "I can't afford to pay for a place for him. I just don't have that kind of money. I don't know what I'd do if Hollywood Haven forced him to move out. So, please, you can't tell anyone about this. I need your help."

Emily's love and concern for her father were obvious. I figured he must have been a really cool dad if they were this close. How nice for them.

"What can I do?" I asked.

"Could you quietly return everything to its proper owner, you know, without making a big deal out of it?" she asked. "I can't trust anyone here to do it and not say anything, and it would look suspicious if I suddenly had all the items and returned them."

"Sure," I said. "I'll take care of it."

"Great. Thank you so much, Haley," Emily said. "I put everything in a box and stashed it in my car. Can you take it now?"

We walked to Emily's car in the parking lot. She popped the trunk and handed me a brown cardboard box. I peeked inside and saw a jumble of items.

"This is wonderful of you," Emily said. "Thanks again."

She hurried back across the parking lot as her dad drifted away from the group of men at the fountain. I carried the box to my car and placed it on the passenger seat.

I figured that returning the items on the sly would be easy. With the gala just days away, I'd be here often and nobody paid much attention to where I went in the facility.

I decided to get started right away. I dug through the items and found the ruby and diamond earrings that I was sure belonged to Shana. I locked my car and went inside Hollywood Haven.

The lobby was busier than usual. Two groups of middle-aged couples were huddled together, no doubt discussing the suitability of the facility for one of their aging loved ones and waiting to take the tour. Sylvia sat on a sofa, with Ida in her wheelchair parked next to her. I spotted Rosalind coming out of her office with a bundle of papers in her hand, headed my way. Karen, of course, wasn't at the receptionist's desk. I figured she'd sneaked out to have a smoke.

I needed to finalize a few things with Rosalind and thought I was lucky to run into her, but she spared me only a glance as she walked past and joined the two groups of visitors. Oh well, I could catch up with her later, I decided.

My biggest concern at the moment was the swag bags. I needed to find the gals who'd promised to help with them. L.A. Affairs had a vendor who routinely provided swag for every type and caliber of event, so I knew I could get the bags prepped and delivered to the gala on a few hours' notice. The gals were a hoot and I wanted to see what they'd come up with. Hopefully the list wouldn't include jean jackets, banana clips, hair crimpers, or Hammer pants.

I headed down the hallway toward the residents' wing and heard piano music coming from the dayroom. Several voices were raised in song, something I didn't recognize. Not that I wanted to sing along but, jeez, it would be nice to hear a tune and some lyrics that were familiar.

At the last moment I changed directions. I really needed to talk to the gals about the swag bags, but that could wait. The rumor Priscilla had told me about this morning could sink the entire event. I had to run it to ground.

I suspected that Mr. Stewart was behind the not so subtle innuendos that the gala would be canceled, so I walked down the hallway to his office. His door was closed. I knocked. When I didn't get a response I knocked again. Another minute dragged by. I pressed my ear close to the door, listening for voices. Nothing.

There was the possibility that Mr. Stewart had left his office, so I knocked once more—a little harder this time—then turned to leave. I'd taken only two steps when the office door opened.

"Yes? Yes? What is it?" Mr. Stewart called.

He looked out of sorts and slightly rumpled standing in the doorway. His hair stuck up in the back and he blinked his eyes as if trying to get me into focus.

Oh my God. Had he been napping?

Mr. Stewart leaned his head back slightly to peer at me through the lower portion of his eyeglass lenses. His expression soured.

"You're that girl from the event-planning company," he said, then waved me away with both hands. "I don't have time for this. I'm very busy. I'm in the middle of something important."

"I'm sure you are," I told him, in my we're-on-the-same-side voice. "That's why I'm here."

"What?" he asked, completely thrown by my answer.

"I know about the rumors," I told him.

"You . . . you do?"

He looked a little nervous now, as if he hadn't expected anyone would approach him about the matter. I hadn't told him exactly what the rumors were about, but he looked as if he already knew—which made me pretty darn sure that I was right in suspecting that he was the one who started them.

"These rumors are detrimental to the future and the reputation of Hollywood Haven," I said.

He waved me away again. "Rumors make the rounds all the time. It's nothing."

"Word is spreading that the gala will be canceled," I said.

"You don't need to concern yourself with this," Mr. Stewart told me.

"It's my job to handle absolutely everything that involves your event," I said. "And I want to assure you that this rumor is absolutely not true. The gala is going forward. Everything is arranged, handled, ready, and on schedule."

He didn't look relieved, as I expected someone in his position would when faced with the collapse of a major event in front of everyone who mattered in Hollywood and Los Angeles.

I wasn't sure why, exactly, Mr. Stewart was so opposed to the gala. At first I'd thought he simply didn't want to fool with it after Derrick was murdered and he thought he'd be stuck with handling the arrangements. But then he'd turned the prep over to Rosalind—along with just about everything else that had to do with the running of Hollywood Haven, it seemed. All I could figure now was that Mr. Stewart knew his job was in jeopardy—probably serious jeopardy—and he didn't want to see Internet and newspaper headlines the day after the event that read, HOLLYWOOD HAVEN CELEBRATES 50TH; HEAD HONCHO GETS AXED.

Not a great way to end a career.

"I'm doing absolutely everything to make Hollywood Haven's fiftieth gala a night to remember," I said.

From the look on Mr. Stewart's face, I got the feeling he wasn't happy to hear my assurances. I also got the feeling that there was little I could say on any subject that would make him happy. So I figured what the heck? Why not press him for some info on Derrick's murder?

I eased a little closer and, using my we're-best-friends-now voice, said, "You know, there are other rumors going around. Rumors about Derrick Ellery's murder. And you."

I expected a startled who-me from him, a flat-out denial, or some outraged indignation, but I got none of that. A confession would have been nice, but I didn't get that either.

"You were seen coming out of Derrick's office shortly before he was found dead," I said.

His gaze zinged down the hallway to the door to Derrick's office, then farther into the lobby. His expression shifted and I knew he'd made the connection. Someone there had seen him.

"It's nonsense. I went to Derrick's office frequently," Mr. Stewart said. "Now, if you'll excuse me I have work to do."

He went back into his office and closed the door.

Huh. That hadn't exactly gone as I'd planned.

Either Mr. Stewart had ice water in his veins, or he was innocent. I didn't know which. Maybe I could get some info from Karen.

I headed back to the lobby. Still no sign of her at the front desk. I'd thought she'd slipped away for a smoke, but maybe she was with Detectives Walker and Teague, giving her statement about seeing Mr. Stewart outside Derrick's office. She'd told me she planned to get a list together of everyone she'd seen that day and call the detectives this morning. Surely, they'd want to talk to her immediately.

Without Karen on duty to tell me which rooms belonged to Delores, Trudy, and Shana so I could ask them about the swag bag items they'd come up with, I had no way to locate them except by mere chance. But I'd run into them several times before, so I figured what the heck.

I took the hallway of the residents' wing—this time the song being played on the piano was vaguely familiar—hoping I could catch one or all of the gals in the dayroom. They weren't there, so I stepped outside.

The grounds surrounding Hollywood Haven were extensive and lushly landscaped, making it unlikely that I could spot them unless they were seated near the door. They weren't.

Just for gee-whiz I headed down one of the walkways, stretching up over the shrubs and short palms—it's great to be tall—hoping I might catch a glimpse of them. I didn't. I gave up and went back inside.

All was quiet in the dayroom. The singers and pianist had abandoned their musical performance. Several groups of residents were clustered together, some playing cards, others working on a jigsaw puzzle.

I decided I'd take one more shot at finding Karen at the front desk. Just as I stepped into the hallway, commotion off to my right caught my attention. I turned and—yikes!—what the heck was going on?

The two families I'd seen earlier in the lobby waiting for the facility tour plodded toward me, Rosalind out in front. Their faces were ashen. Their jaws hung loose and their eyes were glazed.

It looked kind of like a zombie walk.

"What's wrong?" I asked, as I rushed over.

My words didn't seem to register at first, but finally Rosalind looked at me.

"It's Karen," she said. "We found her. On the tour. Out back. Shot. She's . . . she's dead."

CHAPTER 20

"This is quite a coincidence," Detective Walker said. "Wouldn't you agree?"

Even though it was a rhetorical question, I wasn't about to let it pass unchallenged.

"No," I said. "Nothing about it seems coincidental to me."

I was sitting across the desk from Detectives Walker and Teague in an office they'd commandeered at Hollywood Haven, being asked some uncomfortable questions and getting semi-major stink-eye from them.

Rosalind had come out of her I-found-a-dead-body stupor pretty quickly and made the necessary calls. Two patrol units pulled up right away followed in short order by the usual contingent of law enforcement officials, including Detectives Walker and Teague.

I'd hung around—being the first person to leave the scene of a murder isn't usually a good idea. I'd wanted to make sure Karen had talked to the detectives today about seeing Mr. Stewart go into Derrick's office shortly before he'd been murdered. Now, Teague and Walker were eyeing me and giving off a definite we-think-you-did-it vibe.

"You have to admit, Miss Randolph," Detective Walker

said, "it's suspicious that two people have been murdered and you were here, at the scene of the crime, both times."

"I'm working on their anniversary gala," I said, which I'm sure I'd already told them a couple zillion times. "There are numerous things that must be finalized. I have to be here to handle them."

"And those things just happened to require your presence here on the days two people were murdered?" Detective Teague asked.

Okay, when he put it that way it didn't sound so great for me. Obviously, I had to turn this conversation around.

"Karen intended to talk to you today," I said. "Did she?"

"About what?" Detective Walker asked.

"Mr. Stewart," I said. "She saw him outside Derrick Ellery's office shortly before his body was discovered. She said it was unusual. Mr. Stewart rarely went to Derrick's office."

It was kind of bad of me to throw Mr. Stewart in front of the bus like that, but I was only repeating what Karen had told me. Besides, I had my own suspicions about Mr. Stewart.

The detectives exchanged a look. This was news to them. Karen obviously hadn't had a chance to contact them before she was murdered.

I did a mental fist pump—I knew something about their investigation that they didn't.

"You were aware of this new information?" Detective Teague asked.

"Karen told me all about it last Friday," I said. "She was upset because she hadn't remembered it when you'd interviewed her."

"Did she tell anyone else?" Detective Walker asked.

"Nobody that I know of."

"So it was just you. You're the only one who knew she

was about to name names. And now Karen is dead. And you're here again at the scene of a murder," he said. "Have I got that chronological sequence correct?"

I thought it better not to answer.

"I find myself wondering if it was Mr. Stewart that Karen spotted outside Derrick's office," Detective Teague said.

"You were outside that office shortly before his death, weren't you, Miss Randolph?" Detective Walker asked.

Oh my God. Now they were double-teaming me. And, really, what they were insinuating kind of made sense—and made me seem guilty.

I'd had enough of these guys.

I shot to my feet, drew myself up into my mom's I'm-better-than-you pageant stance, and said, "I've answered all of your questions. I've told you everything I know—several times. I've cooperated. If you have any more questions, you can call my lawyer."

I powered my way out of the office, through the lobby, out the front door, and across the parking lot. I absolutely had to get out of there—and I absolutely had to get a lawyer, one of these days.

I jumped into my car and sped away.

Of course, I made for the nearest Starbucks. Thank goodness it was close by. I pulled into the drive-through line, my brain cells bulging with everything that had happened at Hollywood Haven.

Karen was dead. She'd been murdered—shot, just like Derrick Ellery.

It didn't take a homicide detective to figure out that whoever had killed Derrick had also murdered Karen. The motive this time was clear—somebody didn't want Karen blabbing to the cops about the person she'd seen outside Derrick's office the day he was murdered.

I pulled forward with the line of cars and ordered a thought-boosting *venti* mocha Frappuccino.

The obvious suspect was Mr. Stewart. I'd spoken with him earlier and told him that he'd been spotted leaving Derrick's office. Even though I hadn't told him who, exactly, intended to rat him out, it wouldn't have been hard for him to realize it was Karen. After all, the front desk was at the end of the corridor with a direct view of Derrick's doorway.

After I'd left Mr. Stewart's office, could he have found Karen? Confronted her? Then shot her?

It was possible—and I didn't feel so great knowing I might have set that chain of events into motion.

At the pickup window I paid, took a long, much-needed sip of my Frappie, and turned onto Ventura Boulevard. A lot of really unpleasant images of Karen zinged around in my head as I drove.

Then, thank goodness, something else hit me.

Mr. Stewart wasn't the only suspect in Derrick's murder. There were others—and they might have overheard Karen and I talking in the lobby last Friday when she'd blurted out that she intended to contact the homicide detectives today with new information about who she'd seen outside Derrick's office. One of those suspects might have murdered Karen.

I thought back to our conversation in the lobby, trying to remember who'd been there. Emily and Alden the Great. Ida and Sylvia, too. Mr. Stewart had been there. Vida and Rosalind had passed by the reception desk. Delores, Trudy, and Shana were seated nearby filling out the form for Shana's lost earrings.

Three of them were suspects—Vida, Sylvia, and Mr. Stewart. Had one of them shot Karen? If so, they'd have also murdered Derrick. Yet I didn't have any compelling evidence.

Obviously, I was going to have to dig deeper and I was ready to do it—no matter how many mocha Frappuccinos it took.

By the time I'd arrived at L.A. Affairs I'd finished my Frappie and I'd called all the vendors who'd been working hard to put the gala together. I assured them the rumors were untrue and unfounded, and that the event was still a go. Everyone was relieved—especially me when I confirmed that none of the companies had dropped the gala from their calendars and scheduled something else.

I stopped by Priscilla's office to share the good news with her—and so she could notate it in my permanent record, of course. She was seated at her desk, sipping coffee, staring at her computer screen and pecking on the keyboard with one long, freshly manicured fingernail.

Obviously, her day hadn't been as stressful as mine.

"The situation with the Hollywood Haven anniversary gala is under control," I announced from the doorway.

I said it in a slightly breathless, TV-morning-news-reporter kind of way to convey the dire situation I'd just single-handedly averted.

"It's not canceling?" Priscilla asked, a note of caution in her voice, like she wasn't sure she believed me.

As if I'd make an outlandish statement like that if it weren't true.

Well, okay, I might—but luckily I didn't have to.

"I went straight to the director," I told her, like that old geezer was actually on top of things at Hollywood Haven and I hadn't caught him holed up in his office napping when I'd arrived.

"You did?" she asked, sounding impressed.

"He told me he didn't know where the rumor had come from or how it had gotten started," I said, which was true.

I still thought he was lying, but Priscilla didn't need to know that.

"I assured him that everything for the event was handled and would proceed on schedule," I said.

Priscilla slumped in her chair. "That's good news."

"I called all the event vendors and told them that nothing had changed. The gala is a go," I said.

"So, no more problems?" she asked.

I saw no need to tell her about yet another murder at the retirement home. Really, what was the point?

"None that I can see," I told her.

"You're sure?" she asked.

"Positive."

"There's nothing?" she asked.

Okay, now she was kind of getting on my nerves.

"As you know, Priscilla," I said in my I'm-going-to-steamroll-over-you-now voice, "an event is a highly fluid situation. Things change quickly. Problems pop up. But no matter what happens, I will handle it."

She nodded slowly, taking in my words and, hopefully, mentally composing her favorable comments for my job performance review.

I glanced at my watch and said, "I have another appointment."

I didn't, but I thought it was best to look busy—and leave before Priscilla thought up another question about the Hollywood Haven gala.

"Haley?"

I'd taken only a few steps down the hallway when I heard Priscilla call my name. My own personal take on Holt's training kicked in immediately, so I was tempted to pretend I hadn't heard her and keep walking. But with my entire future resting on my job performance review, I turned back.

"About the lightbulbs you had replaced in the ladies' room," Priscilla said.

Damn. I knew I should have kept walking.

"They're too bright," she said.

"They're—what?"

"One of the girls in accounting complained," Priscilla said.

Somebody claimed the lightbulbs in the restroom were too bright? Jeez, how did she manage when she went outside into the sunlight?

"Have them changed, will you?" she asked.

"I'll check into it," I said, and mentally shuffled that task to the very bottom of my priority list.

When I got to my office I opened my handbag and fished out my cell phone, and something caught my eye. I dug past my wallet and cosmetic bag—both Coach in their classic black signature pattern—and spotted earrings.

Shana's ruby and diamond earrings. I'd totally forgotten to give them to her today. And not only that, I realized, I had a box of stuff in my car I had to figure out how to return.

I needed to decide how best to handle that situation but, luckily, my cell phone rang, so I could put that whole thing off for a while.

Then I looked at the caller ID screen. It was Mom.

Oh, crap.

"I've had a brilliant idea," she announced when I answered.

Note: she hadn't said hello or even asked how I was.

"I'm good, Mom, thanks for asking," I said.

She rolled right past that.

"I've decided I should work in a museum," Mom said. "I love art and it fits in perfectly with my educational background."

Mom had gotten her college degree in something to do with art. She'd told me exactly what it was but, honestly, I was never listening.

"I've been thinking, too, about adding my employment restrictions to my résumé," Mom said. "I want a prospective employer to know up front exactly what my requirements are. Don't you think that's a good idea?"

Why had I answered the phone?

"First of all," Mom said, "I can't work mornings. My under-eyes are slightly—very slightly, mind you—puffy first thing in the morning, so I can't go out until my cucumber compresses have worked their magic. And, of course, I can't work during my regularly scheduled hair appointment, or my nail appointment, or my massage, my yoga class, or my spin class."

Why didn't I just hang up?

"Computer work is out of the question," she said. "I simply will not destroy my manicure by pecking on a keyboard."

Because Mom was Mom, that's why.

"You know, Mom, museums are open to the public," I said.

She didn't say anything, but I knew she was mentally recoiling at the thought.

Mom's idea of mixing with a crowd was having Sunday brunch at the Four Seasons.

"All sorts of people go to museums," I said. "Children, too."

She gasped. "Children?"

Mom was semi-okay with her own kids, but not exactly the kind of mother to start a play group.

"Busloads of kids," I said. "They stay for hours. Sometimes they even eat lunch there."

"Oh, dear." Mom drew in a breath. "Perhaps a museum isn't the best place for me, under those circumstances."

"Let me know when you come up with another idea," I said.

I hung up before she could say anything else.

I'm sure she didn't notice.

CHAPTER 21

"Hello? Haley?" Mindy said when I answered my office phone.

I wasn't really up for dealing with Mindy—especially first thing in the morning—but I can push through when I have to.

Besides, my day was off to a good start. I hadn't worked at Holt's last night, so Marcie and I had gone shopping. We'd eliminated three stores from our hunt-for-the-Sassy list, which meant we were closing in on it. Things could only get better.

"Yes, this is Haley," I said.

"Oh? Oh, goodness. Yes, Haley," she said. "Well, first of all, I want to thank you for the fine-tipped pens you got for me. Oh, my, they're so nice. I just love them. Thank you so much."

"You're welcome," I said, and, really, this was the nicest thing anybody had said to me so far today—who'd have thought it would be from Mindy?

"I just love, love, love them," she said.

"I'm glad," I said. "You called for something else?"

"What? Oh, well, no, I don't think so."

"You said 'first of all' when I answered," I pointed out. "So is there some other reason you called?"

There was a long pause, then Mindy said, "Oh! Yes! What was I thinking? You have a gentleman caller in interview room number three. Oh, my, my, my, he's so handsome. He's just about the—"

I hung up.

If a good-looking man was here to see me, I wasn't about to waste time listening to Mindy.

Immediately, I yanked open my desk drawer, dug my cosmetic bag and brush out of my handbag, did a touchup and a fluff, and headed for the door. I couldn't imagine who might be here. Probably a new client, because none of the men I knew would likely be referred to as a gentleman caller, except for maybe—

Ty.

I froze. Oh my God. Was it Ty?

My thoughts scattered. Was Ty here? Waiting for me in interview room number three? Just steps away?

But why would Ty come to see me? To let me know he'd agreed to be interviewed by homicide detectives in the Kelvin Davis murder case, and that he might be arrested? To tell me he knew I'd staked out Brianna King's house so he wanted to explain everything that had gone on between them? Did he intend to admit that he'd left fifty grand and a handgun in my closet?

Or maybe he just wanted to invite me out to dinner?

I started to feel light headed. My heart raced. I shook all over.

Where the heck was Marcie at a time like this? I desperately needed my BFF right now.

Images of Ty filled my head. Private moments, special looks, whispers. His scent, the feel of his arms around me.

I let those pictures play out in my mind, then shook them away. Ty and I were done. Over. I had to remember that.

I pulled myself together and left my office.

When I walked into the interview room, I was kind of disappointed but not really.

Ty wasn't there.

It was Jack Bishop and—oh my God—did he look hot.

He had on a dark Tom Ford suit with a pale blue shirt and a gray print necktie. I'd only seen Jack in a suit a few times and the sight always took my breath away—along with almost everything else about Jack.

I wondered if he had a gun in a shoulder holster under his jacket. Oh my God, how hot would that be?

Jack stood by the window checking his cell phone. He turned when I walked in and gave me one of his killer grins.

"Morning," he said, and tucked his phone into the pocket of his jacket.

I smiled because, really, I wasn't yet able to form words.

"You called," he said.

I had no idea what he was talking about. Nor did I care. I just wanted to look at him.

Jack took a step closer. "Yesterday."

Finally my you-have-to-speak-now brain cell kicked in.

"Would you like a coffee?" I asked.

More than anything, I wanted Jack to say yes. I wanted to walk him to our breakroom. I wanted absolutely everybody in the office to see me with him and be totally jealous.

"We have pumpkin-flavored creamer," I said.

Oh my God, had I actually said that?

I'm such an idiot sometimes—well, usually only when Jack's around.

Jack moved even closer. "Sounds good but I'll pass for now."

He gazed at me, waiting, I'm sure, for me to tell him just why the heck I'd called him yesterday. Then I remembered—which was a complete miracle—that I'd explained what I wanted in the message I'd left on his voicemail.

"Lawsuits," I said. "I need info on anything involving Hollywood Haven."

Jack frowned. "What's that got to do with your ex?"

The last time I'd asked Jack for something it was Ty's phone records so I could find out what connection he had to Palmdale and the murder of Kelvin Davis. No wonder Jack looked confused.

"This isn't about Ty," I said. "It's about another murder."

"You're involved in two murders?" he asked.

"Technically, now it's three," I said.

Jack shook his head. "Stay out of it."

I ignored that and gave him a rundown on what had happened at the retirement home.

"I'm thinking that the employees who were wrongly fired might have filed lawsuits against Hollywood Haven," I said. "If so, the director, Mr. Stewart, is probably named in those suits and he's probably in a world of trouble. I figure it gives him an excellent reason to murder Derrick Ellery."

Jack considered this for a moment, then nodded. "It's a possibility."

"Will you find out about the lawsuits?" I asked.

Jack hesitated, then walked closer. "Are you certain you want me to?"

Oh my God, he'd switched to his Barry White voice.

"Of—of course," I said.

At least, I think I said it. I meant to. But, jeez, I'm totally empty headed when I hear his Barry White voice.

"We'd had a disagreement," Jack said, stopping only

inches in front of me. "I apologized, but you never accepted that apology."

He smelled great, and some crazy heat was rolling off him.

Jack lowered his head and said, "I offered to kiss and make up."

His warm breath puffed against my cheek. His lips brushed my ear.

"Well?" he whispered.

Oh my God, he'd asked me a question—*now?* I couldn't even come up with my own name, at the moment.

Jack stepped back. He gazed at me for a long, hot minute, then walked out of the interview room.

I collapsed into a chair.

The Nuovo store closest to my apartment was near the mall in Valencia, so after work I decided to swing by and check it out. I still hoped Holt's would complete the acquisition before I quit my job so I could take advantage of the employee discount that had been increased to twenty percent, if Jeanette's info was accurate. And, of course, I hoped they would have the Sassy satchel in stock.

Maybe I could get them to hold it for me—and one for Marcie, of course—until my discount kicked in.

I shopped at this mall often. It had a nice mix of upscale and midrange stores. An outside plaza opened at one end that gave way to several blocks of trendy shops, boutiques, art galleries, candy stores, a movie theater, office buildings, and restaurants. The narrow streets and wide sidewalks urged shoppers to stroll while oversized display windows invited them inside.

I nosed in at the curb and got out.

The trees and shrubs twinkled with tiny lights and a sound system played a song that, just like in the dayroom at Hollywood Haven, seemed vaguely familiar.

Memories of Ty flew into my head. Wallace, the boutique he'd opened last year, was across the street, and down the block was the restaurant where we'd had our first sort-of date.

How could I be thinking about Ty? Jack had almost kissed me in the interview room at L.A. Affairs today. Shouldn't I be thinking about him instead?

Heck with both of them, I decided, as I headed down the sidewalk. I was on the hunt for an awesome handbag. I couldn't afford to be distracted.

A chime sounded when I stepped inside Nuovo. The shop had a contemporary feel, with pale hardwood floors, track lighting, and chrome fixtures. The salesclerks were all tall, thin women with full-on makeup, dark hair pulled back in low buns, and dressed in short black dresses.

They looked like they'd just walked out of a Robert Palmer music video.

The racks were filled with designer dresses, skirts, blouses, and coats. Shelves held sweaters, jeans, and—handbags. Lots of handbags. Gorgeous handbags. And every one of them seemed to be calling my name, begging me to take it in my arms, caress it, and make it my own.

Immediately I felt at home.

Of course, I checked out the handbag display first. The selection was excellent—Prada, Dior, Chanel, Gucci, all the best names. I was slightly disappointed that the Sassy wasn't there, but not really surprised since it was the hottest bag of the season.

"May I assist you?" a salesclerk asked.

This place had clerks who actually wanted to wait on a customer? How weird was that?

"I was hoping to find a Sassy satchel," I said.

She smiled a don't-we-all smile—which, I'm pretty sure, she'd practiced in the mirror.

"Perhaps I could order one for you?" she suggested.

"That would be nice," I said, in a calm, even tone, although I really wanted to swing from one of their chrome dress racks and scream like I'd spotted a half-price Birkin on Black Friday.

We walked to the counter and she started tapping on the cash register's computer screen.

"It may take as much as three weeks to receive your bag," she said. "Will that be acceptable?"

No, of course not, but I couldn't say so in a nice place like this.

"It's fine," I said.

"May I have your name?" she asked.

"Haley," I said, and she began typing again.

"Randolph?" She stopped typing and looked at me. "Haley Randolph? An employee of the Holt's chain of department stores?"

Crap.

I didn't want anyone—certainly not the ultra cool clerks at this fabulous upscale shop—to know I worked at that crappy store. How had she known? I was wearing my black business suit from Nordstrom and carrying my Louis Vuitton satchel. I looked like I belonged here. Had some media blitz gone out announcing it to the world?

Of course, there was nothing I could do but channel my mom's sedate, sophisticated, I-dare-you-to-make-something-of-it expression.

"That's correct," I said.

The clerk smiled. "Welcome, Miss Randolph. We're so pleased you chose to shop with us this evening."

Okay, that was weird.

"It seems the Sassy satchel will be available sooner than

I'd thought," she said. "Will the end of this week be satisfactory?"

This place was giving rush service—and being nice about it—to somebody who worked at Holt's? Did they know what kind of store it was?

"That will be fine," I said. "And I'd like two of the bags, please."

"Certainly," she said, and started typing into her computer screen again. "Will there be anything else? Is there another way I can assist you?"

Wow, the service at this place was awesome.

I could never work here.

I thanked her and left the store, then called Marcie as soon as I got to my car. She didn't pick up, but I gave her the good news and told her we'd come back on Saturday for what was sure to be a picking-up-our-Sassy-satchels ceremony orchestrated by the Nuovo clerks, complete with confetti cannons and cascading balloons.

After running into my apartment and changing into jeans and a sweater, I dashed to Holt's. As I jumped out of my car and headed for the entrance, I saw that the Paper-Palooza protesters were still circling, waving their homemade signs and chanting about how Holt's was single-handedly poisoning the planet with our new department.

Apparently, our corporate office hadn't decided what to do about them yet. There were still only a dozen or so protesters, so their movement hadn't gained strength, as Jeanette had feared. Perhaps everybody at corporate was hoping they'd find a new cause to protest or maybe just get tired and go away.

I skirted around them, as I'd done before, but two of the women broke rank and blocked my path. One of them shoved a flyer at me.

"We want you to consider our position, if you're going to shop here," she told me.

"Really, you should take your business elsewhere," the other one said.

They thought I shopped here? At *Holt's*?

I didn't know which was worse—having people think I actually bought stuff from this crappy store, or having them think I worked here.

I cut around them, rushed inside, got to the breakroom, and clocked in a leisurely thirty seconds ahead of time.

Bella and Sandy were already headed for the sales floor. I caught up with them in the women's clothing department.

"Remember that girl who used to work here and is a big soap star now?" Sandy said.

I could never recall her name but she used to stink up the breakroom with her diet meals, lost a ton of weight, went blond, got contacts, and made it big in Hollywood. I'd spotted her in person with an entourage while on vacay.

"She's starting her own line of housewares," Sandy said. "I read it in *People* magazine last night."

"Maybe she'd like to be the spokesperson for the headwear line I'm going to start after I finish beauty school," Bella said.

"I'll bet she shops in Nuovo," Sandy said. "Maybe we'll see her in there sometime."

"That store?" Bella grumbled. "I went in there, you know, just to check it out. Those skinny-ass clerks wouldn't give me the time of day. I felt just like what's her name in that movie."

"Julia Roberts," Sandy, our go-to gal for celebrity trivia, said. "The movie was *Pretty Woman*."

"Yeah, whatever," Bella said.

Okay, that was weird. I'd gotten great service at Nuovo.

"Haley?" Jeanette called.

"I'm out of here," Bella said, and cut into the clothing racks.

"Me, too," Sandy said, and followed.

I was tempted to go after them, but Jeanette was closing in fast—and she was impossible to miss. Tonight she wore a neon yellow maxidress that she'd accessorized with matching costume jewelry.

I'm sure she was visible from space.

"I know you'd mentioned you were resigning," Jeanette said, "but I'd still like you to handle our new-employee orientation."

It hardly seemed like a good idea to let a person who'd announced their departure preside over new hires. But I was sure I could provide essential information to people coming on board. I could share my specialized knowledge—texting undetected by management personnel while crouched on the floor in front of the jeans wall in juniors; hiding out in the shoe department; the most comfy brand of bedding to rest on while in the stockroom pretending to fetch something for a customer.

"Sure," I said.

"Wonderful," Jeanette said. "Oh, and there's something else. I wanted you to be the first to know that the employee discount for the Nuovo stores has been increased. It's thirty percent."

"It was increased again?" I asked.

Jeanette waited, as if she expected me to say something more. But I couldn't think for a few seconds. My brain was busy calculating the huge savings I'd get on all the fabulous handbags and clothing at Nuovo.

"Wow, that's an awesome savings," I said.

"It is," she agreed, then walked away.

The figures circled through my head for a while, then I pushed them out.

Nothing, not even a thirty-percent discount, would get me to keep working at Holt's.

Chapter 22

"**H**aley?" Priscilla called as I walked past her office door.

Here it was, first thing in the morning and Priscilla wanted something already? I'd just arrived and was on my way to the breakroom for my first cup of coffee. What the heck could be so important?

I stopped in her doorway and managed to pull off a pleasant smile, despite my serious lack of caffeine and sugar. Priscilla sat at her desk perusing shoes on the Macy's Web site.

Obviously, I'd made her job super easy by taking over Suzie's events and the duties of the facilities manager. Surely, I'd see that reflected in my job performance review.

"The pumpkin-flavored creamer you ordered for the breakroom?" Priscilla said, sparing me a quick glance as she clicked on the boots icon. "It's the wrong brand."

"The wrong—what?"

I might have sounded kind of grumpy when I said that but, jeez, why wouldn't I?

"Reorder, will you?" Priscilla asked, her gaze glued to the image of stiletto over-the-knee boots.

"There's nothing wrong with the brand I ordered," I told her.

"We want the employees to be happy," she said.

What about me? I was an employee—and I definitely wasn't happy.

Then it hit me. Oh my God, could I possibly get downgraded on my job performance review because of the office lightbulbs and creamer?

I hate being the facilities manager.

"I'll handle it," I told her, and left.

Of course, no way could I go into the breakroom now, not with all the employees in there fixing their coffee and grousing about the coffee creamer. I wasn't going to start my day getting mad-dogged by everybody.

I went to my office and closed the door, figuring I could hide out until the usual morning crowd drifted out of the breakroom, then get my coffee in peace. I wasn't up for doing any actual work yet, so when my cell phone rang I was relieved to see that it was Marcie calling.

"Too cool about the Sassies," she said, when I answered. "We get them this weekend?"

"I have an event on Saturday night," I said. "We'll go in the afternoon, okay?"

"You bet," Marcie said. "Oh, and listen, sorry it took me so long to get back to you about the info you wanted on Derrick Ellery. My friend in that department was out sick."

I'd asked Marcie to check on his bank accounts a couple of days ago. It was a huge favor, so I sure as heck wasn't going to push her for the info.

"Who is this Derrick guy, anyway?" she asked.

I thought it best not to mention that he was dead.

"Why?" I asked.

"This guy is loaded," Marcie told me.

"How loaded?"

"Over two hundred grand," she said.

Detective Shuman had told me that Derrick had been dating a number of women and we'd both wondered how he afforded to take them out in style. I'd never imagined he had this kind of money.

"Where did it come from?" I asked.

"Beats me," she said. "All I can access is the balance—without attracting a lot of attention, that is. I'm still checking for more info, but I'll e-mail what I have so far. The flu bug is going through the building, so a lot of people are out sick. I'll let you know if I find anything else."

"Thanks, Marcie. I really appreciate it."

I ended our call, then drifted to the window and gazed at the Galleria across the street. A Starbucks would hit the spot right now, but I didn't need much of a brain boost to think of the possible ways Derrick Ellery could have come into so much money—legally, unfortunately, which probably wouldn't help find his murderer.

Obviously, Derrick hadn't earned and saved that kind of cash from his job at Hollywood Haven. He could have inherited it or sold some property. Heck, he could have won the Lottery. Maybe he'd been involved in some sort of lawsuit that he'd gotten a settlement from. Or perhaps, like Ty, his family was wealthy.

Still, if any of those things had brought Derrick so much cash, I couldn't help but wonder why he worked. Did he love it so much at Hollywood Haven he didn't want to leave?

I couldn't picture anybody loving a job that much.

Or maybe that was just me.

Other information I was hoping to uncover would come from Detective Shuman. I'd left a message on his voice-mail, asking if he'd learned anything new on Derrick's

murder. I hadn't heard back from him. Sure, he was probably busy trying to solve other murders, but what about
the info I needed?

I was, after all, *me*.

I called him again and he answered right away.

"Morning," he said, sounding chipper.

Obviously, there wasn't a coffee creamer crisis in the
LAPD breakroom this morning.

"You sound great," I said. "Can I attribute that happy
note in your voice to your new girlfriend?"

"Yeah, maybe." Shuman chuckled. "Yeah, definitely."

I was glad to hear things were going well between Shuman and Brittany. Still, I needed whatever info he'd come
up with.

"I hate to spoil your good mojo with a murder," I said,
"but have you heard anything new on the Derrick Ellery
case?"

"The investigation is moving forward, but slowly," Shuman said. "Nothing new has come up. Teague and Walker
are still waiting on lab results, still conducting interviews."

I'd hoped Shuman would tell me the detectives had made
an arrest—especially since one of the interviews they'd
been conducting had been with *me*.

"You heard there was a second murder at Hollywood
Haven?" I asked. "The receptionist."

"I heard."

The playfulness had drained out of Shuman's voice. I
didn't feel so great that I'd caused it.

I asked one more question.

"What about Kelvin Davis?"

"Nothing new on that, either," he said.

"Okay, thanks," I said, and decided to lighten the mood
and maybe restore Shuman's good humor. "And, listen,

you need to get Brittany something really nice for Christmas. I'll take you shopping."

"No way. You'll cost me a fortune," Shuman said, and laughed.

"She's worth it," I told him, and ended the call.

I stood at the window gazing across the street at the Galleria, and I couldn't help but wonder how much time Shuman had spent checking for info on these two investigations. Neither case was assigned to him and he'd only been looking into them as a favor to me.

Honestly, I was okay with that. What I really hoped was that Shuman was spending his spare time with his new girlfriend, having fun and enjoying his life. He deserved it.

Of course, I still needed to find out who had killed Derrick. The gala was only a few days away—plenty of time for Mr. Stewart to cancel. No way was I letting that happen. Not when I was this close to quitting my job at Holt's.

I gathered my things and left the office.

"I need to see some ID," the new receptionist at Hollywood Haven told me.

She didn't say it, actually, more like she barked it. I guess I shouldn't have been surprised, because she had the nobody-messes-with-me look of a bulldog. Actually, she sort of looked like a bulldog, with a compact body, rounded shoulders, and lips that naturally turned down.

I'd already introduced myself, explained my reason for visiting, and flashed my L.A. Affairs portfolio. She'd been totally unimpressed.

Maybe I should have a badge made up, somehow.

I dug through my Tory Burch handbag and presented my driver's license. She took it, stared at it, glanced from the photo to me, then to the photo again, and finally handed it back. She seemed super cautious, which made me think she'd learned what had happened to Karen.

I guess she was concerned about being murdered on the job.

Go figure.

"Sign in," she said, and pushed the log book at me.

I scrawled my name. She looked at my signature and, for some reason, initialed it.

"You can go in now," she told me.

Obviously, she'd gotten her customer service skills from the TSA. But I wasn't going to let that bother me. I had a lot to do and I had to stay focused.

Yet another song I didn't recognize drifted out of the dayroom as I approached. I hoped I would find Delores, Trudy, and Shana there so I could get their list of suggestions for the gala swag bags.

Just before I turned the corner, I spotted all three of the gals exiting a room down the hall and heading my way. I guessed they were going out because they'd all glammed up. Delores had on a maxidress and a turban, while Trudy and Shana were decked out in print pants and jackets. They'd drenched themselves in jewelry and carried large tote bags.

"There she is," Trudy said when she spotted me.

"We were just talking about you," Shana said as they all crowded around. "We need to give you our ideas for the swag bags."

"Great," I said. "I need to get the bags assembled right away."

"Listen, honey," Delores said, "I need you to explain something to me. These Hollywood people who're coming to the gala. What's with them? They're already multimillionaires. They already have everything on the planet. You know what I mean, honey? And if there was one tiny item they didn't already own, they could certainly send one of their personal assistants out to buy it. So what's with the swag? Tell me. What's with it?"

I couldn't give her a good explanation—and I sure as heck didn't disagree.

"So, anyway," Delores said. "You want swag? Let me tell you, we've got swag for you. Trudy, show her our list."

I expected Trudy to pull a notepad out of her tote bag that maybe had a picture of a Rubik's Cube on the cover, but she whipped out an iPad and scrolled through several screens. I braced myself to hear their suggestions, which I was sure would include a Pet Rock, jelly bracelets, Jordache jeans, and OP T-shirts.

"First of all, a fitness smartwatch," Trudy read from the list.

"I just got one," Shana said. "I love it.

"Next, a Bluetooth-enabled ball cap," Trudy said.

"It allows voice control of a paired device," Shana explained.

"Wireless headphones that track health markers," Trudy said.

What the heck was going on?

"Wait," I said. "I've never heard of these things."

"Wearable electronics are hot right now," Shana said, "especially in emerging markets."

"Look here, honey," Delores said, and pointed to a tiny square gadget not much bigger than a quarter that was clipped to the pocket of her maxidress. "It's a life-logging camera. It tracks personal data generated by behavioral activities. I just got it, so I'm trying it out today."

"This is the newest model," Shana said. "Video and audio."

"I'm wearing it on the red carpet Saturday night at the gala," Delores said.

"For YouTube," Trudy said. "I've got Facebook and Instagram, and Shana is tweeting throughout the evening."

"Cloud service providers are driving the IT market," Shana said. "But who cares about IT at a gala?"

"That's why we made these suggestions," Trudy said, and gestured to her iPad. "We've got more, but you get the idea. I'll send it to you."

"Wow, I'm impressed," I said, because, really, I was, and I gave her my e-mail address.

"Perfect," Trudy said, after she'd input it into her iPad.

"We've got to run," Shana said. "We're going shopping for the gala."

"Oh, wait. That reminds me." I dug through my handbag and came up with the ruby and diamond earrings Emily had asked me to return. "Are these yours?"

"Oh my God!" Shana squealed. "I thought they were gone forever!"

Delores and Trudy crowded closer, all of them looking at the earrings.

"Where did you find them?" Trudy asked.

I'd promised Emily I wouldn't rat out her dad and run the risk of getting him kicked out of Hollywood Haven, but I had to give a plausible reason why I had the earrings.

"I found them outside on the grounds," I said.

"You're kidding me. Tell me you're kidding me," Delores declared. "They claimed they'd searched everywhere and hadn't found any of the things that had gone missing."

"Did you find anything else?" Trudy asked.

The women seemed so relieved the earrings had been located, I didn't feel right not admitting there were other items.

"A scarf," I said, because it was the flashiest item in the box. "Red with blue stripes. Does it belong to any of you?"

They all shook their heads.

"I'll take it to Rosalind," I said. "She has the list of lost items. I'm sure she can find the owner."

"You're an angel, Haley," Delores told me. "Sent straight from heaven."

"And this is a miracle," Shana agreed, clutching her earrings. "I can't wait to tell everybody the good news."

"Got to run," Delores said to me.

They smiled and waved as they hurried away.

I stood in the hallway watching them, kind of wishing I was going too. They looked like they were having such a good time.

I knew their afternoon and evening were going to be better than mine. I was positive of it.

Because after work I was going to see Brianna King in Palmdale and find out what had gone on between her and Ty.

CHAPTER 23

I'm not big on suspense.

I wanted to know exactly what was going on with Brianna King in Palmdale, the one phone call between her and Ty, his traffic accident around the time of Kelvin Davis's murder, Ty being named as a person of interest in the investigation, and the cash and gun I'd found inside the closet of my second bedroom. Somehow, it was all connected. It had to be. Nothing was that much of a coincidence.

So I figured that if I learned what had gone on between Ty and Brianna, I'd know more about Kelvin Davis's death.

That wasn't everything, of course.

I had no trouble admitting that to myself as I drove north on the 14 freeway toward Palmdale after my day had ended at L.A. Affairs. Luckily, I wasn't scheduled for a shift at Holt's tonight, so I didn't have to make up a reason for not going in.

I think Jeanette was wise to my touch-of-the-stomach-flu excuse, a personal favorite of mine.

What I really wanted to know was what, exactly, had gone on between Brianna and Ty while we were dating.

The simplest and easiest way to end the suspense was for me to simply ask Ty. But I didn't want him to think I was snooping in his private affairs like some crazy ex-girlfriend. We'd broken up, so, really, it was none of my business.

But, kind of, it was.

He'd made that phone call to Brianna and headed for Palmdale while we were officially boyfriend-girlfriend. He'd kept the whole thing a secret from me. I could think of only one reason he would do that.

I got an icky feeling in my stomach.

If I discovered that he'd been involved with Brianna while we were dating, I'd be devastated.

If I discovered that little girl was his, I didn't know how I'd manage.

Not even weapons-grade chocolate would get me through it.

It was almost dark by the time I exited the freeway onto Rancho Vista Boulevard and drove to Brianna's neighborhood. Streetlights were lit. Windows glowed a welcoming yellow. I flipped a U in the cul-de-sac and pulled up to the curb across the street and down the block from Brianna's place. I killed the engine and my headlights so as not to attract attention from the neighbors.

Brianna's house was dark. She must not have gotten home from work yet—if she worked. I didn't really know. But I wasn't going to sit here without finding out for sure. I jumped out of the car, rang her doorbell, and waited. When I didn't get an answer, I got back into my Honda.

The last thing I wanted to do was sit and stew about my upcoming confrontation with Brianna. Calling Marcie was an option, but I wasn't up to talking about it—not even to my BFF. I killed a few minutes checking my Facebook page and my e-mail, and was tempted to play Candy Crush for a while, but the box of items Alden the Great had lifted from the Hollywood Haven residents took my attention.

I pulled it off the seat next to me, switched on my phone's flashlight app, and peered inside. There were about a dozen or so items and none of them looked anywhere as expensive as Shana's ruby and diamond earrings. I spotted a couple of hairbrushes, a stick of deodorant, socks, a scarf, and other personal items. Nothing of great value, but I was sure the owners wanted them back.

At the bottom of the box I spotted a book. I'd have to return it first, I decided, in case the reader was only half finished and didn't want to be left hanging.

But when I pulled it out, I saw that it was a journal. The cover was pale lavender, faded now with time. The corners were frayed. I opened it and saw that all the pages were filled with graceful, flowery handwriting. They smelled musty and the edges were tattered.

I turned to the first page, but there was no name, no address, nothing to indicate who it belonged to, but I knew it must have been a woman who'd written in it so faithfully.

I glanced at Brianna's house. Still dark.

Not that I wanted to pry into anybody's private life, but surely whoever had put this much effort into recording her thoughts would want them back. I flipped through the journal hoping I could find a name or some indication of who the journal belonged to.

As I turned the pages I realized these weren't accounts of daily life like a diary, they were all poems. Love poems.

I wasn't a huge poetry fan—not that any number of my high school English teachers hadn't tried to convert me—but even I could see that these were beautifully written. Each poem flowed with an outpouring of undying love and commitment, passion and everlasting devotion.

What would it be like, I wondered, to love someone so

much that you'd have those kinds of words inside you? What would it feel like to be on the receiving end of that much love?

The image of Ty bloomed in my head. Tall, handsome, generous Ty. We'd shared so much, yet it had turned out to be so little.

I closed the journal and put it back in the box. Tears sprang into my eyes.

Would anyone ever love me like that?

Why couldn't it have been Ty?

Headlights beamed into my car and I looked up in time to see the garage door on Brianna King's house roll up and a BMW pull inside. The door closed.

Had he loved her like that? Once? Still?

"Enough," I muttered aloud as I shook off the weight of my emotions. I checked my makeup, grabbed my hand-bag, and hurried to the front door.

The lights came on in the living room window as I rang the bell. Mentally, I braced myself for whatever might happen. Brianna could refuse to speak to me, refuse to let me in the house. If she did, really, I couldn't blame her. Still, I had to find a way to get her to talk to me—at least about Ty's connection to Kelvin Davis.

I heard voices from inside the house, then the door opened a few inches. I straightened my shoulders, ready to convince Brianna to let me in—only she wasn't there.

"Hi," a little voice said.

I looked down and saw a tiny girl peeking up at me, her body hidden behind the door.

My heart nearly stopped.

"Would you like to come inside?" she asked.

She had light brown hair.

Like Ty.

"Reese, honey, no." Brianna appeared, blocking the

doorway. "You don't open the door unless I'm here with you, remember?"

Her eyes were blue.

Ty had blue eyes.

"Sorry, Mommy," she said.

Did she have any of his facial features? Did she resemble him in the slightest way?

Her nose, maybe. I couldn't be sure.

Maybe it was my imagination.

"It's all right, sweetie. Just remember next time," Brianna said.

Maybe I should leave.

Brianna turned to me. "Can I help you?"

I could tell her I'd made a mistake, that I was at the wrong house—something so I could leave without arousing suspicion. For a few seconds I was tempted to do that.

But I didn't. I wanted to know the truth. I *had* to know the truth.

Gulping back my emotions, I forced a smile and tried not to come across like I was there to sell her something.

I'd only seen Brianna from a distance the last time I was here—tall, dark haired, pretty, early thirties. Today she had on nice pants and a sweater, and her hair was in a casual updo, as if she'd been at work all day.

"I'm a friend of Ada Cameron," I said, thinking it best not to mention Ty's name yet.

"Ada?" Brianna gasped softly. "Is Ada okay? She's not sick or anything, is she?"

"No, it's nothing like that," I told her. "My name is Haley Randolph. I wanted to talk to you—"

"Haley?" she asked, and her face lit up. "Ty's girlfriend? He told me all about you. Come inside. Is Ty with you?"

Oh my God, what was happening?

Brianna looked past me, craning her neck to see outside.

"No, he's not here," I said.

Brianna stepped back and waved me into the house. The living room was decorated in warm shades of brown with splashes of bright blue. The furniture looked worn but in a good way, as if family and friends gathered here often. A few toys were scattered on the floor in front of the television, and a basket of laundry sat beside the sofa.

"Sit down, sit down," Brianna insisted. "Can I get you something? I have soda, probably—no, I'm out. I didn't get by the grocery store. Would you like coffee?"

A beer might get me through the rest of my visit—not even a mocha Frappuccino would cut it—but I thought it better to keep a clear head.

"No, but thank you," I said, as I settled onto the sofa.

"Mommy, can I play with your iPad?" Reese asked.

Brianna glanced at her wristwatch. "Okay, just for a few minutes. Then it's dinner, homework, bath, and bed."

"Okay, Mommy." Reese gave me a grin and a little wave, and disappeared down the hall.

Brianna sank onto the chair closest to where I sat on the end of the sofa and said, "I should have recognized you, Haley, from all the pictures Ty showed me."

"He told you about me—us?" I asked.

She smiled and rolled her eyes. "I've never seen him so taken with anyone before. Of course, with Ty you have to read between the lines. But I could see he was crazy about you."

Apparently, Ty and Brianna hadn't spoken lately because she didn't know that we'd broken up. Either that or Ty had kept it from her.

"When did you two last talk?" I asked.

She frowned, remembering. "Oh, gosh, it's been a while now. Time gets away from me. The weeks just fly by. Who can keep up?"

I figured her life was a faster pace than mine, with a job, a house, a child to take care of and, apparently, no husband—which meant no help with any of those things.

"So, what's going on with Ada?" Brianna asked. "Frankly, I'm surprised she remembered me, after all these years."

Brianna seemed open and honest, so I couldn't see trying to dance around the situation.

"Ada's fine," I said. "It's Ty I'm worried about. Homicide detectives want to question him in the death of Kelvin Davis."

"Oh, no . . ." Brianna leaned forward, covering her face with both hands. "No, no, no."

"Did you know?" I asked.

Brianna drew herself up and shook her head. "I should never have called Ty. I shouldn't have involved him. But I was at my wit's end and I . . . I didn't have anywhere else to turn."

"I know you and Ty were involved several years ago," I said.

A quick smile parted her lips. "Ada told you that, didn't she? She's such a sweetheart. I think she wanted it to be true, but really, Ty and I were just friends."

"You—you were?" I asked, and swallowed hard.

Brianna smiled and got a little dreamy eyed. "We had a big crowd of friends. We'd all met up in Europe, then came back to Los Angeles and hung out. It was just one big party back then."

Ty? A big partier?

The smile faded from her face. "Then things changed. You know how it is. You have a great circle of friends for a while, then everybody moves on."

Hearing about this different side of Ty and learning that he and Brianna had merely been friends was a lot to take in—and none of it related to the murder of a con man who'd bilked hundreds of investors out of millions of dollars.

"What does this have to do with Kelvin Davis?" I asked.

Brianna looked a little surprised by my question.

"I was married to him," she said.

CHAPTER 24

Icouldn't help it. My mouth fell open.

"Not one of my best decisions," Brianna murmured, then flashed a quick smile. "But I have Reese and she's made it all worthwhile."

I still couldn't say anything. Luckily, Brianna kept talking.

"Kelvin was ambitious and driven, and he had lots of money," Brianna said. "I was young and in awe of him, and completely taken in by his expensive car, his fancy clothes and watches, his condo in Century City, the office he had in Malibu with a view of the ocean. He was always spending massive amounts of money."

"I can see why you were impressed," I said.

"Even though we'd known each other for only a couple of months," she said, "one night in Vegas we threw caution to the wind and got married."

"Just like that?" I asked.

"Big mistake. I regretted it pretty soon afterward, which is why I kept my maiden name," Brianna said.

"You figured out what he was up to?" I asked.

"It wasn't long before I began to suspect that Kelvin's business dealings weren't on the up and up," she said. "I realized how secretive and manipulative he was—not just with his clients, but with me, too."

"That's not good," I said.

"The charge cards he gave me started getting declined," she said. "He began getting strange phone calls at all hours of the day and night. He'd leave for long periods of time and not tell me where he was going or what he was doing. I became suspicious, but I really had no idea what he was up to."

"That must have been awful for you," I said.

"Then I found out I was pregnant."

"Oh my God," I said. "What did you do?"

"Got a divorce. Kelvin didn't fight me on it." Brianna waved her hands around the room. "He bought me this house as a parting gift and took off. I counted myself lucky that I didn't see or hear from him again."

"But you learned about his arrest, the things he'd done, the people he'd cheated?" I asked.

She nodded. "It was all over the news. Thank goodness, nobody made the connection to Reese and me. I was glad I'd had him buy me a house here in Palmdale near my sister, away from Los Angeles."

I sat there for a few seconds, processing everything she'd told me. I didn't think my opinion of Kelvin Davis could sink any lower, but it did.

She'd been through a lot—and with a baby, too.

"And you never heard from him after the divorce?" I asked.

"Well, actually . . . I did." Brianna squared her shoulders and drew in a breath. "After Kelvin jumped bail and disappeared, years went by. Not a word from him. Nothing. Then, suddenly, he showed up here at the house."

"He wanted to see Reese?" I asked.

"He wanted money," Brianna said.

"Jackass," I said.

She nodded. "He was flat broke. He wanted me to sell the house or refi it and cash-out the equity and give it to him. He told me that since he'd paid for it, he was entitled."

I got an icky feeling.

"You didn't do it, did you?" I asked.

"No way. Without a mortgage payment I have some financial breathing room. I've got Reese in private school. I'm putting money in a college fund for her. I wasn't going to give that up for Kelvin," Brianna said.

I was relieved to hear her say those things, and I admired that she put her child first. That couldn't always be easy.

"Then things got ugly, really ugly," Brianna said. "When I refused to give in about the house, Kelvin threatened to go public with our relationship."

"Oh my God, you're kidding."

"He said he would drag me—and Reese—through the mud," she said. "I wasn't going to allow that to happen to Reese. I wasn't going to let her life, and her future, be ruined. Some of the families of the kids she's in school with might have lost money because of Kelvin's swindles. Can you imagine what it would be like for her if word got out about who her daddy was?"

Yeah, Brianna was a great mom, all right.

"And I was afraid that the court might seize my house to pay back some of the people who'd lost money in Kelvin's schemes," she said.

"So you called Ty?" I asked.

"I hated to do it. We hadn't seen each other or talked in years. But I didn't have anywhere else to turn. My family doesn't have the kind of money Kelvin wanted," Brianna said. She smiled and heaved a sigh. "One phone call to Ty.

I drove down to L.A. and met with him, told him everything. He agreed immediately. Not a moment's hesita-
tion."

"That sounds like Ty," I said.

"So I told Kelvin what was going to happen and gave
him Ty's contact information," Brianna explained. "They
met and Ty gave him the cash."

That explained why a note with Ty's info and fingerprints was found in Kelvin's possession when his body was
discovered. Brianna's fingerprints were likely on that note,
too. All I could figure was that her prints weren't in the
system, so the detectives hadn't connected her to the crime
scene—or maybe the detectives weren't that far along in
their investigation yet.

It also explained why Ty was so reluctant to agree to be
interviewed by the cops. He didn't want to implicate Brianna.

"How much money did Kelvin want?" I asked, but I
was sure I already knew the amount.

"A lot," she said. "But he settled for fifty thousand dollars because Ty could get it to him in cash immediately."

"And Ty paid him?" I asked. "You're sure?"

"Positive."

Okay, that was weird. Why was fifty grand in my closet
if Ty had given that amount to Kelvin Davis?

"Ty came by the house after it was done and told me
he'd handled it," Brianna said.

"Were there any problems between Ty and Kelvin?" I
asked.

She shook her head. "No. Ty seemed fine. He stayed
for a while, played with Reese, and showed me the pictures of you."

"And that was it?"

Brianna thought for a few seconds. "Oh, and he told me

he'd been in a minor car accident a few days before—I asked why he was driving a rental—and he said that you two were living together."

Ty had, in fact, stayed at my apartment immediately after his car accident. On several occasions he'd gone out and had been very vague about his whereabouts—so vague, I'd strongly suspected he'd been lying to me.

My thoughts jetted back to those few days, and everything that had happened—including the suspected lies—fell into place in my mind.

Ty had been on his way to Palmdale to meet with Kelvin and pay him off when he'd been involved in the car accident. Ty must have thought the duffel bag with the cash and gun had been stolen by someone during the crash cleanup—he couldn't exactly file a complaint, under the circumstances. Then, not realizing it was in my closet, he'd gotten his hands on another fifty grand—no problem for a man of his means—driven back to Palmdale, paid off Kelvin, then stopped by Brianna's house and told her everything was handled.

After their amicable meeting, had Kelvin attempted to blackmail Ty for more money? Had things gotten heated? Had Ty come back to Palmdale, met Kelvin in that deserted house, and shot him?

He couldn't have, I realized, because the gun was in the duffel bag inside my closet—unless Ty owned a second pistol, which didn't seem likely.

A wave of calm washed over me. I'd always known Ty couldn't have killed Kelvin. Now, after listening to Brianna's story, everything made sense and I knew I'd been right.

"I didn't know the police wanted to question Ty. I had no idea," Brianna said. "He should have told me."

"That's not his style."

"I'll call the police and explain what happened," Brianna said. "I can't stand by and do nothing if Ty's in trouble."

"I don't think it's a good idea for you to contact the cops," I said. "Not yet, anyway."

The homicide detectives investigating Kelvin Davis's murder probably hadn't uncovered the fact that he'd been married. Since Brianna was using her maiden name and they were wed in Nevada, the investigators weren't likely to stumble over that info without a lot of digging.

"Ty was helping me," Brianna said. "I can't sit back and do nothing, pretend I don't know what's going on."

I understood how she felt, but couldn't go along with it. "You can't be sure how the detectives will interpret your explanation," I said. "They might see it in a way you never intended, and both Ty and you would end up in hot water."

"I didn't think about that," Brianna said.

"Don't say anything for now," I said. "And you shouldn't try to contact Ty. The police might be monitoring his calls."

She nodded. "All right, if you think it's for the best. But you'll tell him I'm not going to leave him twisting in the wind over this, won't you? I can't do that—not after what he did for me and for Reese. I'll go to the police and explain everything if he wants me to."

"Sure," I said, though I didn't know when I could see Ty again or how I'd explain that I'd gotten the message from Brianna to deliver to him. I'd have to figure out something, if it came to that.

We were quiet for a few minutes. All I'd been able to think about for so long was my suspicion that Ty had kept his relationship with Brianna a secret while we were dating, and that little Reese might be his.

I didn't feel so great about myself.

But being here now, hearing what Brianna had been through, made me feel even worse about myself.

"This whole thing has been a nightmare for you, hasn't it?" I said.

"One bad decision during a wild night in Vegas," Brianna said, shaking her head. "What was I thinking?"

"You must have loved him," I said, and the words of some of the love poems I'd read in the journal while I'd been waiting in my car floated through my mind.

"At the time, I did," Brianna said.

"You were young," I pointed out.

She nodded. "Seems I was the only one who had any loving feelings for Kelvin, thanks to all the scams he pulled. He was only here in Palmdale for a few days and somebody tried to beat him up. I really think Kelvin believed he could get away with anything."

A few seconds passed before I realized what she'd said.

"When Kelvin came here to get money from you," I said, "somebody saw him and knew who he was?"

"Kelvin was sure nobody would recognize him. He'd put on some weight, his hair had thinned, and he wasn't dressing in those thousand-dollar suits anymore," she said. "But some guy at a bar recognized him and confronted him. He said that because Kelvin had screwed his parents out of their life savings, his dad had killed himself and his mom had suffered a heart attack."

"How awful," I said.

"I think the guy would have beaten Kelvin to a pulp, but his buddies stopped him," Brianna said. "Can't blame the guy."

"Were there others who recognized him?" I asked.

"I don't know, but I wouldn't be surprised," she said.

It seemed likely to me, too. Kelvin Davis had lived a very flashy lifestyle—at the expense of a lot of hardworking people—and his face had been splashed all over the news media after he was arrested.

"I hate what happened to all of those investors," Brianna said. "I wish I could do something to help them."

She had a good heart. It was easy to see why she and Ty had been so close back in the day.

I rose from the sofa. "I'd better go."

She stood and glanced at her wristwatch. "I'd better get dinner started. Reese has homework tonight."

We walked across the room together. Brianna opened the door.

"When all of this is settled," she said, "you and Ty should come up for a visit. We'll have dinner. And I promise you won't have to listen to Ty and me tell our remember-that-time stories all evening."

"Thanks," I said.

I couldn't tell her that Ty and I had broken up.

I couldn't say the words.

CHAPTER 25

"I'm calling with an anonymous tip," I said.

"Haley?" Detective Shuman's voice was kind of loud in my ear coming through my cell phone, and had a definite what-the-heck quality to it.

Not that I blamed him.

I climbed out of my Honda in the parking garage near L.A. Affairs carrying my handbag—a fabulous Fendi tote that perfectly complemented my promotion-worthy business suit—and holding my cell phone to my ear. Cars cruised past me as employees arriving for work searched for empty parking spaces; tires squealed, doors slammed.

Arriving on time for work definitely had its downside.

"It's not me," I told Shuman, and said again, "This is an anonymous tip."

"What's going on?" he asked.

Shuman was definitely in cop mode. I'd hoped he'd just roll with my insistence that what I was about to tell him was not coming from me, but not so, apparently.

Since Shuman hadn't been assigned to the Kelvin Davis investigation he'd have to pass on my info to the investigating detectives, and they would surely question him about where and how he'd acquired it. I sure as heck didn't want my name attached to it, so I figured this oh-so-clever subterfuge was the best way to handle it—if Shuman would work with me, that is.

"The Kelvin Davis investigation," I said, as I headed through the parking garage toward the elevator.

"What are you doing mixed up in that?" Shuman demanded.

"You're awfully cranky for first thing in the morning," I said. "You and Brittany didn't break up, did you?"

"Haley," he said, sounding a little angry. "You shouldn't—"

"I wasn't in any danger," I told him. "I have some information, so listen up, will you?"

Shuman didn't say anything, but I heard heavy, angry breaths coming through the phone, which was kind of hot, of course.

"A guy in a bar in Palmdale recognized Kelvin Davis. Things almost got physical," I said, then related the story Brianna had shared with me last night in her living room.

Shuman didn't say anything for a minute or so and I knew he was thinking, running the story through his cop-trained brain.

"You didn't get a name?" he asked.

"No, but how many of Davis's victims killed themselves and had a spouse that had a heart attack?" I said. "There can't be many—at least, I hope there aren't many."

"Should be easy to check out," Shuman said. "The story probably made the news."

"This guy in the bar was angry about what had happened to his parents," I said. "He wanted to get even with Kelvin Davis right there in the bar."

That's what I would have done—Shuman, too, I was sure.

"I'm thinking he might have followed Kelvin, lured him

to that abandoned house, somehow," I said. "Or maybe forced him at gunpoint."

I couldn't tell Shuman what else I'd envisioned about that meet up, which was that after realizing he was in serious danger, Kelvin Davis, being the weasel that he was, probably showed the guy Ty's info on the piece of paper Brianna had given him. He'd likely claimed he could get money from Ty, if the guy let him go.

"I'll pass it along," he said.

"Thanks," I said, and was ready to change the subject. "So did you and Brittany break up?"

"No, we didn't," he said, and his voice sounded lighter. "And thanks for the anonymous tip."

"What tip?" I asked.

"Right," he said. "Stay out of trouble, Haley."

He ended the call before I could respond, which was wise on his part.

I got into the elevator along with about a dozen well-dressed, carefully groomed people, and rode up to the third floor.

"Are you ready to party?" Mindy exclaimed when I walked into L.A. Affairs.

"It's me, Haley," I said, and kept walking.

Since the pumpkin-flavored coffee creamer I'd re-ordered had arrived—courtesy of rush shipping—and was in place, I figured it was safe to go to the breakroom this morning. Just as I stepped into my office to stow my handbag, my cell phone chimed. It was Marcie.

"Okay, you've got to tell me," she said when I answered. "Who is this Derrick Ellery guy—and is he single?"

I took that to mean Marcie had uncovered additional information about him, as promised.

"Why?" I asked. "What did you find out?"

"Not only has he got tons of cash in the bank," she said, "he owns a dozen properties."

Okay, that surprised me.

"He does? You're sure?"

"My friend in the mortgage department got her contact at the title company to run a check," Marcie said. "It's residential property, mostly. A couple of commercial lots also."

"Oh my God . . ." I sank into my desk chair.

That much property in Los Angeles—or most anywhere in Southern California—would be worth millions. Where had Derrick gotten the money? Probably from the same place he'd gotten the two hundred grand in his bank account, I realized, wherever that was.

"Listen, Marcie, thanks," I said. "I owe you."

"No problem," she said. "I've got to run."

We ended our call and I sat there at my desk for a while, thinking. As I'd figured before, there were numerous ways Derrick could have come into the cash—and now the properties—legally and honestly. I had no way of knowing whether his financial condition had any bearing on his murder.

I really wished Shuman had been assigned to the case. Knowing exactly what Detectives Teague and Walker had learned about Derrick's background sure would help. Maybe if I pressed Shuman, he would dig a little deeper.

I scrolled through the address book on my phone but stopped when I saw Amber's number. Ty flew into my head—but really, he'd hardly been out of it since last night when I'd talked to Brianna.

My anonymous tip about a possible suspect in Kelvin Davis's death wasn't much to give Shuman—and it might prove to be a wild goose chase—so it was very possible Ty could still be implicated in the murder. And even if he was cleared of that crime, he could still be in trouble. After all, by giving that cash to Kelvin, Ty had aided and abetted a fugitive, even if it was for the best of reasons.

It hit me then that I had to see Ty. I had to look at him with my own eyes and see how he was holding up. I had to know exactly what was going on with him. The thought consumed me.

I called Amber.

"I'm wondering," I said when she picked up, "what are Ty's lunch plans for today?"

She didn't hesitate. "A working lunch at the office with all of the department heads."

"Oh."

I was disappointed but, really, I guess I shouldn't have been. Maybe this was a sign that I should steer clear of Ty.

"That's okay. Never mind. Thanks, Amber."

I ended the call, grabbed my things, and left the office.

"These are for you," I said, and dropped the box of items Alden the Great had pilfered onto Rosalind's desk. "You have the lost and found reports. You should be able to return them easily."

Rosalind peered into the box, then up at me.

"Where did you get these?"

I'd promised not to rat out Alden and I wasn't going to do that. But I had no idea who these things belonged to. I could have asked Rosalind to give me the lost and found reports so I could track down the owners, but I was sure she wouldn't because I wasn't an employee of Hollywood Haven—I hoped not, anyway, since the reports contained the residents' personal information.

"I spotted the box under the shrubbery in the parking lot," I said.

One of Rosalind's eyebrows crept up her forehead in

I'm-not-sure-I-believe-you fashion. She stared at me, waiting for me to expand on my story. I didn't, of course. If you're telling a whopper of a lie, it's better to keep it simple—or so I've been told, of course.

"So you'll match up the items with the reports of stolen items?" I asked, anxious to end this conversation.

Rosalind huffed, then dragged the box off her desk and dropped it on the floor.

"I'll get to it when I have time," she said.

I'd figured she wouldn't make the task a priority, so I'd deliberately held on to the journal of love poems. Somehow, it was too personal, too precious, to leave lying in a cardboard box with hairbrushes, deodorant, and rolled-up dirty socks. The thought that Rosalind—or anyone but the poet—might read those beautiful words, written straight from the heart, seemed like the ultimate invasion of privacy.

"I'd like to find out who reported a stolen journal," I said. "I want to return it myself right away."

Rosalind huffed again, pulled open the bottom drawer of her desk, and yanked out a stack of papers. She flipped through them.

"No one," she told me, then shoved them into the drawer again. "Now, if you'll excuse me."

I left her office and headed down the hallway.

As I turned toward the residents' wing, I heard piano music and singing coming from the dayroom. For a change, the lyrics sounded familiar.

Whoever owned the journal must not yet have realized it was missing, I decided, but I didn't want to leave it to chance—or Rosalind—to see that it was returned to its rightful owner. I went inside the dayroom.

A man was seated at the piano and two women were standing behind him, all of them singing. The tune was catchy. The table with the jigsaw puzzle had attracted a crowd. A four-some was playing cards.

I spotted Ida in her wheelchair parked at the window. Sylvia wasn't with her. Ida gazed outside with that same lost, empty look on her face I'd always seen. I wondered if her thoughts had journeyed to her past, to the movie roles she'd played, the parties she'd attended, the days she'd spent with the composer who'd been the love of her life.

Or maybe Ida was just relieved that her daughter hadn't come to visit today, as I'm sure everyone else was.

I crossed the room and checked out the bulletin board.

A flyer announcing a bus trip to the Glendale Galleria that was a week old was pinned in the corner. I pulled it down and found myself bobbing my head to the music as I flipped it over and wrote, "Found, a journal." I added my name and telephone number and stuck it on the board again.

I decided I could do more. I grabbed a flyer for a trip to the movie theater that had already taken place and on the back I wrote: "Lost something? It's been found! See Rosalind," and pinned it to the board.

Rosalind would probably have a snit-fit on a biblical scale when she found out what I'd done but, really, I didn't care.

I was waiting for a traffic break to pull out of the Hollywood Haven parking lot onto Ventura Boulevard when my cell phone rang. It was Jack.

After dealing with Rosalind I wasn't in the best of moods, so hearing from a hot, gorgeous private detective was just what I needed to boost my spirits.

"You can forget about Stewart and lawsuits," he told me when I answered. "He's not involved in any."

It wasn't like Jack to jump right in on business, so I figured he must be in the middle of something way cooler than what I was doing.

"So Hollywood Haven isn't involved in any legal action?" I asked.

I'd thought the employees who'd supposedly been wrongly fired by Derrick had brought lawsuits against the facility, blaming Mr. Stewart for the problem because he'd hired Derrick before completing his background investigation. It made a pretty good motive for Mr. Stewart to murder Derrick. I guess I'd been wrong.

"The retirement home is involved in several suits," Jack told me. "But they all involve Derrick Ellery, not Stewart."

"Who brought the suits?" I asked.

"Some of the residents," he said. "I don't know anything more. I'll let you know when I find out."

"Thanks, Jack," I said.

We ended the call and I sat there for a while thinking. Why would some of the residents sue Derrick and Hollywood Haven? None of the folks who lived there that I'd spoken with had complained about Derrick, except to say that his concern for them sometimes crossed the line and seemed nosy. Nobody really liked the guy, but how could that justify a lawsuit?

My cell phone rang. It was Amber.

My heart rate picked up. Oh my God. Was she calling to tell me that homicide detectives had showed up at Holt's corporate office? Had they arrested Ty? Led him away in handcuffs?

I gulped back my emotions.

"Hello?"

"Yeah, listen, Haley," Amber said. "I thought you might want to know where Ty was having dinner tonight."

Chapter 26

He wasn't on a date—I'd made sure of that when Amber had told me Ty's plans for tonight. No way was I walking in on that.

But his being on a date might have worried me less.

I left my car at a parking lot a block off Figueroa Street in downtown Los Angeles and headed for the bar Amber had told me about. Ty was there celebrating a friend's birthday.

For anyone else, this wouldn't have been unusual. While Ty had lots of friends, he almost never hung out at a bar, seldom joined in on this sort of occasion, and he never—absolutely never—left work this early to do it.

It wasn't quite six o'clock yet and the streets were jammed with vehicles as the office buildings emptied out for the day. Well-dressed business people carried briefcases and messenger bags as they made their way down the sidewalks. I spotted the bar Amber had told me about and moved along with the crowd.

Was Ty at a bar tonight celebrating with friends because he was stressed out about the Kelvin Davis murder investigation? Had he agreed to be interviewed and wanted one bang-up night on the town before he faced the homicide detectives? Was something far worse going on?

Really, it was none of my business.

My steps slowed. What the heck was I doing? Why was I overcome with this crazy need to make sure Ty was all right?

And what would I talk to him about when I saw him?

I couldn't tell him that I'd been investigating the murder myself. I couldn't mention my visit with Brianna and Reese. I couldn't ask him about the duffel bag he'd left in my closet.

Then something else hit me.

Oh my God, what was I going to do with all the money and the handgun?

The cash wasn't mine, so I couldn't spend it—though that might be the saving grace to this whole ordeal.

What would I do with the gun? If I tossed it out somebody might find it and use it in a crime. I couldn't ask Jack what to do with it, since I'd never even told him about it, and no way could I take it to Shuman.

I didn't know the answers to any of these things. I just knew I had to see Ty.

Laughter and loud voices met me as I walked inside the bar. The place was dimly lit and decorated with lots of dark wood. People were squeezed around tall tables and into booths and stood in clusters around the perimeter of the room; all the seats at the bar were taken. Everyone seemed to be in high spirits, especially for a Thursday night crowd.

I paused just inside the doorway.

Why was I here?

I looked around.

Why did it matter so much to me?

The place was jammed.

Why was I putting myself through this?

Spotting anyone from the doorway was impossible, I realized. I'd have to walk through the tables, check out everyone if I hoped to find Ty.

I couldn't do it.

I whipped around and walked outside, my mind spinning and my emotions churning—and I didn't even know why. All I knew was that this had been a mistake.

"Haley?"

Oh my God. Ty.

He jogged around me and planted himself in front of me. I froze.

"I saw you inside," he said.

His collar was open and his tie was pulled down. A few strands of hair fell over his forehead. The worry lines around his eyes I'd noticed the last time I saw him seemed deeper, longer.

"Are you okay? Are you coming back in?" he asked.

Ty looked concerned, or anxious, or—something. I didn't know what. I could barely think.

"I was supposed to meet Marcie," I said, thankful I could come up with a halfway reasonable lie. "But I just got a text from her. She can't make it."

He didn't invite me to join him and his friends, just stood there for a few seconds looking at me.

"So, uh, how are you?" I finally asked.

Something inside me pulled me toward him—was it inside him, too?

"I'm . . . I'm okay," Ty said. "You?"

Did he feel it?

"Busy," I said.

He nodded. I nodded. A really awkward moment dragged by.

I couldn't stand it.

"What's up with you and the Kelvin Davis murder?" I asked. "Are you okay with what's going on?"

Ty hesitated a few seconds, then said softly, "No. I'm not okay."

He sounded lost, confounded. This was totally unlike him.

"I've . . . I've been doing a lot of thinking," Ty said.

About me?

"I believe that maybe . . . maybe I've made some . . . mistakes," he said.

About us?

"I, uh, I . . . I don't know what's going to happen," he said.

I'd never heard Ty talk this way before. He'd always— always—known exactly what to do, exactly how to do it, exactly when to do it.

I wanted to throw my arms around him, comfort him, make everything better for him. Couldn't he feel that vibe? Didn't he sense it? Didn't he want it?

"I'll walk you to your car," Ty said.

I guess not.

We headed down the sidewalk, turned the corner, and entered the lot where I'd left my Honda. I clicked the lock and he opened the door for me.

"Haley?" he said, as I started to get inside.

I turned back. "Yes?"

Ty gazed at me for a while, then said, "I wish . . . I wish things had turned out differently."

"Different how?" I asked.

He shrugged. "I don't know. I just think . . . maybe if . . . I wonder—"

Ty kissed me. He wrapped both arms around me, pulled me against his chest, and kissed me. I locked my arms around his waist and kissed him back. I could have held on forever, but he pulled away.

"I'm sorry," he said, and walked off.

"He was sorry?" Marcie asked. "For what?"

"I don't know," I said.

"For kissing you?"

"I don't know."

"For breaking up with you?" she asked.

"I don't know."

For once, my best friend was being no help at all.

Since I'd seen Ty last night and he'd kissed me, I'd had nothing else on my mind. I'd been so consumed with it that I hadn't even been able to call Marcie until this morning. Now, sitting at my desk in my office, I still didn't understand what he'd meant.

The list of things for which Ty could be sorry was a long one, in my opinion—everything that Marcie had mentioned, plus the things he'd done while we were dating that had eventually driven us apart. I had no idea which of these things, exactly, he was apologizing for.

The only thing I knew for sure was that this sudden, crazy turn in Ty's behavior had been brought on by his involvement in the Kelvin Davis murder. Ty had been hit with a massive, life-changing, oh-my-God-I-can't-believe-that-happened experience and he was questioning a lot of things.

Whether it turned out to be a good thing—or a bad thing—remained to be seen.

"If he meant he was sorry for breaking up," Marcie said, "do you think he'll want to get back together?"

I'd wondered the same thing.

"And if he does," she said, "do you want to?"

I couldn't answer her—because I honestly didn't know.

All kinds of thoughts and emotions were zinging around inside me.

"Think about it," Marcie said. "Call me later."

"Thanks," I said, and ended the call.

I'd spent a great amount of mental energy on Ty since last night—and since this whole thing with Kelvin Davis had started, I realized—and it was wearing me out. Today was Friday. I had a lot to handle for upcoming events, plus a number of loose ends to tie up for Hollywood Haven's gala tomorrow night. I didn't know how I was going to get through the day.

My office phone rang.

"Hello, Haley," Mindy said, when I picked up. "You have a client. Yes. A client. It's definitely a client. It's that Mrs. Potter again."

Since I wasn't exactly on top of my game today, I was relieved that Laronda Bain was the client who'd dropped by. I'd worked some magic putting her son's birthday party together—without the benefit of a wand, by the way—and had put in place every outlandish, idiotic request she'd made. I'd phoned yesterday and left a message with her personal assistant with the news. I guess Laronda wanted to come by today to thank me in person.

Great. Just the boost I needed today.

"Thanks," I said, and hung up.

I found Laronda's event portfolio and headed down the hallway. She was seated in interview room number one, wearing gray everything—dress, shoes, jewelry—and what I took to be the closest thing she could get to a smile. I greeted her, sat down, folded my hands atop the portfolio, and waited to be showered with compliments.

"I'm adding another feature to the party," Laronda announced.

She was—what?

"It's the invitations," she told me.

The invitations were completed. Done. Printed and addressed. Ready to be sent.

"I'd like something different," she said. "Something more innovative."

Oh my God. What now?

"I want the invitations to be delivered to each guest by an owl," she told me.

Obviously, I was suffering from some sort of comprehension impairment this morning, because surely I'd heard her wrong.

"You want them delivered by—what?" I asked.

"An owl. Like in the book and the movie," she said.

I just looked at her.

"An owl," she said again. "A live owl that will fly to the home of each guest and deliver the invitation."

Oh, crap.

Her son's birthday party was two weeks away. How was I supposed to find owls? And how the heck would they get trained to deliver invitations by then?

Laronda kept talking, but it turned into blah-blah-blah.

I'd had it with her, with her kid's party, with having to pull off actual magic to make things happen—and not just for Laronda. It was everything—the pumpkin-flavored coffee creamer, the lightbulbs that were too bright, the clients who were always coming up with some ridiculous event element, my job performance review.

Wait. Hang on a second.

Maybe I could quit. Yeah, I could do that. After all, I still had a job at Holt's. I'd worked there for a year and I'd managed to get by—

Oh my God. *Oh my God.* What was I thinking? I couldn't quit my job at L.A. Affairs and keep my job at Holt's.

That just shows how stressed I was.

And I knew one thing I could do right then to alleviate my stress.

"It's not going to happen, Laronda," I told her. "There's no time to train the owls. And even if it could be done, I doubt the parents of your guests want an owl swooping down on their kids, clawing them or scaring the crap out of them. So here's what we're going to do. We'll hire actors, put them in owl costumes, and have them deliver the invitations."

Laronda froze—and not just her face. She stared at me, blinked twice, then said, "Oh. Well, all right. If you think that would be best."

"I'll get right on it," I said, and rose from my chair.

She picked up on my oh-so-subtle we're-done-here move, got up, and left.

I left too.

I hadn't received a single call about the journal, so after I signed in at Hollywood Haven I headed for the dayroom. A few things still needed Rosalind's final approval for tomorrow night's gala, but I wanted to make sure the flyers I'd pinned to the bulletin board about the stolen items were still there. If Rosalind had torn them down to keep from dealing with the situation, I wanted to know so I could bring it up during our meeting.

Everyone seemed to be in high spirits when I walked into the dayroom. The same guy was seated at the piano and a half dozen women were gathered around him, belting out a lively tune. A group of women had drawn chairs together by the window and were giggling. A foursome at the jigsaw puzzle was doing more talking than puzzle solving, and three men were yucking it up while watching an old black-and-white movie on television.

I hoped that meant everyone was feeling upbeat and excited about the gala—which would also mean it would be more difficult for Mr. Stewart to cancel the whole thing at the last minute.

It would have been nice to see Delores, Trudy, and Shana today, but I didn't spot them. Maybe they were out shopping for more bling to wear during their moment on the red carpet, or were getting their hair and nails done. I wondered if they were busy saturating social media with their prep for the event. I'd have to check out YouTube, Facebook, Instagram, and Twitter to see if they were posting.

As I crossed the dayroom I found myself bobbing my head along with the music. The tune seemed familiar and, for once, so did the lyrics.

The two flyers I'd posted on the bulletin board were still there, I saw as I stood in front of it. Rosalind hadn't taken them down.

I figured there were any number of reasons the owner of the journal hadn't contacted me yet. With everyone busy prepping for the gala, the announcements for upcoming shopping and movie trips weren't high on anyone's priority list. Plus, since most of the events had already taken place, the residents probably didn't check out the notices very often.

The pianist and singers struck up another song and it sounded familiar, too. Not the tune, but definitely the lyrics. How weird was that? Why would I recognize only the words?

Then it hit me—it was one of the love poems.

How could that be?

Then something else hit me—were the love poems actually song lyrics?

Maybe I should have paid better attention when my high school English teachers had tried to make me learn about poetry.

I pulled out my cell phone, Googled song lyrics, and typed one of the phrases from the song the residents were singing into the site's search box. An entire song popped up. I read over the lyrics and realized that yes, it was a match. Then I saw the composer's name. It was Arthur Zamora, Ida's lost love.

Well, at least I'd stumbled across the owner of the journal. Wow, how cool was that?

Someone had mentioned that Arthur had suffered a mild stroke recently, so no wonder he hadn't noticed the journal was missing or been able to check out the notice I'd put on the bulletin board.

Just for gee-whiz, I Googled Arthur Zamora and got a long list of Web sites. I glanced over several of them and saw that he'd been a composer and lyricist to the stars back in the day. He'd written original production numbers for all kinds of television shows and movies—even for the Emmy and Oscar award ceremonies. He'd composed songs for, and had accompanied, some of the biggest names in Hollywood.

I read further and saw that Arthur had also become one of the most beloved entertainers of his era. There were glowing comments from everyone he'd worked with, marveling at the depth and beauty of his lyrics. Arthur Zamora had touched the hearts of millions with his songs.

Ida Verdell floated into my head. Surely, she knew Arthur had composed those songs. Did she hear them and think about their lost love? Did she wonder if he'd written some of those songs for her? Did her heart ache listening to them, wondering what her life would have been like if things had turned out differently between them?

I flashed on her daughter Sylvia. She was cranky and grumpy, a chronic complainer whose argument with Derrick Ellery had escalated into a heated exchange so intense

I considered her a suspect in his murder. Surely, a daughter from Ida's union with Arthur would have turned out differently.

Sadness weighed me down. It was too late for Ida and Arthur now. Their moment had come and gone.

I was glad I could return the journal to him. Maybe looking it over, remembering happier times, would help his recovery. Maybe he'd be reminded of Ida. Maybe he would have a change of heart and want to talk to her—they both lived right here in the same care facility.

Maybe I was being overly optimistic, I thought.

Maybe I was just transferring my feelings for Ty onto them.

Maybe I should leave things as they were—for Ida and Arthur, and for Ty and me.

CHAPTER 27

"**H**ey, where are you going?" Bella asked as we left the breakroom and I headed toward my assigned will-this-horrible-day-ever-end department for my evening shift at Holt's.

I stopped and looked back at her. I recognized that pained look on her face and knew what Bella was about to say.

I was in no mood.

The Friday night crowd of shoppers shuffled past, their arms laden with truly hideous merchandise. Kids ran through the aisles. A baby was crying nearby. The store's music track blared an accordion solo—definitely not a soothing Arthur Zamora song. All of this after dealing with the Paper-Palooza protesters at the store's entrance.

"We've got a meeting," Bella said.

No way could I deal with a meeting tonight. My afternoon at L.A. Affairs had gone from bad to worse, thanks to two new clients who wanted me to plan play dates for their dogs—I mean, really, I like animals too, but social functions for a couple of schnauzers? Then I found out that a bakery I'd ordered three cakes from had gone out of business, a wedding anniversary I'd been putting together for the last two months canceled, and the breakroom microwave had broken—which, for some reason, was my fault.

I was pretty well ticked off at Jack and Shuman. I'd called them trying to get more info on the Kelvin Davis and Derrick Ellery murders, but both of them, apparently, had lives of their own and hadn't called me back.

I hate it when that happens.

And, of course, this thing with Ty was making me crazy. He'd kissed me, then said he was sorry. About what? The kiss? Our breakup? For being a total jackass, at times, while we were dating? Or something else entirely?

"Come on," Bella said, gently urging me toward the training room. "At least we'll be off the sales floor for a while."

That was definitely a plus. Also, the Holt's meetings were no-brainers. I snoozed through most of them, periodically executing a well-timed nod so it appeared I was paying attention.

About two dozen employees were already seated in the training room when Bella and I walked in. I snagged seats for us on the last row, strategically placing myself behind that big guy from menswear. A woman in a no-nonsense Michael Kors business suit—obviously from the corporate office—stood at the front of the room alongside Jeanette, who was dressed in a where-the-heck-did-she-find-that-thing dress. Two bins filled with packets of papers were stacked nearby.

Oh, crap. Handouts.

I was ready to bolt for the door when Jeanette started speaking.

"We're very fortunate to have Constance Dodd from the corporate training department with us tonight," Jeanette announced. "We've all been very concerned about the protesters outside our store and Ms. Dodd is here to address that issue."

This was about the protesters? I was going to have to sit through a butt-numbing, mind-draining meeting because of them?

"Our corporate office training department has worked feverishly to put together this workshop," Jeanette said.

A workshop? As in we'd have to work?

"Constance is going to take us through the company-approved procedures for dealing with the protesters," Jeanette said.

Procedures?

"With the help of the entire corporate training team, she's put together workbooks and a PowerPoint presentation," Jeanette went on.

Death by PowerPoint?

"Then she will lead us through some role-playing," she said.

What? I was going to have to actually participate in this meeting?

"And afterward," Jeanette said, "there will be a quiz."

A—what? A quiz? I was going to have to actually sit here, stay awake during a presentation, get up in front of everyone, and act out what I'd supposedly learned, then take a quiz? All because of those protesters?

No way.

I heard grumbling and some groans—and they weren't coming from me.

Jeanette waved her hands for calm.

"I understand this isn't something any of us want to do," she said. "But until those protesters are gone, we'll have to proceed with the training and learn how to properly deal with them."

My day had been crappy—and now it was getting worse. I couldn't handle it. I couldn't.

I shot to my feet.

"You want those protesters out of here?" I demanded.

Everybody turned. Constance Dodd gasped. Jeanette definitely looked worried.

"Fine!" I said.

I stormed out of the training room, plowed through the crowded aisles, and burst out the front door. The protesters were walking in a circle, waving their signs and chanting. I yanked my cell phone out of my pocket, activated the video feature, and started recording.

For a few seconds I was afraid they would see what I was doing and hide behind their signs before I captured their faces—too bad I didn't have one of those tiny, inconspicuous life-logging devices Delores planned to use at the gala—but their chant got louder and they waved their signs higher as they paraded in front of me. I zoomed in on every face.

"Hey! Listen up!" I shouted.

I guess they never expected anyone to drown them out, because they all stopped chanting and walking, and stared at me.

"You think Holt's is poisoning the planet with the Paper-Palooza?" I screamed. "What do you think your signs are made of? Paper! And the sticks holding them are wood! From trees!"

They exchanged troubled looks. A few of them lowered their signs.

"If you don't want to end up on YouTube as the world's dumbest protesters, you'd better leave right now!" I told them, and held up my cell phone. "Otherwise, I'm posting this."

They all dashed across the parking lot to their cars. I noticed then that most of the employees from the training room had followed me, along with Jeanette and Constance Dodd, who looked stunned.

Apparently the procedure I'd just executed was nowhere in her handouts or PowerPoint presentation.

Everybody stood frozen, staring at me—except for Jeanette.

She walked over. "I'd like to speak with you in my office, Haley. Now."

"This arrived for you today," Jeanette said, as I followed her into her office and sat down in the chair in front of her desk.

I expected to get fired—which, believe me, would have been okay with me—but instead she presented me with a large box. It was addressed to me here at the store and was marked "hand deliver."

"What's this?" I asked.

Jeanette shrugged as I ripped open the box. Inside was yet another box, this one a gorgeous pale blue, tied with a huge silver bow. I unwrapped it, and inside were—oh my God—two Sassy satchels.

Where in the heck had these come from? Who'd sent them to me—here at Holt's?

Then it hit me. They must have been from Nuovo. I'd requested the bags and they must have come in early so they sent them to me. But how had they known I worked at this particular Holt's store? Was it in their computer?

"Beautiful," Jeanette said, as I took the bags out of the box.

I hugged them, feeling the buttery softness, breathing in the scent of the leather, my mind racing with images of all the places I could take my Sassy and exactly which look would go best with it.

Wow, this was just the boost my day needed.

"Nuovo sent them," Jeanette said, pointing to a label I hadn't noticed on the side of the box. "I didn't realize they delivered."

I couldn't wait to tell Marcie.

"I received an e-mail from corporate about the Nuovo acquisition," Jeanette said. "The employee discount has been increased."

Increased? Oh my God. I didn't know if I could take any more good news right now.

"It's fifty percent," Jeanette said.

"Fifty percent?" I might have said that kind of loud.

"Off everything in the store."

"Everything?" Yeah, I definitely said that too loud.

"It's a fantastic benefit of working for Holt's," Jeanette pointed out.

Wow, it sure as heck was. I could hardly take it in.

"Do you think you might want to stay?" she asked.

"I'm tempted. I mean, I'm really tempted," I told her, as the idea raced around my brain. "But no, I'm still going to resign."

Jeanette didn't look happy—which was kind of weird because, believe me, I'm nowhere near an ideal employee—but she didn't say anything.

I figured it was better if I got out of there before she turned her attention to my oh-so-clever method of dispatching the protesters. I put the Sassy satchels back into the box and left her office.

Bella was waiting in the hall. She gave me a big smile and said, "You rock, girlfriend."

Nice to know somebody appreciated how I'd not only gotten all the employees out of a coma-inducing training session, but rid the store of the protesters as well.

I should take my show on the road.

"Somebody's looking for you," Bella said.

Oh, crap. Was it Constance Dodd? If so, I'm sure she didn't intend to offer me a position at the corporate office in thanks for making her job easier, although after tonight, I was sure my name would make the rounds there.

Probably not in a good way.

"That detective," Bella said. "The good-looking one. Shuman."

Wow, could my evening get any better?

"Where is he?" I asked.

"Over by the jewelry counter," Bella said.

"Great. Thanks," I said as I walked away.

"Find out if he has a brother," Bella called.

I dashed into the breakroom and got my car keys out of my handbag, then wound through the shoppers, my box of Sassy satchels tucked under my arm. I spotted Shuman checking out the jewelry. Something for Brittany, I figured, and my heart warmed a little knowing that he was happy enough to shop for her.

He seemed to sense my approach—I have that effect on people—and looked up. He smiled. Not that goofy grin I'd seen him favor Brittany with, but it made me smile in return.

"I have to take this to my car," I said, and held up the box. "Walk out with me."

Of course, I could have spoken with Shuman standing there at the jewelry counter. But Bella was right, he was good looking so why wouldn't I want to parade him through the store with me so everybody could see us and be jealous?

Yeah, I know, I'm kind of shallow sometimes, but that's the tool kit I'm working with.

There was no sign of the protesters when we left the store. The parking lot was nearly full, customers coming and going. The security lighting struggled against the darkness.

"So what's up?" I asked when we reached my car.

"I passed along your anonymous tip," Shuman said.

I clicked the remote on my key chain and unlocked my car doors.

"Did the detectives believe you?" I asked.

Shuman opened the door, gave me a little grin—which looked totally hot in the parking lot's low light—and said, "I embellished a little about the source of the anonymous tip, made the story believable."

"Are they going to run with it?" I asked.

He shrugged. "Yes, but I'm not sure how high on their priority list it is."

I placed the box on the seat, squared it up, gave it one last loving look, then shut the door.

"Did you hear anything new about the Derrick Ellery investigation?" I asked. "Something about lawsuits he was involved with, maybe?"

Jack had told me Derrick and Hollywood Haven were being sued by some of the residents. Detectives Teague and Walker must have learned about them also.

"Lawsuits?" Shuman thought for a few seconds. "No, I haven't heard anything about lawsuits. What were they about?"

"I don't know," I said. "But it seems weird, doesn't it? Derrick had over two hundred grand in the bank, plus all that property."

I filled Shuman in on the info I'd gotten from Marcie—without mentioning her name, of course—about the millions of dollars' worth of real estate Derrick owned.

"Where would he get that kind of money?" Shuman mused.

"And why would the residents of Hollywood Haven sue

him?" I said. "Nobody there liked the guy, but that's not grounds for a suit."

Shuman shifted into serious cop mode. "Why didn't they like him?"

"I asked around. All anybody ever said was that he was too chummy with some of the residents," I said. " 'Nosy' is what some of them called it."

"You mean like asking personal questions?" he said. "Questions about their finances, maybe?"

"I guess, but—"

Hang on a second. Had Derrick's supposedly casual questioning actually been a cover for something else?

Shuman must have realized it at the same moment, because our gazes locked in an I-figured-this-out expression.

"Some of the residents don't have any family to watch out for them," I said.

"Derrick was in a position to know who those people were," Shuman added.

"A lot of them suffer from dementia and Alzheimer's," I said. "They don't always know what's going on around them."

"And he could have exploited that," Shuman said. "He could have convinced some of the residents to sign over their money and property to him."

"Since they didn't have any family," I said, "nobody would know, nobody could have stopped him."

"The worst kind of elder abuse," Shuman said.

I thought about it for a few more seconds, then shook my head.

"But it doesn't make sense," I said. "Everybody I suspected of murdering Derrick was an employee of Hollywood Haven—except for Sylvia."

I gave Shuman the info I had on Ida's cranky daughter and the complaints I'd heard she'd made to Derrick.

"Maybe Derrick attempted to get Ida to sign all of her assets over to him, but Sylvia found out," Shuman suggested.

Was that what she'd complained about? Was it the root of the heated argument she'd had with Derrick in his office shortly before his murder?

"But why would Sylvia kill Derrick?" I asked. "There are some pretty strong laws dealing with elder abuse. Even if Ida had already signed everything over to Derrick before Sylvia found out about it, she could have gotten a lawyer and fought it. The court could have forced him to give it back, right?"

"I'm not a lawyer," Shuman said, "but what you're saying makes sense."

"So why was Derrick murdered?" I asked. "What he did was really despicable but, if it could all be undone, why would Sylvia kill him?"

"I have no idea," Shuman said.

"Me either."

CHAPTER 28

It was go-time for Hollywood Haven's fiftieth anniversary gala and I'd been busy all day straightening out a few minor wrinkles and confirming that everything was in place.

Tonight, the residents, celebrities, and industry insiders would walk the red carpet at the iconic Hollywood Roosevelt. The Blossom Room, where the Academy Awards were held back in the day, had been booked. It was a huge ballroom done in classic Spanish revival with a gorgeous handcrafted ceiling, arched doorways, and wrought iron chandeliers. The tables were set with gold and white and splashes of red.

The menu included smoked salmon, prime rib, a sushi and shellfish station, vegetables that looked too good to be actual vegetables, and a dessert bar so divine it might have been beamed down from heaven.

Tiberia March from Distinctive Gifting had delivered the swag bags. Even though I hadn't given her a lot of time, she'd made it happen. All the electronic gadgets Delores, Trudy, and Shana had suggested were in the bags, along with tons of other fabulous gifts.

Marcie dropped by and we spent a few minutes oohing and aahing over our Sassy satchels, planning their first outing and what we'd wear for the occasion, then left.

With everything in place and under control at the venue, I headed to Hollywood Haven. I wanted to make sure there were no snags getting all the residents into the fleet of limos that had been hired and to the hotel on time. Plus, I needed to change into my evening wear.

I pulled into a parking space, grabbed the event portfolio, my garment bag, and tote—a roomy Coach—and went inside.

A few of the male residents dressed in their tuxes milled around in the lobby; the women, of course, weren't ready yet—good to know some things didn't change with age.

Mr. Stewart, who stood with the men, asked, "When will the limos get here?"

Seemed he'd gotten over his ill feelings about the gala. He'd insisted on being among the first to arrive at the hotel. I'm sure he intended to chat up whoever would listen to make sure everyone knew who he was and what a fabulous job he was doing—according to him, anyway.

"I just confirmed with the limo service," I reported. "They're on schedule and will arrive in twenty minutes."

His expression soured, as if this didn't suit him—I had no idea why, nor did I care. Twenty minutes was the window I needed to change clothes and get back in time to check off the names of the residents as they climbed into the limos.

The receptionist—who was still taking her job way too seriously—had me sign in and show my ID, then I headed for the ladies' room just off the lobby.

I slipped into one of the stalls and changed into the cocktail length little black dress and peek-toe pumps I'd brought with me, then went to one of the mirrors, freshened my makeup, sprayed my updo, and put on some conservative jewelry.

Technically, I was the hired help and wasn't supposed to be decked out as fabulously as the party guests, so my yes-I-can-answer-your-question look was just right for the occasion.

The finishing touch—as it should be for every outfit—was a Gucci suede mini clutch with a crystal closure and a discreet over-the-shoulder chain. I definitely needed a hands-free bag for tonight. My cell phone, car keys, and lipstick fit inside perfectly, along with a credit card and a little cash.

I left the ladies' room and spotted Delores, Trudy, and Shana in the hallway. They shrieked a greeting and hurried over.

Trudy had on a gold gown with leopard trim. Shana had gone with red to coordinate with her ruby and diamond earrings. Delores was in silver and white, and while Trudy and Shana had crafted intricate up-dos, Delores had on a white bejeweled turban.

"Wow, you ladies look hot," I said.

They preened and giggled.

"And look at you," Delores said. "You look adorable. Doesn't she look adorable?"

"You look adorable," Shana said.

"Very adorable," Trudy agreed.

"Come over here, honey," Delores said. "Huddle up close. Trudy, get a picture. You need to update Facebook."

"Shana has been tweeting all afternoon," Trudy said, as she took her cell phone out of her evening bag.

I dropped my belongings on a nearby chair and stepped between Delores and Shana. We all smiled as Trudy snapped a photo.

"Let me get one of the three of you," I said.

Trudy handed me her phone and I took a few pics of them.

"Are you ladies ready to head to the hotel?" I asked, returning the phone.

"Oh, no," Delores told me. "We're going last. We're going to walk the carpet and make our entrance when the place is full."

"It makes for a much better video," Trudy said.

I gathered up my things and said, "Great. I'll see you at the entrance in a bit."

They waved and disappeared into the dayroom.

By the time I made it back to the lobby it had filled up with residents and was humming with excitement. All the women were wearing fabulous gowns and sparkling jewelry. Some of them were dressed in classic old Hollywood fashions—although I'm pretty sure some of them thought they were still in style.

Oh well, it was their night.

I stowed my garment bag and tote behind the front desk—I didn't have the receptionist sign for them but I was tempted—grabbed my portfolio and wound my way to the entrance. I peeked outside. The limos were just pulling up.

Everyone seemed positively giddy as I checked off their names and they went outside. Not all the residents would go, unfortunately. Some were too frail or too ill to leave the facility. I wondered if they recalled a time when they'd walked the red carpet and attended gala events in their younger days, or if those memories had disappeared.

Alden the Great would spend the evening here at Hollywood Haven. I figured Emily was concerned that the change in surroundings would be too confusing for him. Ida Verdell's name wasn't on my list either. I wondered if her crabby daughter simply hadn't wanted the hassle of dealing with her wheelchair, though Sylvia didn't seem like the kind of person to turn down a free meal.

I sent the last of the gathered residents out the door with a big smile, then checked the guest list. About a half dozen names remained, including Delores, Trudy, and Shana. I figured they were still in the dayroom tweeting and posting to Facebook, so I headed down the hallway. I'd have to round up the others somehow.

The dayroom was empty. I'd never been in there when it was so quiet. It was dark outside, so the space was dimly lit without the usual sunlight that beamed in through the huge windows.

I crossed to the patio, thinking maybe the gals had gone outside to film a segment for their YouTube video, but they weren't there. I went back inside and headed for the hallway. As I approached the bulletin board, someone stepped out of the shadows and blocked my path.

"You're Haley, aren't you."

It was more an accusation than a question. I blinked in the dim light and saw that it was Sylvia. She didn't look happy.

"Aren't you?" she demanded, and stepped closer. "Don't bother denying it. I asked around. I know who you are."

Okay, that was weird—in a really creepy way.

"You have something that belongs to me," Sylvia said, then dug into the huge tote bag on her shoulder. She pulled out a piece of paper and thrust it at me. "See? Right here?"

It was the flyer I'd pinned to the bulletin board about the journal I'd found.

Something wasn't making sense. Sylvia was obviously confused.

"That journal belongs to Arthur Zamora," I said.

"No, it doesn't!" Sylvia screamed, gnashed her teeth, and flung both arms out. "It belongs to me! To my mother!"

Oh my God, what the heck was going on?

"It's not his! It's not! It's not!" she yelled.

"It's his lyrics journal," I said, trying to sound calm and hoping she'd get over whatever the heck was wrong with her.

Sylvia's breath came in short, furious puffs, and her nose flared.

"Those aren't lyrics!" she said. "They're poems! Poems my mother wrote!"

Now I was the one who was confused.

"She wrote those poems to Arthur," Sylvia said. "Then he took them and turned them into songs—and made a fortune off of them!"

"Oh my God," I said. "You're kidding."

"I found that journal in my mother's things two months ago," Sylvia told me. "I read it. I recognized the songs. She didn't want to talk about it—him being the great love of her life—but she finally confessed. So I marched right into his room and confronted him."

I figured this had to have been before Arthur had his stroke.

"I told him he was a fraud," she said, her anger growing. "Mr. Beloved Composer and Lyricist. Ha! I told him I knew he never wrote one word of any of those songs, that he stole every single one of them from my mother. And what did he do? He laughed in my face, that's what he did."

"He denied it?" I asked.

"No. He copped to it. Said it was true," Sylvia said. "And then he told me there was nothing I could do about it. My mother had written those poems for him, sent them to him unsolicited, so he could do what he wanted with them."

"You couldn't have sued him for copyright infringement, or something?" I asked.

"That's exactly what I told him I was going to do!" Sylvia declared. "My mother wrote those poems that he turned into lyrics, and she—and the rest of the family—deserved our share of the royalties he was raking in."

Obviously, I was missing something here.

"Okay," I said, "so why are you upset?"

"Of course I'm upset!" she screamed. "Why wouldn't I be upset!"

Just past her in the hallway, I saw Delores, Trudy, and Shana step into view. They saw us, stopped, and stared.

"I could have had that money! It was due me, after all I had to put up with over the years," Sylvia said. "And I'd have had it, too, if it hadn't been for that bastard Derrick Ellery."

Now I was even more confused.

"Derrick?" I asked. "What does—oh God."

It hit me then what had happened.

"Derrick was always chatting up the residents, asking about their personal lives, as if he was just being friendly," I said. "But he was actually coercing them into signing over their assets to him. That's what he did to Arthur Zamora, wasn't it?"

"That stupid old fool," Sylvia said. "That's what he gets for dumping my mother, making her life—and mine—miserable, and for stealing what didn't belong to him. He ended up alone and sick, stuck in this place with nobody to watch out for him."

"So Derrick stole all of Arthur's money and his property?" I asked.

"Damn right he did," Sylvia said.

I realized then that while everyone at Hollywood Haven thought Sylvia was always complaining to Derrick about conditions at the facility, she was actually confronting him about how he'd stolen Arthur Zamora's assets.

Then it hit me—that last argument they'd had in Derrick's office that had been overheard must have escalated into something far worse and been the final straw.

"You killed Derrick, didn't you?" I said.

Sylvia glared at me, seemingly unfazed, then reached into her tote bag again. She pulled out a handgun and pointed it at me.

Oh, crap.

Behind her, I saw the gals get wide eyed, then step back around the corner.

"You did, didn't you? You killed Derrick?" I said.

Delores's face poked out from the corner, her bejeweled turban sparkling in the dim light.

"I could have gotten money from Arthur," Sylvia said. "But he'd signed everything he owned over to Derrick."

"You killed Karen," I realized. "You were in the lobby that day. You overheard her saying she was putting together a list of people she'd seen outside Derrick's office."

"That was unfortunate," Sylvia said, and had the good grace to look somewhat contrite. "I liked Karen."

I figured Sylvia had no reason not to kill me, too.

I wasn't all that concerned about Sylvia's situation— only my own, at the moment—but I thought it was a good idea to keep her talking.

"You could have gotten a lawyer," I said.

"A lawyer," Sylvia smirked. "Like I've got money for a lawyer."

Delores kept watch. I wished she'd disappear down the hall with the other gals. I didn't want anything to happen to her.

"It was worth a try, wasn't it?" I asked.

"Sue Arthur, when he had no money?" Sylvia uttered a bitter laugh. "And I suppose you think I could sue Derrick, too? How? I'm not related to Arthur. I've got no standing in a suit on his behalf. The whole thing was a tangled legal nightmare that would have dragged through the court for years."

I couldn't disagree with her reasoning. The situation did seem hopeless.

"I want that journal back," Sylvia said. "It's my evidence, my ticket to serious money. I'm going to sell this story to all the tabloids, the talk shows—anybody who will listen—and make them pay for the rights."

Delores was still watching us. I decided it was better to leave the building before Sylvia realized she'd seen and heard everything.

"It's in my car," I said.

Sylvia waved the gun. "Let's go get it."

Thankfully, Delores drew back as I headed for the hallway. I walked slowly, giving all the gals time to get to safety. I crossed the lobby with Sylvia on my heels. Nobody was there, except the receptionist, who didn't bother to look up.

Outside, the last limo was still waiting at the curb. Three residents were inside while the driver stood by the front fender.

He seemed like a strong, sturdy guy, but since he wasn't armed and I didn't know how well he could handle himself if something went down—plus, I didn't want to put the residents in danger if Sylvia opened fire—I didn't let on that the woman behind me was holding a gun on me.

"I'm waiting for the last three people," I said to the driver as we walked past. He nodded and I kept walking.

We crossed the parking lot to my car. The security lighting here wasn't much better than at Holt's. Sylvia held the tote bag in front of her. One hand was inside, holding the gun.

I dug the keys from my bag and clicked the locks, then glanced back at Hollywood Haven as I opened the door.

Oh, crap.

Delores, Trudy, and Shana had followed us out of the building. The three of them were huddled together near the entrance, watching every move we made.

"It's inside," I told Sylvia, and pointed to the journal lying on the seat.

"Get it," she told me. She pulled the gun from her tote and waved it around.

I leaned in, grabbed the journal, and gave it to her.

"Go ahead and tell whoever you want about our little conversation," Sylvia said, with a smug smile. "Nobody is going to believe you. There are no security cameras inside the dayroom. You have no proof, no evidence. And those three?"

Sylvia nodded toward Delores, Trudy, and Shana, standing near the entrance.

"Yeah, I know they were listening," she said. "But they're old. Nobody is going to believe them. They'll all be dead long before any sort of legal action happens. Understand?"

I nodded.

"Good."

Sylvia dropped the journal into her tote bag and backed away. When she reached her car, she jumped inside and took off.

Delores, Trudy, and Shana rushed over.

"Talk to me, honey," Delores said. "Are you okay?"

"We were so afraid for you," Trudy said.

"You were very brave," Shana added.

"I'm okay," I said, even though I was kind of shaking on the inside.

"She killed Derrick?" Trudy asked. "And poor Karen. Such a shame."

I opened my bag and got my cell phone. "I'm calling the cops. She's not going to get away with this."

"Don't worry," Shana said. "We've got this."

"I've got everything right here," Delores said, and pointed to her head.

I thought she meant the incident was committed to her memory, but then I realized she was pointing to something else—the tiny life-logging camera she'd attached to her turban.

CHAPTER 29

"I've had a brilliant idea," Mom announced when I answered my cell phone.

I'd just left the parking lot at my apartment complex and turned right onto Via Princessa—the light I ran if I was late for my shift at Holt's, which, for some crazy reason, wasn't the case this morning. It was early to talk to Mom, but I figured it had to be good news.

After last night, I was definitely on a roll.

"Remember when I mentioned that I was considering seeking employment at a museum?" she asked.

Like I could ever scrub that image off my brain cells.

"I've been doing more thinking," Mom said, "and I decided you were right."

Wow, it was worth answering the phone just for that.

"I've thought of a new way to combine my extensive knowledge of beauty and fashion, and my love of art," Mom said. "So I've decided to put together a museum exhibit devoted to beauty queens."

I couldn't think of one darn thing to say.

Luckily, Mom kept talking.

"I think it will be fabulous," she said. "Don't you?"

What could I say? Mom was Mom.

"Sounds great," I told her.

The best part of her idea was, of course, that I wouldn't have to write her résumé.

"I need to get all of my pageant gowns out of storage and start assembling my exhibit," Mom said. "Got to run, sweetie."

I ended the call as I turned into Holt's parking lot. Since the store hadn't opened yet, only the employees' cars were there. No sign of the protesters.

An early shift wasn't my idea of fun, especially after a late night, but since I sleepwalk through most of my day here I figured it would be okay. Besides, everything that had happened at Hollywood Haven was still looming large in my thoughts, so it was better to stay busy—well, kind of busy.

After Sylvia had driven away with the journal last night I'd called Detectives Teague and Walker. It took some patience—something I don't have much of—but I finally reached Teague. He seemed skeptical of the info I gave him—it was good to know I wasn't the only person who hadn't known what life-logging was—but he finally agreed to contact Detective Walker and meet me at the Hollywood Roosevelt.

Delores, Trudy, and Shana had been all over the detectives when they arrived. They backed up my story, then explained how the life-logging device had captured both audio and video of my confrontation with Sylvia. The detectives took it into evidence and said I could expect to hear back from them.

I wasn't worried.

The gals were excited about their part in solving two murders. I was pretty sure it was all over social media this morning.

Once Detectives Teague and Walker viewed the life-logging

content, I knew they would get a search warrant, question Sylvia, and find all the evidence they needed to close the case. I didn't know if that meant a happy ending all the way around. I thought of Ida alone in Hollywood Haven after Sylvia went to prison. She wouldn't have her daughter there looking out for her, but maybe Ida's life would be more peaceful without Sylvia around.

I swung into a parking space and killed the engine. The big neon blue Holt's sign looked down on me. For once, I smiled at the sight.

The fiftieth gala had come off flawlessly. Not one hitch, bump, or hiccup. Everything went smoothly, everyone had a fabulous time. Compliments rained down from everywhere.

I would ace my job performance review. No doubt about it. And finally—finally—I could quit my job at Holt's.

As I got out of my Honda, a car whipped into the next space. It was a cherry red convertible Ferrari Spider, and inside was—Ty?

What was he doing here? And what the heck was he doing in that flashy sports car?

He shut down the motor and looked at me for a moment, then climbed out. His hair was windblown. He hadn't shaved. He had on jeans, a loose white shirt with the tail out and the sleeves rolled up, and flip-flops.

Oh my God, where was my *real* ex-boyfriend?

Ty walked around the car and stopped in front of me.

"Nice ride," I said.

He shrugged. "Impulse buy. Last night."

I guess if he could spend over two hundred grand on a whim, it was okay for me to have a go at the fifty thousand dollars he'd left in my closet.

He nodded toward the far end of the parking lot and said, "I was waiting for you. I got some news."

"Good news?" I asked.

"My attorney called yesterday. I'm no longer a person of interest in the Kelvin Davis murder," he said. "They found the guy who did it. He confessed."

I felt as if a ton of weight had been lifted from my shoulders.

"That's great," I said. "What happened?"

Was it my anonymous tip I'd given Detective Shuman?

"I didn't ask," Ty said. "I don't know, and I don't care."

Honestly, I didn't care either. The only thing that mattered was that Ty was cleared.

He glanced away, then back at me again, and said, "I've been doing a lot of thinking lately. You know, taking stock of . . . things."

Was I one of those things?

"I need to make some changes," he said. "I'm taking some time off, a leave of absence from Holt's, and I wanted . . ."

He wanted me to come with him? He wanted me to jump into that new car? Just the two of us? And let the road take us wherever?

"And I, well . . . uh," Ty said, "I just wanted you to know."

Oh. I guess not.

I gulped down my emotions and managed a nod. Ty walked back around the car and dropped into the driver's seat.

I heard the motor rev as I hurried into Holt's. I didn't look back. I didn't want to watch him drive away.

Jeanette intercepted me just inside the entrance. Employees were opening the registers and straightening the racks, readying for the day ahead.

"I have some good news, Haley," Jeanette said, "and I wanted you to be the first to know."

I was in no mood.

I couldn't imagine that anything Jeanette said to me would fall into my own personal this-is-fantastic category. Not now. Not after what had just happened.

"The Nuovo acquisition has gone through," Jeanette said. "I'm pleased to report that the employee discount has been raised to eighty percent."

Eighty percent? Eighty percent off designer clothes, accessories, and handbags?

"Did you say *eighty*?" I asked.

Jeanette beamed me a huge smile. "Isn't that wonderful?"

This wasn't wonderful. It was horrible.

No way could I walk away from that kind of discount, and that meant—oh my God—I was going to have to work at Holt's *forever*.

"Hey!" someone shouted.

I turned and saw one of the salesclerks standing by the entrance, pointing outside.

"Does anybody know a hot-looking guy driving a red convertible?" she called. "He just pulled up outside."

My heart nearly jumped out of my chest.

Ty came back? For *me*?

Was he going to ask me to go with him?

Would we ride up the coast with the wind in our hair, crank up the music and sing along? Run through the surf, stroll through a winery, spend our nights under the stars?

Would we talk—really talk—about hopes, dreams, and our life ahead?

Did I want that? Or was I better off leaving things as they were?

Should I take a chance and go with him?

Oh, crap.